"Did you ev... the first gentleman I've kissed.

He hadn't, not at all, but that guileless confession kept him painfully hard. And might all the lords of the admiralty forgive him, he was kissing her again. She parted her lips freely for him, exploring him as much as he was her. He slid his hands along the narrowing curve of her waist, inside her dressing gown so there was nothing but the gossamer-weight linen between him and the quivering fullness of her breasts and *this had to stop*.

He released her and forced himself to step away from temptation. Her hair was mussed and tousled, her cheeks flushed, her nightclothes askew and, damnation, he'd never wanted any woman more than he wanted this one, whom he'd no right to have.

"Oh, my," she murmured. "That was not pretending, was it?"

"No." The blood was still thumping through his body, demanding to be obeyed. "That was as damned real as it gets."

* * *

Princess of Fortune
Harlequin Historical #721—September 2004

Miranda Jarrett

Princess of Fortune

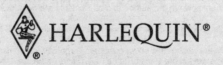

HARLEQUIN®

TORONTO • NEW YORK • LONDON
AMSTERDAM • PARIS • SYDNEY • HAMBURG
STOCKHOLM • ATHENS • TOKYO • MILAN • MADRID
PRAGUE • WARSAW • BUDAPEST • AUCKLAND

ISBN 0-373-29321-6

PRINCESS OF FORTUNE

www.eHarlequin.com

Printed in U.S.A.

Please address questions and book requests to:
Harlequin Reader Service
U.S.: 3010 Walden Ave., P.O. Box 1325, Buffalo, NY 14269
Canadian: P.O. Box 609, Fort Erie, Ont. L2A 5X3

For Mary Jo,
A most excellent friend, and a writer who always
inspires, with affection and admiration.
And who else can remain so cheerful
when the fire siren wails at 6:00 a.m.?

Chapter One

Kingdom of Monteverde, 1796

Who would have dreamed that London—wicked, wealthy, barbarous London—would become her only sanctuary?

London. Oh, dearest saints in heaven, whatever were her parents thinking?

Isabella forced herself to take another deep breath as she stared out the window of her bedchamber, striving to master the panic and fear knotting in her chest. She still could not quite believe she was leaving this view, this room, this house, and this life, with no guarantee that she'd ever return. Usually so full of activity, the palace now seemed forlornly silent, her father and brother already gone and most of the servants fled to the hills.

Next—last—to go would be Isabella. Earlier her trunks had been taken away, and as her lady's maid fastened the rows of buttons along the sleeves of her jacket, she felt these last minutes here in her home slipping away more relentlessly than the grains of sand in an hourglass. Inside her kidskin gloves her palms were already moist with anxiety, and her heart raced with dread for what lay before her.

But she was the only daughter of the King of Monteverde, and a Fortunaro princess must be strong as a lioness, full of courage and pride like the fierce, noble beasts that graced the family's arms. Yes, yes, a lioness of gold: that was what she was, and with fresh determination Isabella drew in her breath and raised her head to what she hoped was a more regal angle.

"Isabella, hold still," scolded her mother with her usual impatience. No one would ever guess that Mama, too, would be fleeing tonight—which was, of course, the point. Mama was as exquisitely dressed and coiffed as she was every evening, her favorite rubies around her throat and her still-beautiful face with the heavy-lidded eyes so artfully painted that, by candlelight, she could pass for Isabella's sister instead of her mother.

"If you continue to fidget, daughter," she continued, looking down her famous nose at Isabella, "and do not let Anna dress you properly, I shall turn you over to the French and that vile little Corsican instead of to the English."

At once Isabella went still, letting the maid finish dressing her in her traveling clothes. Mama was right: she was eighteen, far too old for such childish restlessness. If it weren't for General Buonaparte and his ridiculous war turning all the royal houses upside down, a suitable marriage would have been arranged for her long ago.

"That it should come to this, Your Highness," said the Marchese di Romano grimly, the last of her father's advisers left in the palace, and one of her mother's closest friends. He was an older man whose eyes now seemed to wander in opposite directions and who relied weightily upon his gold-headed walking stick, but no one at court had ever doubted that his mind remained as sharp and clever as any fox's. "That a Fortunaro princess should be forced to scurry away like a low skulking thief, to snivel and beg for mercy from those heathen English—"

"Oh, hush, Romano," said Mama mildly. "She is going to England because it is the only country that Buonaparte cannot capture. There is no other place where she will be as safe."

Idly the marchese tapped his stick on the polished floor. "The English will adore our dear princess, you know," he said, studying Isabella with a connoisseur's eye. "They are all penny-gallants for a pretty face in distress."

"She is more than simply a pretty face, Romano," said her mother sternly. "She is my daughter, and a great beauty."

"Of course, of course," said Romano softly, soothing. "She will have no equal among those milk-fed English ladies."

Though Isabella kept her head proudly raised, as if already confronting those English ladies, her unhappiness was mushrooming. Didn't Mama plot and plan as expertly as any general? Hadn't she already explained every detail to Isabella, how it was her duty to be the one Fortunaro to go into exile in London? Isabella wasn't a fool, and she didn't need Romano to tell her how to behave. The Monteverdian army had already been pounded and swept by the French in battle after battle, the few remaining troops now poised at the gates of the city for the same surrender that had humbled Florence, Naples, Venice, even great Rome herself. How could Isabella not fail to understand her role as the last proud symbol of her family's defiance, there under the protection of the King of England?

But why must it be her *duty—her fate!—to be the only one sent so far, far away for safekeeping? Why was she standing here in this near-empty palace, her clothes weighed down by the gold coins and jewels sewn into the seams and her heart made even heavier at the thought of the dangerous, lonely voyage before her?*

As if to answer, the rumbling roar of the guns began again, closer now than ever before.

"It is time," said Mama briskly, arranging her cashmere shawl more elegantly around her arms. She took Isabella by the shoulders, her face so close that Isabella could see how the powder settled into the lines around her mouth. "You must go, my brave little lioness. We cannot let the English change their mind, can we? You will go, and you will always remember who you are, what you are, and bring nothing but honor to our name."

Isabella gave a quick jerk of a nod, not trusting her voice to answer. She must be brave and daring like Mama, and she must not weep and wail like a baby who'd not gotten her way. She turned each cheek for Mama to kiss, then kissed her in return, the quick brush that Mama had always preferred.

"I—I'll miss you, Mama," she said with a gulp, blinking back her tears. "God be with you, and with Father and Giancarlo, too."

"Of course He will, my darling," said Mama, her smile brilliant as she patted Isabella's cheek. "He always watches over us Fortunari, doesn't He? Now Romano and I must go, and so must you. Farewell, Isabella. Farewell!"

And as quickly as that, Mama was gone, leaving only the fading scent of her perfume and the click of her lacquered heels on the marble floors, followed by the fainter tapping of Romano's stick. Swiftly Isabella turned away. She did not weep, of course, because Mama wouldn't want that, but inside she felt as empty and abandoned as the palace itself.

She wished that when they'd said farewell, Mama had spoken less of duty and honor, and more of love. She wished that same farewell had been longer, warmer, sweeter, something for Isabella to remember on the perilous voyage to England, instead of the quick, formal parting before Romano. She wished she could admit her fears, instead of always having to be brave as a lioness. She wished—she wished for many things that couldn't be, things that even a Monteverdian princess had no right to desire.

"Bah, Her Majesty has no heart," muttered Anna, purposefully just loud enough for Isabella to hear. "No heart at all."

"Enough, Anna," said Isabella sharply. It didn't matter that the older woman had become her lady's maid by default, one of the last few servants who hadn't panicked and fled the palace, or that Anna would be her one link with her old life as they traveled together. Isabella's mother insisted that such familiarity should never be tolerated, no matter the circumstances. "It is not your place to fault my mother, unless you, too, wish to be branded a traitor."

"Traitors, traitors," muttered Anna, linking her finger and thumb together in the sign against evil. The gesture made her look even more like an ancient little crow, dressed in black from her stockings to the kerchief tied beneath her chin. "What does loyalty mean these days, eh, with the French devils at our gates?"

"Base-born rabble, nothing more," countered Isabella, automatically repeating her father's description of the tawdry French army. To her family, such upstarts were below contempt, unworthy to be even an enemy of their own ancient kingdom. "Our brave army will not waver before such a mob."

Anna sniffed loudly, that sniff saying much about the pitiful chances she gave the brave Monteverdian army. "Your bonnet and gloves, my princess."

Isabella lifted her chin so Anna could tie the bonnet's silk ribbons in a bow, then took the gloves herself, unwilling to let Anna see how her fingers were trembling. Weren't the Fortunaro women as famous for their strength as for their beauty? Couldn't she prove herself worthy of her mother's faith in her to do what must be done?

"Her Majesty said for you to make every haste, my princess," insisted Anna. "Her Majesty said—"

"It is not your place to speak with such freedom, Anna," said Isabella curtly, a perfect echo of her mother's reprimands. "Do you see me disobeying my mother? Do you see me dawdling? Rather it is you and your clumsy old fingers that have delayed me with my dressing."

"Forgive my clumsiness, my princess," mumbled Anna, bobbing her head up and down by way of apology. As she did, a rough little pendant slipped free of her bodice: three twigs lashed with red thread into a triangle and strung on a black cord.

"What is that around your neck, Anna?" asked Isabella suspiciously. "You know heathen charms and talismans are not permitted in the palace."

Quickly Anna tucked the pendant back into her bodice. "It's naught to do with the devil, nor with the priests, my princess. It's a family sign, that is all."

"It still has no place here, and I do not wish to see it again. Now come, bring that lantern, so we might be on our way."

For the last time, Isabella hurried down the marble staircase, the weight of the treasure stitched into her clothes slowing her steps. Down one flight, then another, into the dark, narrower hallway that led to the lower gardens and the beach. She'd never come this way by night, and certainly never with only a single servant holding a lantern against the darkness. Cobwebs brushed and clung to her clothes, and as she heard the mice scrambling to keep clear of the light, she whispered a quick prayer to guard her against whatever dangers might lie within the murky shadows.

Oh, that bats and rats and spiders and cobwebs might be her only threats!

"This way, my princess," said Anna, puffing with exertion as she unbolted the last door for Isabella. "The English sailors will be waiting for you on the beach."

Isabella nodded, holding her heavy skirts to one side as she slipped through the door. Vines had been allowed to grow over the door to disguise it, and as she shoved them aside, the lacquered heels of her slippers sank into the soft sand. The air was cooler here near the sea, and Isabella could taste the sharp tang of salt as she nervously licked her lips. At the water's edge, perhaps thirty feet away, she could make out the dark shadow of a longboat pulled up on the shore, with men sitting waiting at the oars and two others standing aft, doubtless looking for her. Large men, lowborn and rough, speaking quietly among themselves.

Englishmen.

"Go ahead, Anna," she said, striving to hide her anxiety as she hung back in the shadows. "Tell those men to come greet me properly."

But Anna didn't move, her wizened face inside the black scarf as set as a wooden mask. "You tell them yourself, my princess. I'll go no farther, not with you."

Isabella stared at her, stunned. "How dare you speak to me with such insolence? Come here at once, Anna, and do as I say!"

But Anna only shook her head, jutting out her pointed chin for emphasis. "I will never leave Monteverde, my princess," she said, hissing the words like a curse, "and never with a spoiled little bitch like you."

Isabella gasped with shock. No other servant had ever spoken to her like that; no, no other *person* in her memory ever had. "Anna, how *dare* you—"

But Anna had already slammed the door shut against Isabella.

"Wait!" Isabella grabbed the doorknob, frantically jiggling it with both hands. "Anna, open this door at once, I say! At *once!*"

But all she heard through the heavy door was the sound of the bolt in the lock scraping into place, and the echoes of Anna's footsteps fading away down the hall, abandoning her to her fate alone.

"Anna!" she shouted, her fear rising by the second as she thumped her fists against the door. "Anna, come back *now!*"

"Miss?"

Instantly she turned around, her heart racing in her chest. She could make out little of the English sailor's face in the shadows, but there was no mistaking how he loomed over her, the prow of his cocked hat pointing downward as he addressed her. The long, dark boat cloak he wore made him seem larger still, but from the braid on his hat and the brass buckles on his shoes, she guessed he must at least be an officer, and perhaps what among the English passed for a gentleman. Beside him was another man with a long pig-tail down his back, dressed in rough canvas trousers and a worn, striped jersey that marked him clearly as a common sailor.

And these two were to be her saviors. Oh, Mama, what have you done?

"I'm sorry to have frighted you, miss—er, that is, *signora*," said the officer. "But I do need to know if you are—"

"I am the Princess di Fortunaro," she interrupted in imperious English, drawing herself up as tall as she could. She must be brave and proud, and hide her fear for her family's sake. "I am not a 'miss.' You must address me as 'my princess.'"

"Very well, then," said the officer heartily as he touched the front of his hat, and also obviously relieved that she spoke English. "I am Lieutenant Goodwin, at your service, my princess."

Isabella nodded but didn't answer. She wasn't precisely sure what to say in return, true, but she was also waiting for him to show proper regard and respect, and to bow low to her. Wasn't it enough that she'd made the effort to address him in his own language? But she must recall that he was English, and the English were widely known to have no manners whatsoever. Barbarians, all of them, from their Hanoverian king on down.

"You have, ah, any followers who will be joining you?" he asked, looking past her to the closed door, and cheerfully unaware of how much of a barbarian he was. "Servants?"

"No," she said, already feeling more alone than she'd ever been before. "There are none that I can trust."

"No abigail to tend to you?" he asked with surprise. "You'll be the first lady the old *Corinthian* has ever seen, you know, there among all us hoary sailors."

She regarded him with chilly disdain, wishing to put more distance between them. "Not a lady, Lieutenant. A Fortunaro princess."

"Aye, aye, quite right you are," he said quickly. "I warrant you're ready to come aboard, my princess? We've already stowed your dunnage, and we're ready to shove off whenever it suits."

Isabella frowned. She had worked hard at her English lessons, particularly hard once Mama had decided she must go to London, but these words, these expressions— aboard? stowing? dunnage? shoving off?—had not been in her tutor's primer. Whatever *was* this Englishman asking of her?

Gruffly he cleared his throat. "We cannot keep the ship waiting much longer, my princess, not if we wish to get you away safely. We'll lose the tide."

The ship, and the tide. That much Isabella could understand. She looked beyond the man and the longboat, and farther out in the bay she now could make out the dark silhouette of the English ship, outlined by the lights from its lanterns. At such a distance it seemed small, as insubstantial as canvas scenery for a saint's day pageant, and hardly sturdy enough to carry her and these men clear to London.

To *London*.

"My princess?" The lieutenant was offering the crook of his arm to her as support, as gallant a gesture, she supposed, as an Englishman could muster. "You are ready?"

Oh, please, God, please, grant me find the courage to be strong and brave and worthy, to be a true Fortunaro princess!

She took a deep breath, holding her head as high as if she were wearing her best diamond tiara instead of a plain plush bonnet for travel. She *could* do this, and she would, one step at a time. Ignoring the lieutenant's arm, she bunched her skirts to one side to lift them from the sand, and began walking—one step, then the next, and the next after that—across the sand to the waiting boat.

To her future, and to London.

Chapter Two

For Captain Lord Thomas Greaves, all his dreams of glory and golden plunder crashed in the instant the porcelain monkey shattered against the east wall of the Countess of Vaughn's drawing room.

Not, of course, that Tom realized it then.

"Ah, the ladies," said Admiral Edward Cranford pleasantly in the next room, as if this were all the explanation necessary for crashing statuary. "My sister Lady Willoughby and the others shall be joining us presently."

Thomas nodded, striving to match the admiral's pleasantness even if it didn't make a damned bit of sense. It was most unusual for an admiral like Cranford to summon a captain to call upon him socially like this, here at his sister's house in Berkeley Square instead of the navy offices at the Whitehall, and more unusual still for any ladies to be included.

But Tom would overlook it. Desperation could do that to a man, and God knows he was desperate.

"You were saying you'd found a new commission for me,

sir?" he asked, trying to steer the conversation back to more profitable ground. "What ship is it? When can I join her?"

Cranford hesitated, an ominous sign. "Not a commission, exactly," he hedged. "Not a new ship, but a special assignment from the admiralty. One that is, I believe, uniquely suited to your talents and experience, as well as your rank by birth."

Disappointment rose sharp in Tom's throat, and he fought to keep the bitterness from showing on his face. He could guess what was being offered: a regulating captaincy in the impress service, little better than being a kidnapper, and rightly loathed in every seaport town. Or perhaps they'd granted him a plum place in one of the dockyards, sitting day after day on a tall stool at a desk and growing fat like any other countinghouse drone.

But what else could Tom expect? It didn't matter that he was only twenty-eight, or that he was the fourth son of the Earl of Lerchmere, or that he looked and felt as fine and fit as ever, and quite sufficient to earn the ladies' approval. What did matter was that the navy had judged him to be an invalid officer, and the navy never changed its collective mind.

For over a year he'd been landlocked, impatiently recuperating from the wounds that had nearly killed him, but he'd beaten all the odds. He'd survived, hadn't he? He was ready, more than ready, to offer his life again in the service of his country. He was a captain in the greatest navy in the world, his dark blue uniform coat bright with gold lace and brass buttons and hard-won medals on his breast, but none of it was worth a brass farthing without a ship and crew.

"I appreciate the special consideration, Admiral," he began, trying to keep his words civil. "But I do not believe

I require any such preferential treatment. I would prefer that my record stands upon its own merits or lacks."

The admiral puffed out his cheeks and frowned, the thatch of his white brows bristling across his ruddy-brown face. "You know it wasn't my decision to make, Greaves."

"But surely you have influence to change it, sir," said Tom. He'd spent more than half his life in the navy, and he knew the peril and consequences of speaking too forcefully to a superior, yet he was struggling to keep his temper in check. How could he do otherwise, when his whole life and future were slipping from his grasp? "A sloop, a ketch, anything with a sail! Given that the country's at war, there surely must be some suitable command—"

"Not for a man in your condition, no."

"For God's sake, sir, all you must do is look at me!" For proof Tom held his arms away from his sides, strong and steady and without the slightest tremor. "I've mended good as new—better than new! Those infernal surgeons at Greenwich said I was as close to a miracle as they'd ever seen, Lazarus himself, and if that doesn't make me fit for a new command, why, then I—"

"What the surgeons said was no active duty for two years," said the admiral sternly. "Two years at the least, to see what course that musket ball takes within your chest. The navy cannot afford to have captains in command whose physical well-being is not to be trusted, especially not one carrying a chunk of French lead next to his heart."

"But I'm not some damned cripple!" Tom thumped his fist three times on the table beside him, desperate to prove his words. "Look, sir, I'm strong as an ox, aye, and I can thrash any man who dares say otherwise!"

"Damnation, Greaves, then you'll have to thrash me," countered the admiral sharply, "because I'll not let you take that risk, or risk the lives of your men in the process, not when—"

But before he could finish, the double doors between the two rooms flew open and a small, furious woman charged through them, her hands clenched into tight, tiny fists bristling with rings on nearly every finger. Although she was dressed extravagantly for so early in the day—even Tom knew that wine-colored velvet lavished with gold embroidery was not customary at this hour for Berkeley Square, nor were the lavish necklace and bracelets of rubies and pearls—her thick black hair had not yet been brushed, a mass of tangled, knotted curls that bounced against her back with each indignant step.

"Admiral Cranford!" she called, marching directly to the older man, who bowed low in return. Her English was filtered through another language, her accent without apology. "Thank the saints you are here! These women know nothing, worse than nothing! You tell them, Admiral, tell them what imbeciles they are!"

Belatedly Lady Willoughby came hurrying after, the head of the hurled porcelain monkey in her hand as evidence, and her mouth puckered with distress, as if fearing the wrong words would once again slip out.

"The girl came with the best of references, ma'am," she said plaintively, setting the grinning monkey head on the edge of the mantel. "She has dressed the hair of the Duchess of Kent, and all her daughters. How was I to know she wouldn't suit?"

"But I am not this Duchess of Kent, am I, eh?" said the

young woman, tossing her hair back over her shoulders. "Nor am I one of her daughters, or sons, or small, yapping terriers, either. Ah, perhaps that is what your pretend-maid truly is, a groom to lapdogs! Admiral, Admiral, you see how I am treated, how little respect they show to me!"

Astounded, Tom watched and listened as if it were a Drury Lane farce. The admiral had said that they'd be joined by ladies; he should have warned him instead of this high-handed little harpy. Here he'd been struggling to control himself before his superior, while this chit felt free to rage at Admiral Cranford like a Billingsgate fishwife.

"The maid tends only to fine ladies, not to dogs," insisted poor Lady Willoughby, wringing her hands. "Brother, I assure you no insult was ever planned or wished for!"

"'No insult,' ha," repeated the younger woman darkly, lowering her chin so her heavy-lidded eyes seemed to smolder with righteous fire. "Would you have me as bald as a pigeon's egg, then, with every hair ripped from my head? Is that how you would show me honor and respect?"

"Oh, come, ma'am, I'm sure my sister meant no insult," said the admiral with a forced jollity. "We all want what's best for you, you know. I'm sure your hair can be set to rights in no time."

With an exasperated sigh, the younger woman flung her arms in the air, beseeching heaven to take her side and showing a good deal of her breasts in the process.

"Fools and lackeys, every one," she muttered in Italian. "Toss all their wits together, and it still would not half fill a thimble!"

And that, for Tom, was enough.

"Their manners are worth a bushel of your so-called

wit," he answered in Italian, automatically using the same curt tone that served to humble disrespectful crewmen. "These fine people don't deserve such rubbish from you. I'd say a dog groom was what you damned well do need, for I've never heard any other bitch carry on like you are now."

The young woman gasped and swung around to face him, lifting her chin high. "Who are you, to dare address me so?" she asked suspiciously, continuing in Italian. "Do you not know who *I* am?"

"I am Captain Lord Thomas Greaves, miss," he said with a smile and a brusque bow. "And as for your name, miss, I do not know it, nor do I particularly care if ever I do."

"There now, Greaves, I knew you'd charm the lady by speaking to her in her own lingo," said Cranford heartily in English. "But high time I made the proper introductions, aye? Your Royal Highness, might I present Captain Lord Thomas Greaves, the captain I told you about, and a hero if ever there was one. Greaves, the Princess Isabella di Fortunaro of Monteverde."

"Your Royal Highness. I am honored," said Tom, though he didn't feel honored at all. He felt tricked. A *princess,* and from Monteverde at that. What in blazes was Cranford up to, anyway? Monteverde might be the oldest of the Italian monarchies, but it was also regarded as the most indolent and decadent, with more blissful corruption packed inside its borders than in the rest of the Continent combined. How could one of their princesses come to surface here, in poor Lady Willoughby's drawing room?

He took a deep breath to control his temper, then another. "Your servant, ma'am."

But though it was her turn to answer, she didn't. She

simply stared at him, just stared, reluctantly tipping her head back so she could meet his gaze. She *was* short, true, not that any man would notice her height once he'd seen how seductively rounded her small figure was beneath the red velvet.

She wasn't pretty, either, not in the agreeable pink-and-white, strawberries-in-cream way that English girls were pretty. Her features were strong, her profile the kind minted into ancient coins. Framed by that tangle of black hair, her skin was golden pale, with a deeper rose to stain her cheeks and lips. And she seemed unable to keep still, constantly shifting and turning and twisting and gesturing, with an actress's instinct of how best to keep all eyes firmly on her.

No, decided Tom, she wasn't like English girls. Her beauty was richer, more opulent, like strong claret after milky tea, and likely just as apt to cause a headache and regrets the morning after.

"Your English is most accomplished, ma'am," he said at last, falling back into Italian. If she was going to insult the others again, at least he could spare them hearing it. "I compliment you."

Her smile didn't reach quite her eyes. "*Your* Italian, Captain, is fit for the barnyard," she said, reaching up to touch a finger to one dangling ruby earring. "However did you pretend to learn it?"

Well, then, he could smile, too, if that was the game. Any good frigate captain worth his salt recognized a challenge when given, even if it came from a princess intent upon drawing attention to her breasts by tracing her fingertips idly along the edge of her neckline.

"When I was a boy," he explained, "my father indulged

his interest in Vitruvius, and moved our family to Rome for three years. I learned Italian while there, and having often been stationed in the Mediterranean, the language has proved a useful skill."

"Rome," she said scornfully with a little flick of her fingers. "That explains so much."

"Ah, but *Monteverde*," he said easily. "That explains even more."

He half expected her to slap him. If he were honest, he was almost disappointed that she didn't. Instead she limited herself to a sibilant hiss of frustration between her clenched teeth, and an extra twitch of her dark red skirts away from him.

"I'm so glad you are here, Captain," gushed Lady Willoughby, her relief so fervent she was nearly weeping from it. "The princess has been *so* lonely here, without anyone to speak with, and the condition makes her *intemperate*. You shall make such a difference in her life in London. How happy she must be at last to meet someone like you!"

But the princess did not look happy, nor, for that matter, was Tom himself feeling exactly cheerful. He'd come here at the admiral's invitation, full of hope for new orders and a ship to match, and now it seemed he'd leave with neither.

"I am glad to oblige, my lady," he said, switching to English in deference to the confused Lady Willoughby. He was determined to go now that there seemed so little point in staying. "But if you shall excuse me, I'll say my farewells and—"

"You may not leave my presence without my permission, Captain," said the princess tartly. "And I do not wish you to go."

He stared at her, incredulous. "I am an officer in His Majesty's Navy, ma'am, not one of your wretched subjects."

"If you were, my father would have you whipped for your insolence," she said, folding her arms over her chest. "But no matter. You are to be my escort, Captain, my guard while I am exiled here in London. You are to put your life before mine to protect me, and keep me safe from the villains who would wish me harm."

"Oh, aye, and who wouldn't?" scoffed Tom. "What makes you believe I'll take orders from you?"

"Because they do not come from the princess, Greaves, but from your own superiors," said Cranford sharply, catching Tom's arm to draw him aside, away from the women and into the corner.

"Blast you, Greaves, haven't you figured this yet?" Cranford said, lowering his voice as he continued. "Princess di Fortunaro was rescued from Buonaparte by a British navy vessel, and as long as she chooses to stay in England, she will remain under the navy's protection. That's His Majesty's own wish and decision, Greaves, not the princess's, not mine, and most certainly not yours. It's the *king's,* mind?"

"Aye, aye, sir," said Tom, his shoulders squared at attention and his expression studiously blank, the only acceptable response for a sailor being dressed down. "I know where my duty must lie, sir."

"Very well." Cranford's voice was flinty, leaving no chink for argument. "These are your orders, Greaves. You will be quartered here in my sister's house, for as long as the princess also remains as a guest. You will accompany the princess whenever she leaves the house, you will be armed, and you will be ever watchful for her safety and well-being."

"I am to be the princess's bodyguard, sir?" This was worse than being a mere clerk in the dockyards. Far, far worse. "Those are my orders, sir?"

"That, and more," said the admiral. "Because you're a lord in your own right, you'll be her escort, invited to attend the same parties and balls and whatever other folderol pleases the princess, and to the palace, of course."

"She is in such danger, sir?"

"She is a vibrant symbol of resistance to Buonaparte's forces," said Cranford firmly, "and in these unsettled times, symbols matter a great deal. Her life could be at constant risk, and yet it is important that she be seen about London, seen by the very scoundrels who would kill her."

"Aye, aye, sir," said Tom with gloomy resignation. He would rather face any odds in battle at sea than suffer through this on land.

The admiral clapped him on the shoulder. "Buck up, Greaves," he said. "It's not so bad as all that, is it? How many times in your career will you ever receive orders as agreeable as these? Squiring a pretty young princess about London at the height of the season?"

Tom didn't agree. To be chained to the side of that spoiled creature through an endless round of noisy, crowded parties—damnation, why didn't he just put the pistol to his own head now, and finish what the French had begun?

He glanced past the admiral's shoulder. The princess was standing before the fireplace, studying her reflection in the looking glass as she smoothed and braided her hair, using only her fingers. She caught his eye, paused, then looked back into the mirror.

"I had no choice but to learn to dress my own hair while I was trapped upon that verminous warship," she explained as she deftly coiled the braid and tucked it into a neat knot on the top of her hair. "There was no proper lady's maid there, either."

Stunned, Tom watched as she took her bonnet from the waiting maidservant and settled it on her head herself. But it wasn't just seeing how capably she could braid her own hair after she'd made such a fuss. It was the way she was finishing dressing here in the middle of the drawing room. There was an unsettling intimacy to her movements, a seductive balance between royal propriety and nonchalant display, and almost too late Tom realized he'd been staring at the way her breasts pushed higher when she lifted her hands to place her hat.

"If only I had known, ma'am," began Lady Willoughby, unable to keep the plaintive exasperation from her voice. "If only you had told me you could do—that is, that you knew how you liked your hair dressed, why, surely we could have—"

"Just because I *can,* Lady Willoughby, does not mean I *should.*" The princess held out her arms so the maid could drape a paisley cashmere shawl over her shoulders. "Pray recall who I am before you make another such suggestion. Now come, Captain Greaves. The carriage should be waiting, or at least it shall if that has not been bungled like everything else."

"You are leaving, ma'am?" Tom uneasily realized he was to be included in her plans. "You have an invitation?"

She folded her arms before her, the long tassels on her shawl hanging down nearly to her knees. "I am going anywhere outside this prison of a house. Beyond that, I neither know nor care."

Without waiting for Tom's answer or even to see if he followed, she swept grandly from the room and toward the front door, leaving Lady Willoughby to once again scurry along in her wake.

"Women." Cranford shook his head, as if that single word could sum up all the world's real ills. "You'll need a pistol before you accompany the princess, Greaves. Unless, of course, you are carrying one at present."

"No, sir." Tom could not believe that these really were his new orders from the admiralty, to trail around London like an armed nursemaid after a spoiled princess. Damnation, he didn't *want* to believe it.

"These shall see you through." Cranford opened the top drawer of the sideboard and took out a long pistol box, holding it open for Tom to choose which gun he preferred. So all of this had been planned from the start, even his acceptance, and as he lifted the nearest gun from the case, he wondered if even that, too, had been preordained. There was nothing fancy about the gun, a standard-issue pistol such as any sailor would carry into battle, yet Tom found the familiar feel of such a gun in his hand oddly comforting. At least something in this morning was as it should be.

"I do not expect you to train that upon every greengrocer's window, Greaves." The admiral watched with approval as Tom raised his arm to test the gun's sight. "After all, we're in London, not the Peninsula. It's more a precaution than anything, a way of letting the rest of the world know you are serious about the princess's well-being. Most of the villains who could bring her any real danger are cowards, anyway, and simply being at her side should be enough to scare them away."

"I shall follow my orders, sir." Tom took the plain leather belt that the admiral offered, buckled it low around his waist and hooked the pistol to the ring on the side. It wasn't exactly the height of London fashion, hanging there over his waistcoat, but it would serve the purpose that the admiral wished.

The admiral nodded. "I never doubted you'd do your duty, Greaves. You're an officer of the king, and you'll do whatever is necessary. While you are out with the princess, I'll have word sent to your lodgings to have your dunnage packed and sent here. You have a manservant?"

"John Kerr, sir. He has been with me since my first command." Old Kerr would be as disappointed about these new circumstances as Tom was himself, and just as unhappy that they wouldn't be returning to sea.

"Then I shall make certain my sister has a place for him here, as well." The admiral unstopped the decanter of port on the sideboard, poured it into two glasses and handed one to Tom. "Here you are. You might need a little fortifying, eh?"

Tom took the glass, the sun turning the liquor golden between his fingers. The surgeons had advised him against drinking, fearing the toll that alcohol might take on his heart, but when he thought of the woman waiting for him in the carriage outside, he decided the risk was worth it. If the port did kill him, then he wouldn't have to join her after all.

"Long live the king." Cranford lifted his glass, and Tom did, too. "And confusion to the French."

"Confusion to the French," echoed Tom, "especially in Monteverde."

He downed the port in one long swallow, feeling its heat ripple through him. He stood very still, glass in hand, and waited for the shock, or stabbing pain, or whatever it was that the liquor was supposed to do to him.

But nothing happened. The songbirds in the garden outside were still chirping among the roses, the admiral's nose was still red, and he, Captain Lord Thomas Greaves, was still very much alive.

"Best you were off, Greaves." The admiral set down his glass, wiping his mouth with the length of his finger. "The princess will not like to be kept waiting."

No, she wouldn't. Tom didn't need to reread his orders to know that, and with a last bow to the admiral, he headed toward the front door, the pistol heavy against his hip and the prospect of guarding Princess Isabella di Fortunaro a burden he couldn't escape.

Chapter Three

Isabella stood exactly in the center of Lady Willoughby's front hall and tried hard—very hard—to keep from losing her temper. It was hot in the airless space, with the doors and windows closed tight and the afternoon sun streaming in through the fan light overdoor. Inside Isabella's black lace gloves, her hands were sweating, and the long curving feather on her bonnet kept tickling the nape of her neck in a most annoying fashion. The tall case clock ticked away each second with a solemn finality, counting off the wasted minutes that Captain Lord Thomas Greaves was making her wait.

She did not like waiting. She never had, and she never should, considering her rank, but she was determined to give him the benefit of the doubt for this first time. It might not be his fault. Likely the admiral was keeping him with some sort of nonsense, the foolish old man. She would be gracious, and grant the captain the favor of her patience.

But if he ever dared keep her waiting like this again— ah, she would not forgive him, ever.

"I am sure the captain will here shortly, ma'am." Lady Willoughby gave Isabella her usual watery smile. "He seems like a very nice gentleman."

Isabella sniffed. "He has not been brought here to be *nice*. He is here to keep me safe."

Once again she looked out the long window beside the door. Lady Willoughby's glossy green carriage with the matched grays was sitting there waiting at the curb, taunting her with the freedom it represented. She didn't care if the others believed she was exaggerating: she *was* a prisoner. This was the closest she'd been to leaving this house since she'd been brought to it in the middle of the night, three weeks before, and she could not wait to feel the warmth of the sunlight and the breeze across her skin, and to see more of the city beyond this single boring square.

"I am very sorry, princess," Lady Willoughby said, as if she could read Isabella's thoughts, "but I cannot let you go alone. For your own good, you see. You must wait for the captain to escort you to the carriage."

Isabella frowned, glancing pointedly at the two large footmen standing ready to barricade the door if she tried to escape.

"Oh, yes, of course, you silly goose," she muttered in Italian, as much to irritate the other woman as to keep her own comments safe. "We cannot tax the gaolers hired to keep me caged like an animal, can we?"

"Yes, just so." With no notion of what the princess had said, Lady Willoughby smiled again, even as she wrung her hands with despair. "I'm sure when the captain comes, you shall have the nicest drive imaginable."

Isabella smiled in return and kept speaking in Italian.

"True, true, true, quite the nicest, once you give the captain my leash to hold for himself."

She couldn't play such tricks on Captain Lord Greaves. How could she have known that Cranford would have found even a single man in this country to speak Italian so well? Tears had started to her eyes when she'd heard the familiar, rolling words, she'd been that struck with sudden homesickness, and for one horrible moment she'd gasped aloud from the shock. But after that she'd managed to hide her feelings, the way a princess always must. She hadn't let the captain know how surprised she'd been or how lonely she'd felt, and she certainly hadn't revealed that she'd found him passing handsome, too.

He wasn't like the other English sailors she'd met on the interminable voyage here, rough, ill-spoken men with dreadful battle scars and missing teeth, and he wasn't like the sorry old warhorses the admiral had first introduced her to, either. This captain stood straight and proud, his dark blue uniform tailored to show off his broad shoulders and flat stomach. He had fire to him, too, a challenge in his blue eyes and a bite to his smile, and he hadn't been afraid of her. That was rare, and she liked it.

To be sure, he hadn't shown her one iota of the respect due her rank, but she could teach him that. He was English, and even an English lord like Captain Greaves could not be expected to understand the finely detailed etiquette of the Monteverdian court. But he seemed clever enough. After these last long, lonely weeks, she would welcome any such challenge, an amusing way to pass the days until Buonaparte was defeated and she could sail for home.

Behind her she could hear his measured footsteps at last

coming down the hall to join her, just as she could hear
Lady Willoughby's little birdlike exclamations—such a
meek and spineless creature!—as she rushed to greet him.
But Isabella didn't turn, not at first, keeping her face well
hidden inside the curving silken arc of her bonnet's brim.

His first lesson would be simple enough. She would not
jump for the delight of his company. He must come to her,
and be grateful for her notice.

"What detained you, Captain Greaves?" she asked at last,
without turning. "You knew that I wished to leave directly."

She knew he couldn't ignore her, not only because of
his orders, but because she'd taken care of exactly where
she stood. She'd learned that from watching her mother,
another of royalty's little tricks. The sunbeams slicing
through the fan light must be making the red velvet of her
gown glow like a flame against the stark black and white
of the marble floor. How could he possibly be looking
anywhere else? It was difficult being a small woman, particularly here in England where the females seemed all to
be great gangly storks, and she must rely upon such careful planning to keep attention focused on her.

And for extra emphasis, she let his silence stand for another half beat before, at last, she broke it.

"You have no answer for me, Captain?" She turned,
just enough to look over her shoulder, and she did not
smile. "No explanation for your delaying me?"

He bowed, his wavy hair falling forward over his brow.
"Is there any explanation that would be acceptable to you,
ma'am?"

"No. There is not." She was surprised that he'd answered her question with a question, and surprised, too,

that he wouldn't tell her the obvious reason, that he'd been with the admiral. Unless he hadn't—a possibility that annoyed her even as it piqued her curiosity. "But no explanation is no excuse, either."

"I didn't claim that it was, ma'am." One of the footmen handed him his gold-trimmed hat, and he settled it squarely on his head, as if preparing for battle. "Is the carriage here, Lady Willoughby?"

"Yes, Captain my lord." Nervously, Lady Willoughby peered out the window, just to be certain, as if the carriage might have somehow been whisked away by thieves when she wasn't looking. "But at my brother's request, I have kept the princess within the house until you joined her."

"'Within, within!'" Unable to contain her impatience, Isabella flung one end of the tasseled shawl over her shoulder. "You have done nothing *but* keep me within, Lady Willoughby, ever since I came here! You might as well have locked me in your darkest dungeon, behind bars of iron, for all that I have been your prisoner!"

"If that is the case, ma'am," he said, taking her by the elbow without waiting for permission, "then we had better go without."

She began to pull her elbow away, not liking such familiarity, but then the two footmen blocking the door parted for Isabella and the captain like Moses at the Red Sea. The door swung open, too, and they were outside, on the steps—free!—and Isabella forgot all about the hand at her elbow.

She looked up at the sky and blinked at the brightness. The London sky lacked the brilliance of the one that covered Monteverde, and unlike that perfect enameled blue, this sky was muffled by a haze of coal smoke. But it was still the sky, not the ceiling of a drawing room, and she couldn't help smiling at the difference as the tassels on her shawl rippled in the breeze.

Yet the captain didn't share her pleasure. "Come along, ma'am," he said, steering her down the steps as if her elbow were the rudder on some small boat. "It's not wise for you to stand out here in the open."

With an unhappy little sigh, she let him hurry her into the carriage. Not that she had much choice: even with no more contact than his hand on her elbow, she was conscious of how much larger, how much stronger, he was than she. This is what he was supposed to do, watch out for her welfare, but she'd never before had to consider herself a target.

"You ordered this closed carriage, didn't you, Captain?" she asked as she climbed inside, the leather squabs and polished brass trim warm from waiting in the sun. "After all I've been through, you knew I would wish for an open carriage, so I might feel the air, but you chose a closed one instead."

"Then we'll keep the windows open." His glance swept over the quiet square, searching for any sign of something or someone that didn't belong. "And I believe it was the admiral who suggested the closed carriage."

"Open windows aren't the same."

"No, they're not." His expression was stern, all business, as he sat across from her. "I won't pretend otherwise, ma'am. But I agree with the admiral's choice. In an open carriage, you would be far too vulnerable to any sharpshooter with a good eye."

She had not heard that word before—sharpshooter—but

she'd no trouble deciphering its meaning. Instantly she pictured herself as she'd appear in that open carriage, a bright patch of red and black, visible from every window and every rooftop they would pass. She knew she should be grateful for the captain's experience, but the reality behind it frightened her. Though her parents had tried to keep the worst news from her, she knew what had happened to the French royal family. A crown didn't grant the same omnipotence it once did; Isabella had only to consider how she herself had been sent away to understand that.

Yet she didn't want to be a villain to those who supported Buonaparte, or a symbol for the English who didn't. All she wished was to be herself, and for the captain to be the way he'd been inside the house, bantering with her in Italian and not searching shop windows for lurking assassins with chilly English efficiency.

The footman latched the door shut, and at last the carriage rumbled to a start, the iron-bound wheels scraping over the paving stones as they left the square and headed along the city streets. She leaned forward, eager for even a glimpse of the city.

"So where are we bound, ma'am?" The buildings and streets they were passing would mean something to him, neighborhoods and districts he could recognize, while to her everything had a blurry sameness through the window. "Did you or Lady Willoughby tell the driver a destination?"

"I didn't know one to tell him." She felt foolish and lost, having earned the freedom she'd craved without any sense now of what to do with it. "I have been too much a prisoner to learn of anything beyond those four grim walls."

"Ma'am, you were a guest in a Berkeley Square town

house." The captain's smile was patient and obligatory, a smile guaranteed to make her feel even more foolish and lost. "No one would honestly consider Lady Willoughby's house to be a prison."

"It was the same as one." Her chin trembled. "They allowed me no liberty, no privacy."

"You allowed them no peace," he countered. "Nothing Lady Willoughby might have done to you merited that tantrum over your hair. When I was a boy, my mother would have taken a hairbrush to me or my brothers or sisters for behavior like that, and she wouldn't have used it on our heads, either."

She'd thought he'd understand, but he didn't, or at least he was pretending not to, with this nonsense about his mother's hairbrush. "*Your* mother wasn't a queen."

"No," he said, pushing his hat back from his forehead with his thumb, "but she was an English countess, which amounts to much the same thing."

She frowned, wondering what exactly her mother would do or say in this circumstance. "But Lady Willoughby and her servants have been unkind to me, Captain. They did not treat me like a guest. They searched through my trunks and mussed my gowns."

"How else could they be sure that no enemy could have hidden something harmful in your belongings?" he asked, the logic perfectly clear to him. "They meant only to protect you."

She sniffed. "They have intercepted my invitations and letters of welcome from my cousins, your English King George and Queen Charlotte, and kept them from me."

"Lady Willoughby wouldn't do that, especially not with

correspondence from His Majesty. More likely His Majesty has been occupied with affairs of state, and has not yet, ah, found the time to write to you."

"No, Captain, that was not it at all." She lowered her voice in confidence, even though they were alone. "Because I am a foreigner, and not English like them, the persons in this house will not trust me. They will not even *try*."

He raised one skeptical eyebrow. "I don't believe that. It's rubbish."

"You should believe it, rubbish or not, because it is so," she said, switching back to speaking Italian. She leaned closer to him, close enough that she could see the darker flecks of blue that sparked his eyes. She clasped her hands before her, beseeching as the shawl slithered off her arm. "Can *you* trust me, Captain?"

But though she waited, he didn't answer. Instead of listening, he'd let his eyes follow the shawl as it slipped from her shoulders and came to an abrupt stop there on the neckline of her gown. Monteverdian ladies were not ashamed to display their figures to the best advantage possible, and Isabella had soon realized she wore her gowns cut much lower over her breasts than Lady Willoughby and her dour friends did. Now the captain must have realized the difference, too, his English efficiency scattered to oblivion.

So this, then, was how her mother would have ruled the captain, but the thought gave her no satisfaction. She didn't want him to be like every other man, whether English or Monteverdian. She wanted him to be better.

"I have trusted no one since I left Monteverde, Captain." She pulled the shawl back over her shoulder, willing to put aside her disappointment and give him another chance.

"No one at all, and certainly none of your English. But you, Captain—truly, I might be able to trust you, if you can but trust me."

He cleared his throat, and at last looked back at her face. And he knew he'd erred. She could see the chagrin in his expression, which was, she supposed, *something*.

"I'm an officer of the king, ma'am, sworn to act with honor," he said. "You should be able to trust me."

"You are a man first," she said, thoughtfully stroking one of the shawl's tassels between her fingers. To her he'd always be a man first, and what a shame it was that he didn't seem to think of himself that way, too. "And you are a man who hasn't answered my question. Can you trust me, Captain, so that I might trust you?"

"I told you, ma'am, as an officer—"

"Oh, Captain, not again," she said. "How can you say that to me, when the others were officers, too?"

"Others, ma'am?" he asked with wary surprise.

"Oh, yes, there were three other captains before you, all old men with white hair, puffed up with their own self-importance and gold braid." She waggled her fingers over her shoulders to mimic the heavy gold fringes on their epaulets. They had each tried to dictate to her what was proper and what wasn't, as if they meant to replace her father. They'd lectured her about her behavior and how she'd dressed, and now—now they were lecturing someone else.

He frowned. "What became of them, these other captains?"

So the admiral hadn't told him he hadn't been the first choice. She was sorry for that. When she'd told him about the others, she'd only wanted him to realize how superior he was to them, not to make him feel as if he were fourth-rate. Ah, a man's pride was such a delicate thing!

"Oh, they did not please me," she said with airy nonchalance, trying to make light of the other men to save his feelings. "I told the admiral to send them away, because I could not trust them."

"You dismissed them?" He sounded shocked. "Older officers, white-haired gentlemen who deserved respect for their rank and years of service? *You* dismissed them?"

"I didn't," she said, surprised he would be so upset. At least he had some pretense to a title and noble blood. The others had been disagreeable commoners, underlings, and surely his inferiors. "The admiral did. But I do not see why I am not entitled to—"

"You sent those other officers away," he said, "and because of your whims, they've failed their orders. Because of you, ma'am, their lives and careers must be in rare shambles."

"Their failure is hardly *my* fault!"

"Who else could be to blame?" he demanded. "How in blazes could you do that to those men, ma'am? It's bad enough when you berate poor Lady Willoughby, but for you to ruin three honorable gentlemen officers because they did not *suit* you—"

"I thought I could trust you, Captain," she said defensively. "I thought because you were as unhappy as I am, you could understand me."

"Who in blazes says I'm unhappy?"

"You don't have to say it, Captain!" She sliced her gloved hand through the air as if to cut through his protests. "You do not have to speak one word, either in English or in your barbarous attempt at Italian. You make all perfectly clear. You are no more pleased to be in London than I. You would much rather be back on one of your great smelly navy boats with a ruffian crew of thieves and cutpurses."

"Ships, ma'am." He was biting off each word. "In most cases, an English vessel of war is a ship, not a—"

"Very well, then, Captain. A *ship*. You would rather be in one of your great smelly navy ships than here in this carriage with me. And I see no reason to disoblige you."

She stood upright, swaying unsteadily in the moving carriage, and thumped her knuckles on the roof of the carriage. "Driver, stop! Here, now! Stop at once!"

The captain grabbed her by the arm, trying to pull her back down on the seat so she wouldn't fall as the carriage rumbled to a halt. Through the windows Isabella could see other carriages and chaises and shops with stylish ladies and gentlemen strolling along the pavement, enough for her to realize they were on some fashionable street. To Isabella's satisfaction, many of those passersby were already turning to look at the commotion inside Lady Willoughby's glossy green carriage.

The captain, of course, thought otherwise. "A moment now, ma'am," he ordered as he tried to maneuver her back to the seat. "A moment to calm yourself."

She gasped with indignant shock. She could not recall the last time anyone had dared restrain her like this against her will.

"I will not calm myself," she sputtered, "because I do not need *calming!*"

"I won't let you go until you agree to be reasonable,

ma'am." He held her lightly, almost gently, but there was no mistaking his strength. "I don't want you hurting yourself."

"The only one who'll harm me is you," she said, trying to wriggle free. It wasn't easy. His hands were bigger than she'd first realized, his fingers easily spanning her arm in a way that was daunting, but oddly exciting, too. "I order you to release me, Captain, release me at once!"

"My orders from the admiralty must come first, ma'am." He was working so hard to stop her without hurting her, that, under any other circumstances, she would have laughed out loud. "Damnation, why won't you show a little sense and stop this?"

"Because I am a Fortunaro princess, Captain," she said furiously, her temper finally spilling over, "and the Fortunari do whatever they please."

Abruptly the carriage halted, throwing the captain off balance, and swiftly Isabella jerked her arm free of his grasp. She unhooked the latch on the door and shoved it open, the ribbons on her bonnet blowing up across her face as she teetered on the edge. She'd come too far to change her mind now, and before the captain could pull her back, she stepped from the carriage, her head regally high.

But she'd neglected to wait for the footman to open the step for her, and instead of descending grandly from the carriage, she pitched forward through the empty space in a tangle of red velvet and landed hard on the pavement on her hands and knees, without any grandeur at all.

"Ma'am!" At once the captain was there at her side, kneeling on the pavement beside her. "Are you injured? Should I send for a surgeon?"

"Of course I am not hurt," she snapped, scrambling

back to her feet and brushing him away as well as the two footmen. The palms of her hands stung inside her gloves and she was quite sure her knees were bruised and scraped, but she would never give him the satisfaction of admitting it. Even if a Fortunaro princess might be foolish enough to leap without looking, she would keep the resultant suffering to herself. "I am not some piece of delicate porcelain, to be shattered with such ease."

He looked relieved. "Then let me help you back into the carriage."

"Why should I do that?" She straightened her bonnet, retying the ribbons, and looked up at the sign over the shop before her. At least they'd stopped before one she'd plausibly visit, the windows filled with an enticement of bonnets, gloves and ribbons. "We shall go inside here, Captain, to—to Copperthwaite's Millinery. Yes, that is my wish. A fine shop is not like an open street. There can be no danger to me inside. I shall be quite safe."

She smiled, proud that she'd made her mouth bend around those awkward English words. Walking forward toward the shop took effort as her bruised knees protested, but through sheer will she kept her smile in place and didn't wince. Other people were watching, curious and listening, eager to be able to describe any mistake she might make, and she was determined to earn their admiration, not their contempt.

"You can't do this, ma'am," said the captain in an impatient whisper as he walked beside her. "It's not wise."

"Then *I* am not wise, because I cannot see reason or cause for not entering this shop." She was enjoying herself now, relishing the attention of the growing well-dressed crowd on the sidewalk around them, and she raised her voice so the others might hear her. "How am I to earn support for my dearest Monteverde here in London if I never show myself to the English people?"

An excited murmur rippled through the crowd, and she smiled just enough to acknowledge it. This was a part of being *her* that she'd missed, a part that the captain couldn't understand, and how could he, really?

One of the footmen hurried to open the shop's door for her, and she sailed inside. Because Mama had always insisted upon having the dressmakers and jewelers and everyone else come to her at the palace, Isabella had no firsthand experience with shops, and she gazed about this one now with unabashed curiosity.

One long room was lined on either side with pale green counters, and cushioned chairs for customers. While most of the goods were hidden away in the drawers of the tall cabinets behind the counters, special selections had been artfully arranged here and there to catch a buyer's eye: wide-brimmed leghorn hats with silk flowers, pastel kidskin gloves, veils and ribbons and stocking and garters. Isabella couldn't imagine having such a selection to choose from, and for once it actually did seem as if the common women might have the advantage over her and her mother in the palace.

With the gracious smile still on her face, Isabella stopped just inside the doors, waiting to be properly recognized and greeted. Every shop girl had already turned to look, as had every customer, and Isabella beamed at the attention. Surely in such a center of fashion as this she would be recognized; surely no assassins could be lurking here.

An elegant older woman glided toward Isabella, the curled ribbons on her cap floating gently around her cheeks. She dipped a genteel curtsy, and Isabella nodded in return.

But Mrs. Copperthwaite wasn't noticing. "Good day, Captain Lord Greaves, good day! We are so honored to have you visit us—a gentleman of your heroic reputation!"

Beside Isabella, the captain bowed. "Thank you, ma'am," he said. "You're far too generous with your praise. All I did was for my country, nothing that any officer of the king wouldn't have done in my place."

"Oh, no, Captain my lord, I would dare differ!" exclaimed Mrs. Copperthwaite. "You are a hero, Captain my lord, and I will not have you argue!"

Mrs. Copperthwaite sighed and clasped her hands before her breasts in a way that Isabella found annoyingly overwrought. A hero, a hero, thought Isabella crossly. If this captain were such a great war hero, then why was he mired here on land, making her life so miserable?

Mrs. Copperthwaite sighed again, at last recovered. "Pray, pray, what shall you have this day, Captain my lord? How might we oblige you?"

"Nothing for me, ma'am," said the captain. Even with the shopkeeper so shamelessly fawning over him, he was still watching out for Isabella's safety, his eyes roving all over the counters and cabinets and other customers as he looked for danger. "Though likely my sisters would disagree."

"Then for—for your *friend*." Finally Mrs. Copperthwaite turned to Isabella with a distinctly slighter curtsy. "How might we serve you, miss?"

The shop owner's expression was respectful enough, but

her appraisal was so open—taking in everything from Isabella's heeled slippers to the plume on her hat, and especially the un-English velvet and gold gown in between—that Isabella knew at once what lay behind it. Because she wasn't dressed like a milky-mousy English lady, she must be a—a harlot.

"I am not this man's *mistress*." Isabella drew herself up with regal disdain. "I do not know what should give you such a ridiculous idea."

Beside her, the captain made a growling grumble deep in his throat, and already she knew what that meant, too. He wanted her to *behave*.

"Mrs. Copperthwaite has said nothing of the sort." His voice had a forced lightness to it, more warning for Isabella. "She intends no insult to you. She doesn't know who you are, that is all."

Isabella didn't deign to look at him. Most likely he was right about this Mrs. Copperthwaite—if the woman wished to keep her trade, she could ill afford to make any judgments about her customers—but Isabella had no wish to admit to the captain that she'd been wrong. Royalty never did that.

"Then tell her who I am, Captain," she ordered. "Tell them all."

His dark brows came together, and the little muscles along the line of his jaw twitched. "That would not be wise."

"Oh, you are too stubborn!" Without thinking, she lapsed into Italian, flinging her shawl over one shoulder, tassels flying. "Haven't we already determined that I shall never be a wise woman, not by your preposterous standards?"

Not only was his jaw twitching, but along that same jaw

a mottled red flush was now spreading from the immaculate white linen of his shirt.

"Your wisdom, or lack of it, is not my affair," he said, also in Italian. "Your welfare and safety are. Few in London know you are here, but if you choose to announce yourself like this, in the middle of Copperthwaite's, then I'll guarantee the scandal sheets will be filled with it tomorrow."

"Saints in heaven, what if they are? It will still be your duty to protect me, won't it?"

"It will," he said, "but you'll also make it a damned sight more difficult. Now come, you've done enough damage here. Back to the carriage before—"

"Oh, Your Royal Highness," cried a startled voice in the same Italian. "It is you! Praise the merciful Mother, it *is* you!"

A small, dark woman in a plain seamstress's cap and apron rushed from behind the counters toward Isabella. Her round-cheeked face and her singsong dialect could have belonged to any woman in a Monteverdian market, and because of it Isabella smiled, touched by such an unexpected reminder of home.

But before the woman came closer, the captain lunged forward and grabbed her around the waist, jerking her back against his chest. The woman shrieked and fought him, struggling to break free as he caught her right hand and held it firmly in her grasp.

"Maria!" Mrs. Copperthwaite said sharply. "Maria, stop this at once and explain yourself!"

Still the woman plunged and kicked, while only Isabella and the captain knew that she was spewing out the vilest, most profane insults imaginable against every member of the Fortunaro family. She kept the fingers of one hand clenched tightly, and as she tried to twist around toward the captain, the light caught a flash of a polished blade. Shocked, Isabella could only stand and watch, her welcoming smile now frozen on her face.

"Drop it now." His voice was harsh, efficient. "Save yourself, and surrender."

"To the devil with you, you English bastard!" she cried, breathing hard with desperation as she tried one last time to twist free. "You deserve to die for defending the royalist bitch!"

But the woman's strength was spent. The captain pried the woman's clasped fingers open, and a sharp-bladed pair of sewing scissors dropped to the floor with a clatter. Gasps and ladylike murmurs of horrified surprise rippled through the other customers and shop girls, while the other seamstresses crowded in the doorway to the workroom they were never supposed to leave.

"Send for the constable," said the captain. "Now." Obeying instantly, one of the shop girls ran into the street.

Two of the footmen had hurried to relieve him, each taking one of the woman's arms to hold her until the constable came. Calmly the captain collected the scissors from the floor where they'd fallen, and wrapped them in his handkerchief before he slipped the little bundle of evidence into his pocket. He ignored the woman now, her cap gone and her hair bedraggled and tears of fury streaming down her face as she continued her stream of curses and threats.

But Isabella didn't have the power to ignore it. She felt the woman's hatred wash over her like a wave, the intensity of it shocking and confusing, too. Then she noticed the crude necklace that had slipped free of the woman's kerchief when she'd struggled with Tom. Only Isabella had recognized the tiny triangle of twigs bound with red thread on a black cord.

Isabella knew the symbol, yet she didn't: a family sign, Anna had told her. But what kind of family—what kind of violence—would link Anna to this woman, and now to Isabella herself?

She felt shaken, her knees trembling and weak beneath her. She'd always believed her father was a good man, and a good king, as well. Buonaparte was the despot, not Father, and as soon as the French could be driven out, the people would rejoice and welcome Father back to his throne. That was the truth, wasn't it?

Wasn't it?

Because of Father—because of her entire family—this woman had wanted her dead, and if the captain had not jumped between them, she would have succeeded. Isabella had never seen anyone risk their own life for hers, and the responsibility of it scared her, too. What if the captain had been hurt or even killed trying to save her, simply because she'd insisted on being unwise?

Yet when he came to her now, she saw only concern for her welfare in his face: no reproach, none of the blame that she knew she deserved.

"You are unharmed, ma'am?" he asked her in a gruff whisper. He still spoke in Italian, for her, and that small thoughtfulness was nearly enough to make her weep. "You'll be safe enough from her now, you know."

"Oh, Captain my lord, I am so sorry this has happened!" Mrs. Copperthwaite was flushed and distraught, seeing a scandal that could destroy her business. "How was I to know the creature was mad? She has not been a fortnight in my employ, and I only took her in from pity, and because her stitching was so fine, but now—now the only place fit for her will be the gaol!"

"The woman must be tried under your English law." Isabella spoke again in English. She knew she must be strong and calm, a Fortunaro lioness, and not let anyone see the terror that still hammered in her chest. "Then I am sure she will receive the punishment she deserves."

"You show great character and courage, miss." Mrs. Copperthwaite's smile had a desperate edge. "No wonder Captain his Lord Greaves counts you among his acquaintance, miss."

The seamstress twisted again in the footmen's grasp, just enough so she could spit at Isabella's feet.

"Ha, she is no *miss!*" she shouted in English, making sure everyone would hear. "You do not know who she is? You do not *know?*"

"Quiet," ordered the captain sharply. "You've said enough."

But the woman only laughed, even as the two men that held her half dragged her toward the door.

"She is the only daughter of the villainous royal oppressor of the Monteverdian people!" she shouted over her shoulder. "She is the Princess Isabella di Fortunaro, may she burn forever in the hottest flames of hell!"

Chapter Four

Mrs. Copperthwaite gasped, audible to all in the suddenly silent shop. It was equally evident that she was reappraising the princess, trying to shift her opinion of the young woman's flamboyant dress from that of a gaudy actress or mistress to exotic, eccentric royalty.

"Is this—is this so?" she asked tentatively. "Are you truly—"

"Yes," the princess said softly, her voice scarcely more than a whisper. "I am."

"Oh, my goodness." Mrs. Copperthwaite's hand fluttered over her chest. "Oh, Your Royal Highness, forgive me!"

She sank into a deep curtsy before the princess, her head bowed and meek. One by one, all the other women in the room followed, graceful dips of crushing pale linen and silk.

It was like nothing Tom had ever witnessed, a scene better suited for the boards at Covent Garden than a Bond Street milliner's: a melodramatic capture, the princess's true identity revealed by her would-be assassin, and then in unison every person in the whole wretched shop dropped in an awestruck curtsy. The princess herself couldn't have choreographed it for more self-centered grandeur.

And yet Tom saw at once that she wasn't enjoying the spectacle at all. Although he'd easily thwarted her attacker, the surprise and shock had shaken the princess in ways he hadn't expected. She wasn't accustomed to real danger like that he'd encountered all his life, and it showed. She'd turned uncharacteristically silent, for one thing, and inside the black brim of her bonnet her face had gone as white as bleached linen, her dark eyes enormous with fear and her mouth pinched. All of her imperious mannerisms had fled, and what was left made her seem very young and very, very vulnerable. She'd stopped being the grand royal Monte-verdian princess, and become like any other young woman abruptly confronted with her own mortality.

Thomas held his elbow out for her to take, and when she didn't, he gently captured her little gloved hand himself and tucked it into the crook of his arm. Following his orders, he had wanted to remove her from the store before anyone learned she was a princess. Now, with that secret gone, he realized how much more important it was for the woman herself that he extricate her from this situation as soon as he could.

"Shall we leave now, ma'am?" he asked. "The carriage is just outside."

She nodded, and took a shuddering breath as she turned toward Mrs. Copperthwaite. "You may rise. No such ceremony is necessary."

"Oh, but it is, ma'am!" The older woman straightened, her eager smile proof of how much she wished to gain a royal customer. "It's not every day we have a great lady of your rank honor us with your custom. What pleases you, ma'am? What might I fetch to show you?"

"Another time, perhaps. I find I am no longer in the humor for such diversions." She raised her chin, a bit of her customary demeanor returning. "Captain, I am ready."

"Good day, Mrs. Copperthwaite." Tom bowed solemnly, then led the princess from the store to the carriage. She managed her exit with a sweeping grace, her free arm angled from her body to show off the drape of her shawl, but only he was aware of how heavily she was leaning on his arm for support.

"You were brave, ma'am," he said as the carriage drew away from the pavement. "That wasn't easy for you, I'm sure. You did well."

"I did not." Unhappily she slumped back against the squabs. "I wasn't brave. I was unwise. You said so yourself."

"That was before, ma'am."

"Saints in heaven, such a mortal difference." She sighed and pulled off her bonnet, letting it drop onto the seat beside her. Even in the warm carriage, the color had not returned to her cheeks, leaving her with a drained, forlorn pallor. She leaned her head back and closed her eyes. "I do not wish to speak of this morning again, Captain."

"I am sorry, ma'am, but you must." Though he was trying to be kind, there were simply too many unanswered questions about this morning to pretend it hadn't happened. "You can't pretend this didn't happen. I will send for a surgeon to attend you once we return to the house if that will—"

"I told you, Captain, I am not fragile, and I do not require any of your surgeons' attendings." She sighed again, wincing as she rubbed her palms together. "Now I wish quiet to contemplate."

Thomas frowned. The princess did not strike him as a contemplative woman by nature, but if that would help her recover, he could scarcely object.

"Very well, then," he said softly. "We shall speak later."

"Later," she mumbled, her eyes squeezed shut. "Not now."

Tom suspected she was only pretending to sleep, just as she was pretending to contemplate, but he would grant her that, too. He could use a bit of contemplation himself. Although he had already realized that nothing concerned with the princess would be easy sailing, even so he couldn't have predicted the disaster they'd found in that infernal ladies' shop.

What incredible odds had placed the Monteverdian seamstress in Copperthwaite's? Monteverde was a tiny country. There couldn't be that many refugees making their way to England, let alone living and working at a skilled trade in London while they plotted revenge against their former king. How much more were those odds compounded by the preposterous coincidence of the princess impulsively stumbling from the carriage into that particular shop at that particular time? Not even the most confirmed gamblers at White's could have predicted such a sequence.

And now it would be up to Tom to guess what would happen next, with the princess herself as the stakes.

He watched her as she slept, or contemplated, or whatever it was she was doing to escape his questions. Though her face was at ease, there was a fresh wariness clouding it that hadn't been there earlier, and he was sorry that he hadn't been able to spare her that change. The admiral hadn't told him much of her history, or even the details of how she'd escaped the French to come to England. He didn't know what had become of her family. War was never a good place for a young woman, and he wondered grimly how many other things she'd witnessed or experienced that she wished never again to discuss.

And he'd meant it when he'd called her brave. When the woman had come at her with the scissors, she hadn't fainted or screamed or tossed her petticoats over her face, the way too many young ladies would. Perhaps that kind of nonsense was bred out of princesses. True, he'd known no others for comparison. But this princess had stood her ground, with a rare courage and grace that he could understand and respect.

He studied her now, her dark lashes feathered over the curve of her cheeks. Her breathing was deep, making her mostly bare breasts rise and fall above the low neckline of her gown, and with an honorable effort he forced himself to look back to her face. She wasn't priggish or overly modest, he'd grant her that. Earlier he'd judged her handsome at best, not pretty, but the more time he spent in her company, the more his opinion was changing. She *was* pretty. Too pretty, if he were honest, and he shook his head as he considered all the trouble such thoughts could bring him.

Her eyes fluttered open, and she stretched her arms before her, relishing the motion like a waking cat. "We have reached the Willoughbys' house, Captain, have we not?"

He hadn't even noticed the carriage had stopped. "Ah, it seems we have." He leaned from the window, swiftly scanning the front of the house and down each side of the street. "Here, let me help you down."

But she drew back, her chin down and her arms folded over her chest. "I should prefer you to go first, Captain. To make sure that all is as it should be."

He nodded, understanding, and privately pleased that she'd put her trust in him. Once more he scanned the quiet square, then held his hand out to her.

"All's snug, ma'am," he said gallantly. "Come ashore whenever you're ready."

But instead of taking his hand, she slipped past him unassisted, dangling her bonnet from her wrist by the ribbons. She hurried up the steps by herself, leaving him once again feeling chagrined and in the uncomfortable position, for any captain, of following instead of leading.

Perhaps, he thought, they'd not made such progress, after all.

"How was your drive, ma'am?" Lady Willoughby was asking as the princess handed her hat to a maid. "Was it pleasant?"

"'Pleasant' is not the word I should choose." The princess paused before the looking glass, patting and plucking at her hair where the bonnet had flattened it. "Unless, of course, your English definition of pleasure is to be beset by murderous anarchists. Isn't that so, Captain Greaves?"

"We did have our adventure, Lady Willoughby," Tom said. The countess looked bewildered, yet also clearly relieved that she was no longer the one responsible for the princess's "adventures." "But no real harm was done, as you can see. You are certain about not summoning a physician, ma'am?"

"No, no, *no.*" The princess frowned at his reflection behind hers, clearly displeased that he'd been considerate enough to ask again. "You will come with me now to the garden, Captain."

She was leading again, and again he was left to follow, this time down the hallway through the house, and he did not like it. He did not like it at all. "Where in blazes are you going now?"

She stopped and turned to face him. "I am going to the garden, Captain," she explained with the kind of excruciating patience reserved for small, simple children. "You are joining me. There we shall speak to one another. Then when we are done, we shall leave."

She glanced past him, back to the hovering maidservant. "I want a pot of chocolate brought to me in the garden, a plate of toast, browned on one side only and the crusts cut away, and a small pot of orange marmalade. I will also require a basin of cooled water—cooled, mind, and not cold, or warm, or scalding, or I shall send it back—and a linen cloth for drying."

So the old princess had returned, ready to demand the sun and the stars, and expecting to get there, too.

Not that he was above giving orders himself. "Another place, ma'am. Not the garden."

She stopped again, so abruptly they nearly collided. "The garden is safe. The admiral said it was. There are tall brick walls on three sides, and the house on the fourth has the only entrance."

"I've had men on my crews who could scale a twelve-foot wall like cats," he said. "They'd be over a garden wall in less time than it takes to say it."

"Ohh." Her bravado faltered as her face fell, and again

he glimpsed the princess from the carriage. "I have sat there for weeks and weeks, not knowing. Now, however, I see that such a place would not be—would not be wise."

"No, ma'am." He didn't elaborate, and he didn't have to. "Surely there's another room in this house, a parlor or library."

She nodded, and turned the knob on the nearest door. "This is the earl's library." She went to stand in the center of the room, before the empty fireplace. "You must understand, Captain, that I have not been here before. So many books depress me. Do you care to read, Captain?"

The room was little used and gloomy, with the louvered shutters over the windows closed tight against the sun's damage to the bindings. There'd be little threat to her in here, that was certain.

"I do," he said. "On blockade duty, or a tedious voyage with foul weather, a book is often my best companion at sea."

"I have never found the patience for reading." Even now she was pacing, short steps that crossed and recrossed the patterned carpet. "I haven't the concentration. But that is not what we must discuss, is it?"

"Why don't you sit?" He held a silk-covered armchair for her. "I don't intend this to be a trial for you, you know, and I—"

"My father is a good king." Her words were coming out in a rush, as restless as her pacing. "He is fair, and just, and *good*. I do not know why that—that woman would say otherwise, because it is not true. You must understand that, Captain. You *must*."

"I put no weight in what she said, ma'am." He was careful of what he said, too. He knew little about her father either as a king or a man, but since a country takes its character from its leader, Tom had his doubts about the King of Monteverde, no matter how his daughter pleaded for him. "Every country has its malcontents, and always has. It's the French and Buonaparte that's made them bold now."

"I thank you for your understanding, Captain." She bowed her head and spread her fingers in a graceful fan of acknowledgment. It wasn't hard to imagine her at home in a court's ritual formality, just as he could easily picture her in the thick of that same court's self-indulgence and flirtation. What was difficult was seeing her so sadly out of place here in London, a bright exotic bird trapped among the dry leather spines of the earl's library. "And I thank you also for saving me as you did. I thank you with all my soul and my heart."

He cleared his throat, uneasy with such lavish gratitude. "I was but following my orders, ma'am."

The wariness remained in her manner, but there was a dare there, too. "You could have followed them without risking your own life. It was all so very fast, you know. No one there would have faulted you. To have seen me die would have likely pleased them more, to see if my foreign blood was as red as this velvet."

"Don't jest like that," he said sharply. "I'd no intention of letting you be murdered."

"No?" She stopped pacing and looked directly into his eyes, though he could not tell if she were teasing, or taunting, or simply seeking the truth. "You would have been free of the nuisance of me, Captain. Has that no appeal for you?"

"None," he said firmly. "Not only did my orders oblige me, but my conscience, as well. And no more of this talk from you, mind?"

Her smile spread slowly, lighting her eyes as she turned her face up to his. He'd never expected her to be shy, but that was there, too, an unmistakable undercurrent to the vulnerability he'd glimpsed earlier.

"You did not have to save my life, yet you did," she said, her voice low and breathless. "I did not have to thank you, but I did. Is it such a marvel that I trust you, Captain, like no other in this whole English country?"

She was so close to him that her scent, orange blossoms and musk and female, filled his nose, so close that he could see the flecks of gold in her dark eyes, so close he could not miss the sheen of excitement on the twin curves of her breasts, there in the caress of red velvet.

It occurred to him that she expected him to kiss her. It also occurred to him that as much as he would like to oblige her—damnation, as much as he'd like to oblige *himself*—to do so would be purest madness, and disaster for his career.

He took a step away, clasping his hands behind his back. That was his habit from walking the quarterdeck, but for now it was also the only sure way he'd keep himself from reaching for what she was offering. Even in a wanton place like Monteverde, there had to be other ways of showing trust.

He cleared his throat again. "I am glad that you trust me, ma'am. That should make it easier for you to answer my questions."

"Your questions." Her cheeks flushing nearly as red as her gown, she ducked her head and turned away from him. "I had not forgotten, Captain."

Damnation, he hadn't intended to shame her, especially when he'd wanted the same thing. Promptly he looked away, too, his own face growing warm, and instead concentrated on a blank-eyed marble bust of Homer that stood on a pillar in the corner.

"There were far too many coincidences this morning for chance alone, ma'am," he began, striving to be all business. "Have you contacted anyone else from Monteverde since you arrived in London? An ambassador, a friend?"

"The ambassador returned home months ago, before I'd left, to guard his estates from the French," she said. "I do not believe Father replaced him. Everything was already too unsettled. And as for friends or acquaintances—I have not a one in London, else I would have gone to them instead of here."

He could not imagine being so entirely adrift in a foreign country. The navy had always been there to support him even if his family and friends had not, and he marveled at the strength this small young woman must possess, forced to depend upon strangers for so much.

"Is there any reason beyond politics that someone would want you dead?" he asked. "Did you bring with you anything of great value? Gold, jewels, paintings?"

She sniffed with indignation. "Lady Willoughby could tell you that. Recall how she and her staff have searched my belongings."

True enough. That search would have served its purpose, even though Tom didn't like the notion of her having so little privacy. If anything of real interest had been discovered, then the admiral would likely have relayed it to him.

"Well, then, another reason. Someone who is jealous of your position or rank, or the fact that you escaped while they were forced to remain?"

"No," she said sadly. "My life has not been so interesting as that. Besides, most Monteverdians would consider my escape a banishment, not something to be envied."

"There is no one?" He hesitated, wishing he did not have to ask this. "No, ah, no fiancé, or lover?"

"By all the saints in heaven, of course I had no lover!" Her indignation was rising to such heights that he half expected to smell smoke where she'd scorched the carpet. "No Monteverdian princess would dare take a lover before she was wed, and before she'd given her royal husband a legitimate heir."

"I understand, ma'am," he said hastily. "You don't have to say more."

"But I do," she insisted, "because you do *not* understand, else you would never have asked. To risk bearing a bastard child of impure blood, to lose all my value as a bride to any respectable royal house, to sully my family's name, to be forced to surrender my dowry—I would not do that, Captain, never. *Never.*"

Oh, hell. Now he'd made a right royal mess, hadn't he?

"I didn't say that you had done any of that, ma'am," he said, wishing desperately for a way to withdraw that particular question. "I was only trying to, ah, to learn if there was anyone else who might wish you harm."

"Harm, ha," she said darkly, and muttered some black, incoherent words in Italian that he was certain must be a curse. "*I* could show you harm, which is what you deserve for that. Because I know exactly what you meant. I may be a virgin, but I am not a fool."

He felt himself flush again, something that had not happened since his voice had cracked at age twelve. But then, he could not recall ever having had any woman, young, old, or in between, speak to him so frankly of her virginity.

No wonder he was feeling mortifyingly out of his depth, and sinking fast.

"I assure you, ma'am, there was no disrespect—"

"No more of your assurances." Suddenly she was standing between him and Homer, her dark eyes full of sparks and a fierce tilt to her chin that had nothing shy about it. She snapped her fingers before him, as if to flick away the word itself. "No *more* of your harms, and your coincidences, and— and no *more* of your ridiculous 'ma'am's,' either. It is the insipid sound a nanny goat makes, and it does not please me."

He frowned down at her. He'd always respected titles and ranks, whether it was a senior officer, or his father the earl, and he wasn't sure why anyone would choose to do otherwise.

"But 'ma'am' is the proper way to address you. Even our own queen is called 'Your Majesty' only for the first greeting, and 'ma'am' after that."

"I am not your queen, am I?" Her frown matched his. "I am different. *You* are different. You are the only Londoner who has spoken to me in my own language, and it seems most barbarously wrong of you not to call me by my given name while we converse."

"Call you by your Christian name?" he asked, incredulous. His experience with ladies might be limited, but he did know that most did not wish to be addressed after a few hours' acquaintance with the same jolly familiarity used with a drinking crony in a tavern. Here he'd been worrying that he'd been too free, yet she was offended instead by his being too formal.

"Yes, yes. It will give me great comfort, and be so much better than the nanny-goat bleat." She nodded with satisfaction, as if everything had been decided. "Whenever we are alone, or speaking Italian as we are now, you will call me Isabella. I give you leave. We will speak as friends, eh?"

How could he possibly refuse her when she'd no other real friends in the entire country? How cruel would it be to turn down such a humble request?

She snapped her fingers again, now less from annoyance than for emphasis. "In turn I shall call you whatever your name might be instead of 'Captain.' You do have another, don't you?"

"It's Thomas," he said reluctantly. "Tom for short. But I'm not certain this is—"

"Thomas," she repeated, testing the sound of the name. "Tom. *Tomaso.* That will do. Ah, here is that lazy maid at last with my chocolate. Set it down there, on that table."

Tomaso: no one had called him that since he'd been a boy traveling the Continent with his family. Yet from her lips it sounded different, a silky, luxuriant ripple that couldn't possibly refer to him.

So how in blazes was he supposed to say her name? "Ma'am" might sound like a goat's bleat to her, but at least it had none of the sinuous, sensuous entrapment of *Isabella.*

He was saved for the moment as the servants entered with her requests, and he watched her dictate to them with appalling precision. The maid must place the silver tray with the chocolate pot and toast here, squared to the edge of the table. The footman must present the basin of water, holding it steady while she dipped one fingertip into the surface to judge the temperature, and then place it before the wicker-backed chaise, with the linen cloth folded in half over the arm.

"I know you judge me to be too picky, Tomaso," she said once the servants left. "Perhaps I am. But there is a proper way for things to be done, and an improper one, as well. If standards aren't kept, why, then, civilization is meaningless, and we should just as well go back to grunting and rooting about naked in the dirt like little piglets."

"Yes, ma'am." The unbidden image of her naked made him forget her request.

"Isabella," she corrected him, fortunately unaware of his true thoughts as she sat on the settee and swung her legs up before her. "You will call me Isabella. Now be an honorable gentleman, and look away while I tend my sorry knees."

But it was already too late for honorable discretion. Without waiting for him to oblige, she'd pulled her skirts up high over her garters and bent over to inspect her bruised, scraped knees.

She winced as she dribbled the cool water over them, then glanced up at Tom through her lashes.

"I told you to look away," she said, wrinkling her nose and mouth at the sting of the cold water. "You are not being honorable."

"Damnation, you have not given me the chance before you go and hike up your skirts!" he sputtered. She was wearing yellow lisle stockings with dark blue garters, the ribbons embroidered with red roses that, unfortunately, matched the scrapes on her knees—pale, plump knees which, scraped or not, were still quite fine to look upon. "What honorable lady would do such a thing, I ask you, let alone ask a gentleman to ignore it?"

She blinked, not at all embarrassed. "But I am not an honorable English lady, Tomaso. I am a princess, and I am entitled to ask whatever I please."

He took a deep breath, making himself once again look at her face, an event that seemed to be happening far too frequently with her.

"Not that, ma'am," he said as firmly as he could. "My orders regard your safety and well-being, not your—your modesty."

"My *modesty*. How very English that sounds!" She grinned, and widened her eyes for emphasis. "Well, then. You have reasoned this better than any periwig judge. Since we are in England, I rescind my order. Look at my sad little knees if you wish, and I shall not protest."

With a groan of frustration he dropped into the chair across from her, wondering if even one of those great admiralty lords had any idea of what he was going through.

"Why the devil aren't you having one of the lady's maids tend to you? What reason could you have for doing this here instead, except to plague me?"

"Because you are the only one who knows how it happened," she said, dabbing at her knees. "I was impulsive and—and *unwise*. Stepping from a carriage without waiting for the step is something a simpleton would do, not a princess. The maidservants in this house whisper about me enough. They do not need to see that I have skinned my knees like a clumsy child. But you—I cannot have such a secret from you, can I?"

He hadn't expected that. "You are fortunate you weren't more badly hurt," he said gruffly. "You could have broken your leg, or worse."

"I'm fortunate in a great many ways, I suppose." She dried her knees and flipped her skirts back down, smoothing them around her ankles for good measure. "I could also have been stabbed with a pair of embroidery scissors which, given my ineptitude at handwork, would have been most ironic."

He frowned grimly. He supposed it was good that she could make light of it, but he could not. "'Ironic' isn't the word I would have chosen."

"It is better than the alternative, yes?" Her smile turned wistful. "What happened today in that shop was not your fault, Tomaso. You couldn't have stopped more than you did. I have lived most of my life with the whole world watching, and I know no other way."

"But I shouldn't have let you go into that infernal shop in the first place."

"That's because you believe the best way to keep me safe is to lock me away, but that won't do for me, not at all."

She smoothed a stray lock of hair behind her ear, her smile turning bittersweet. "On my family's crest are three lions, brave and fierce and ready for any challenge. That is how I am, too, Tomaso. Why else would I have come all this way on my own, away from my family and my home? I would rather face life with a roar than hide and quake with my hands over my eyes. Can't you understand that, Tomaso, even being English?"

He grumbled, but he nodded, because it was the easiest reply, if not the best.

But he understood, all right. He understood that he was becoming more and more tangled in the complicated life of this small, fierce lioness, and there wasn't a blasted thing he could do about it.

* * *

With her legs curled up beneath her, Isabella sat in the center of her bed and listened. She'd always been good at listening, particularly like this in the dark. There were a great many things that could be learned that way, stray bits and scraps of interesting information that others tossed away without a thought, information that could prove most useful.

Consider all she'd learned of Lord and Lady Willoughby and their establishment in the few short weeks that she'd been their guest. Simply by listening, she'd learned that the earl stayed downstairs drinking long after the countess had retired, and that when he finally came upstairs—his footsteps unsteady, muttering to himself—he'd go not to his wife's bed, or even his own, but up another flight of stairs to the servants' rooms, where he'd make the kitchen maid's iron bedstead squeak off and on all night.

Isabella herself did not care about the earl's proclivities. She'd certainly overheard worse things in her parents' palace. The earl was a man, and a lord; he could do what he pleased. But because all the other servants seemed to know, too, the house was closed for the night far earlier than was fashionable, the fires banked, the candles doused, and everyone in their beds. But for Isabella, the moment she heard the earl's footsteps meant the moment she knew she'd be undisturbed. Until morning, there'd be no more servants knocking at Isabella's door, no more invented reasons for the countess to come chirping into her rooms, hoping to discover who knew what. Locking her bedchamber door was useless, for the countess held the keys to all the rooms in the house, and had no reluctance to use them.

So in the dark Isabella listened, straining her ears, and smiled when she finally heard those last footsteps of the day. The door upstairs opened and shut, and Isabella hopped off her bed. Barefoot, so she'd make as little noise as possible, she lifted the chair from her dressing table to the top of the trunk at the end of her bed. Then she climbed up first onto the trunk and then the chair, steadying herself with one hand around the bedpost. Her heart was racing with excited dread, and she had to remind herself to take care, and not fall again as she had earlier.

Now she could see over the top carved wooden frame that supported the bed's curtains. The bottom of the frame was lined with the same brocade as the curtain, gathered into a showy sunburst over the mattress, but the top, here where no one would ever see, was covered by a stitched piece of coarse muslin, tacked into place only in the corners. Using a butter knife that she'd kept from her breakfast tray for the purpose, Isabella pried the tacks free, slowly peeled back the muslin and sighed with relief.

There, sandwiched between the lining and the muslin, lay the quilted linen petticoat of her traveling clothes, the skirts spread out in a fan so the outline wouldn't show from below. Gently she touched the petticoat, reassuring herself that it hadn't been touched, and again whispered thanks to her mother for suggesting such a clever hiding place. No one, certainly not foolish Lady Willoughby, would ever think to look here.

Lightly she traced one quilted channel, her fingers following the lumpy outlines of the treasure stitched within for safekeeping. Scores of gold coins, each stamped with the Fortunaro lions, were only the beginning. The real prize was the oval rubies, big as pigeon's eggs and set in hammered gold, that had been in her family since the first Fortunaro had stolen them from the Caesars in Rome and made them the centerpiece of the crown jewels, a symbol of everything grand in her country.

On the voyage to England, the sheer weight of the petticoat and its hidden treasure had been a constant burden to Isabella, but that was nothing compared to the responsibility that had pressed upon her every minute since she'd left Monteverde. Not even her father the king had known she had the jewels, and Mama had made her swear terrible oaths never to tell another.

Isabella's fingers stilled over the largest ruby, the one etched with the Fortunaro lion. Captain Lord Thomas Greaves had asked her if she'd anything that someone would kill her for. She hadn't answered him honestly about that, nor had she told him how she'd seen the little triangle made of twigs around the woman's neck. She couldn't, not without raising too many other questions she'd no wish to answer. But he'd listened to her, anyway, and the readiness with which he'd accepted her evasion had saddened her no end.

How could it not? He was appallingly masculine in a rough English way, and if she were a sleek Italian lioness, then he was surely the model for the blustery wild lion that stood behind the British throne. No wonder she'd been drawn to him the moment she'd entered the drawing room, and no wonder, too, that she'd wanted to kiss him this afternoon, a giddy, foolish impulse that she'd regretted at once.

Flirtation was not why she'd been sent on this journey. She was not here to amuse herself with the man assigned to watch over her, no matter how broad his shoulders might be, or that he alone in London had made the effort to speak her language. In the long, long lineage of the Fortunaro, she was an insignificant nothing, except for what she might do now for her family's honor.

As if to remind herself, she touched the jewels one last time before she pulled the muslin back in place and pressed the tacks back into the corners with her thumbs. But instead of climbing down to the floor, she slumped wearily on the chair, her hands resting on her bruised knees and her bare legs dangling over the chest.

She liked Tom Greaves, and she trusted him, and if they'd been born any other two people in this world, then that would have been plenty. But not only were those rubies hidden in the canopy reason for someone to pursue her; for a Monteverdian princess, they were also reason to die.

With a little sob, Isabella buried her face in her hands, and gave in to the unfairness that had become her life.

Chapter Five

Tom walked down the empty street toward the river, wanting no other company than his own. He'd given up trying to sleep any longer in his unfamiliar bed in Lady Willoughby's guest room, and had set out from the silent house when the skies were still dark, or at least as dark as they ever were in London. Now the first light of dawn was pinking the horizon, and heavy-eyed linkboys were going from light to light, dousing the night's flames for the coming day.

The early morning was chill, damp with dew that had fallen like a silvery haze over the dark wool of Tom's uniform coat, and his breath showed before his face. Yet still he walked on, lengthening his stride in the foolish hope that exercise alone would be enough to ease his restlessness.

The princess had been in his life for barely a day, and she already threatened to overwhelm it, and him. He'd always thought of himself as a strong, honorable man, proud to do what was right yet able to do what was necessary. Not even the surgeon's grim predictions had been able to change that.

But in a single day, the princess had managed to shake all his careful notions of what was right. There was much of her that *wasn't* right, not at all: she was illogical and demanding and impetuous. Yet she'd also shown herself to be brave and clever and far, far too charming for any male's peace of mind. The worst trial for Tom was that for the life of him, he couldn't begin to predict which side of herself she'd decide to show next. The only certainty seemed to be that she'd do exactly as she pleased, with no concern for the outcome.

That, and that she was his responsibility.

Damn. Damn, damn, *damn.*

When it had only been a matter of grabbing the seamstress with the scissors, he'd acted from instinct and training. That had been easy. If guarding her were no more challenging than that, he'd be sleeping peacefully now, not stalking about London like a lunatic.

But what in blazes was he supposed to do when she turned her face up to be kissed? How was an officer of the king to respond when she'd lifted her skirts and dared him to look at her knees? Exactly where in those infernal orders did it tell him when he was allowed to be a man first, and an officer second?

He didn't realize how loudly he was grumbling to himself until he saw the stray dog skitter out of his path, tail between his legs and the fur bristling on his neck. Wonderful. Next he'd cause small children to weep and their mothers to faint.

At least he'd reached the Thames. The river was hardly the sea, but to Tom any water was a better vista than another brick wall. He always liked this time of day at sea, too, when the water was just beginning to come to life. The dawn's pale light dappled the surface, and boats of every size and shape were already cutting across the water, carrying geese to the market, bales of tea from the East India men, a party of drooping revelers bound for their beds and a solitary navy officer being rowed in his ship's gig to the steep steps of the offices at Whitehall. This last made Tom sigh with frustration, and stare longingly down the river to where the oceangoing ships were moored.

Someday one of those ships would be his again. Someday he'd have another command, a ship and crew and a gig of his own.

Someday, that is, if the Princess di Fortunaro weren't the death of him first.

With one last muttered oath, Tom pushed open the heavy door of the Anchor, a coffeehouse that catered to navy officers from the nearby Admiralty offices. It was early here, too, but the Anchor kept seagoing hours, even marking the time for its patrons in watches rather than landsmen's hours and minutes.

He breathed deeply of the welcoming scents of roasting coffee beans and steaming chocolate, mingled with the richer tang of frying bacon from the kitchen. Even so, the room was still nearly empty. Tom liked it that way, especially in his present mood. He took a place at a table near the window, one with the day's first newspapers waiting in a neat pile for customers, and set his hat on the table beside it. A boy brought him an earthenware mug of coffee, and resolutely Tom reached for the topmost paper, determined to find first the news that he dreaded the most.

He didn't have far to look. Directly after the war reports from the Continent and a debate in the House came the story that most of London would devour with their tea and eggs.

The list of beautiful & noble refugees to our shores has acquired a new & most notable addition, viz. Her Royal Highness Isabella, Princess di Fortunaro of the Kingdom of Monteverde. Though the princess is said to have resided in Berkeley Square for several weeks, a guest of the Countess of Vaughn, only yesterday did she boldly venture forth to explore the amusements of the highest *ton*. She is in truth an original beauty of rare style & rich elegance, her ancient blood granting her regal carriage & distinction.

Alas, her first outing in our fair city was marred by an attack against her person by one of the tyrant Buonaparte's handmaidens, one Maria Corelli by name. Only the courage & agility of Captain Lord Thomas Greaves, son of the Earl of Lechmere and already an honored HERO in the service of his country, saved the princess from certain death & tragedy. While others could but quake with terror, the captain, at great risk to his own person, intercepted the villainess, & disarmed her before any violence was wrought. Though faint with terror, the princess was most gracious in her gratitude.

We can only pray that the Captain will continue to attend her & guard her, and offer to us the instructive & pleasurable image of BEAUTY & BRAVERY joined together.

Rubbish, all of it. The princess hadn't been "boldly venturing forth" into that shop, unless those were the words that news scribblers preferred to "tripping" or "falling."

He'd agree that she was an original beauty, though even he knew that was a backhanded way of complimenting a lady whose appearance fell outside conventional tastes, but who was also too well-born or powerful to insult.

But this nonsense about him being a hero, and gallantly saving her from death and tragedy, and uniting beauty and bravery—well, that was about the most stupid cock and bull he'd ever read, and with another oath of disgust he turned to the next paper.

This one was worse. Here he'd "laid down his life to save the swooning princess." He'd done no laying, and she'd done no swooning. In fact, when he recalled how hard the princess had fought him in the carriage, she probably could have dispensed with the seamstress herself, without any assistance from him.

The third paper turned Mrs. Copperthwaite's shop into a scene of Shakespearean carnage, with wounded footmen spurting blood, screaming women, and the Brave Heroic Captain wrestling the Foreign Villainess to the floor before the woman stabbed herself fatally through Her Very Heart.

But despite how far-fetched these stories were, each one contained the same troubling truths. They announced the princess's arrival in London. They told the world exactly where she was staying. They made her sound wealthy. And they announced to every vainglorious or violent dimwit in London that the surest path to seeing his or her name in the papers was to attack the Princess di Fortunaro.

"Ah, Greaves, I didn't expect to find you here!" Without waiting for an invitation, Admiral Cranford settled himself into the chair beside Tom's. He waved at the newspapers, his wide, ruddy face beaming. "Reading about your glorious escapades, are you? Didn't I say you were the proper man for this assignment?"

But Tom wasn't beaming in return. "Forgive me, sir, but I do not see the glory in this. If I had done my duty, I would never have let the princess go into that wretched shop in the first place."

"You cannot keep her a prisoner, Greaves." Cranford shook his head. "If we'd wanted that for her, we would have locked her away ourselves. No, no. I thought I'd made that clear before. It is important for her to be seen about the city. Your role is to show her off, and to be there if she needs you, just as you did yesterday at that dressmaker's shop."

"But if she hadn't—"

"Not a word more, Greaves. You're doing splendidly, and that's an end to it. The other lords at the admiralty are most pleased, too, you know." He tapped the pile of papers. "This is priceless for our cause. You and I both know that a cutting-out mission on the French coast smokes this for danger and risk, but this kind of adventure is what the public wants to read, and it makes the whole service shine in their eyes. A bona fide hero saves a pretty princess—it might as well be one of those ladies' storybooks, eh?"

Not to Tom, it didn't, not by half. "What of the princess? I thought her welfare was to be my first concern."

"The princess?" The admiral seemed surprised Tom had asked. "Was she in fact injured yesterday? Your message said she was unharmed, and certainly these reports—"

"She's as well as any lady can be, under the circumstances," Tom said. "But what of the next time? Every lunatic hothead with a grudge will make her a target after this, yet I am to continue to put her in peril."

"Not in peril, man." Cranford drummed his fingers impatiently. "Don't play the doomsayer. As long as she has you to watch over her, she's not in peril."

"One man against an entire city?"

"One British navy captain!"

"One man," Tom said softly. If he'd learned anything from his last wounds, it was a regard for his own mortality. "She told me her belongings had been searched by Lady Willoughby's staff."

"By my orders." The admiral nodded, waving to the boy to bring him a mug of his own. "A minor precaution for my sister's well-being."

"No doubt." Tom leaned forward, lowering his voice though no one else was within hearing. "Was anything of special interest found? Any keys to dangerous acquaintances here in London, or jewels of great value that would put her at higher risk?"

"Nothing of the sort at all," Cranford said. "Except for her gaudy tastes in dress, everything was exactly as to be expected for a young lady of her rank. As for acquaintances, there are none, at least none that have been found."

"What of her family?"

The admiral snorted with disdain. "She's had nary a peep from that sorry bunch of rascals. For all we know, Buonaparte's men may have used them for shooting practice, and the princess is the last ignoble Fortunaro left on this earth. Which is why, Greaves, I don't want to hear another word about her being in any danger that you cannot navigate, else I'll begin to doubt your capabilities."

"No, sir," Tom answered curtly. There was no other acceptable answer to that, even if Tom did doubt himself. He had to continue to keep those admiralty lords happy and pleased, or else he'd never set foot aboard his own command again.

Yet he still couldn't help but feel sorry for the princess. It was bad enough to be cast adrift in a strange country, but how much worse not to know if your family still lived, or if you were the last and only survivor.

"Good." The admiral relaxed and sipped at the coffee the boy had brought him. "Now that all the lady-hostesses will read about the princess, I'll wager she'll be flooded with invitations, especially at this time of year."

"The only one she cares for would come from His Majesty."

The admiral shook his head. "Not likely, not likely. It's not the princess herself, you understand, but His Majesty's advisors must choose his alliances and public favors with care."

"Surely asking her to tea by way of welcome wouldn't unsettle the rest of his allies?"

"Ah, but it could," the admiral countered. "A Monteverdian princess is entertained at the palace, and suddenly the ambassadors from Parma and Naples and Rome are up in arms, threatening this and that like some damned Punch and Judy play. It's a tangle."

With reluctance Tom could understand, but he doubted the princess would. To her, King George and the rest of the Hanovers were family, albeit remote cousins, and she'd be bound to take his silence as a personal slight. Tom couldn't blame her, either.

"But mark this, Greaves," Cranford said, hurrying to leave that subject behind. "I've heard Lady Allen's giving some sort of ball tomorrow night. That would be a splendid place to show the princess to good advantage. She'd take to that, wouldn't she?"

"Lady Allen, sir?" Tom couldn't keep the dismay from his voice. Even as removed as he was from the fashionable *ton,* Tom had heard of the Duchess of Avery's entertainments, exclusive, infamous affairs notorious both for the excessive wine and gaming in the house and the seductions in the garden outside, parties that often could last clear through the night and almost until noon of the following day. "I'm not certain that would be the best introduction to London for the princess, sir."

"I can think of none better." The admiral's smile turned into almost a leer. "And London, be assured, will thank you for it. You forget that the lady was raised in the Monteverdian court, Greaves. I'd lay you a guinea she could teach even Lady Allen herself a few new tricks, eh?"

Abruptly Tom rose. It wasn't that he didn't believe what the admiral was saying about the princess—given her manner, it was impossible not to—but that still didn't make Tom want to sit here and listen to it.

Damnation, when she'd turned that little chin up toward him and smiled with her lips apart—she'd done that for him, hadn't she? She said she'd trusted him like no other, because he'd saved her life, because she liked him. She'd *said* that. She wouldn't go and look that way at another man for no reason, would she?

Would she?

And why the devil should he care?

"Forgive me, sir, but I should take my leave," he said, tossing a few coins to the boy for his coffee. "They will be expecting me at the house."

"Ah, my sister never rises before noon, and I doubt the princess will, either." The admiral narrowed one eye, watching him closely. "Don't make an ass of yourself over this woman, Greaves. Stay your course. Think of her as a troublesome convoy you must see from one port to the next, and nothing more."

Tom nodded, eager to be done with this conversation, and squared his cocked hat on his head. He wasn't making an ass of himself over the princess; he was following his orders.

But there was only one suitable reply to a superior's advice, and Tom made it. "Thank you, sir."

The admiral coughed irritably, recognizing Tom's haste for what it was.

"I mean what I say, Greaves. I've given you a great plum of an assignment. Don't let it spoil and rot in your keeping. Now good day, sir, and shove off, before I give you a good kick myself."

A plum or a kick, thought Tom grimly as he plunged back into the street. Accepting a challenge, or turning away from it. The kiss of a beautiful princess, and the promise of another ship just out of his reach, or rotten fruit lying on the ground at his feet.

Damn, damn, *damn.*

"Here he is at last!"

Isabella kneeled on the window seat and threw the sash open. She shoved aside the curtains and leaned forward, leaning her elbows on the sill.

"Captain Greaves!" she shouted and waved, striving to get his attention. He was still across the street, crossing the square, but she'd recognize him anywhere. So why didn't he look up to *her?*

She cupped her hand around her mouth and raised her voice, her long braid falling over her shoulder as she leaned farther out the window. "Captain Greaves, here! Here, in the window! Look up at me!"

He stopped and looked up, exactly as she bade him, his handsome face so full of concern that she caught her breath. "Hurry, Captain, hurry! I need you here at once!"

"Hold there now, Princess," he shouted back. "I'll be there directly."

He jammed his hat more tightly on his head and came running across the street.

"Oh, ma'am, he won't like that." The countess shook her head, struggling unsuccessfully to hide a yawn behind the sleeve of her dressing gown "No gentleman likes to be summoned like that."

"He doesn't have to like it." Isabella slipped from the window seat and hurried across to the looking glass, her nightgown fluttering around her bare ankles. "He only needed to come now, as I asked."

"But when he learns the reason, ma'am, why—"

"Why, when he learns it, he shall understand completely." Isabella glanced at the invitation that she'd already tucked into the corner of the looking glass's frame. "He has agreed to guide me in everything while I am in London, and I require his guidance in this matter."

"His guidance for choosing which gown to wear to a ball, ma'am?" Pointedly the countess glanced at the two elaborately embroidered gowns, brought with her from Monteverde, laid across the bed. "Forgive me, ma'am, but

I do not believe the captain will see such a task as part of his duties to you."

"He will, because I wish it so." There was more to it than the gowns, of course, not that she'd ever confess it to a ninny like whining Lady Willoughby. But when Isabella had awakened early, before the sun was even in the sky, her first thought had been of Tom, which had surprised her no end. She'd slept better knowing he was under the same roof. She'd wanted to see him at once, to tell him so; no, she'd *needed* to see him.

Yet when she'd summoned him, the sleepy, shamefaced servant could only tell her that Captain Lord Greaves had gone out, leaving no word of his expected return. At once Isabella had panicked, and hurled her hairbrush at the unfortunate messenger as he'd fled. Alone in her bedchamber, her agitation had mushroomed, anxiety twisting in her chest.

Tom Greaves was the only one in London who cared for her, who understood her. After what had happened at the shop, she'd never feel safe without him beside her. She'd been regarding him as her hero, but now that she thought of it, other people had been calling him that even before yesterday. She didn't really know much about him at all, because, being a princess, it hadn't even occurred to her to inquire. She just *assumed* he'd always be there.

What if she'd driven him away, and back to whoever else had claimed him as a hero first? He'd praised her for being brave, and she'd treasured the compliment, but he'd also told her she was spoiled and rude. What if for him the rudeness had outweighed the bravery, and he'd decided never to return? One moment she resolved to reform, the way he wanted, if he'd only come back; then she'd vow to tell him exactly what she thought of his own ill manners, and throw another hairbrush at him to make her point.

The countess herself had come to try to calm Isabella, bringing the newly delivered invitation from the Duchess of Avery to distract her. But as pleased as Isabella had been to be invited to a ball, the pasteboard card had also reminded her again of how much she needed her captain.

And now he was back, her relief so strong she felt almost drunk with it. He hadn't forgotten her; she hadn't driven him away. Quickly she smoothed her hair with her palms and pinched her cheeks to make them rosier. As fast as Tom was running, she wouldn't have time to do much more, but she did want to look as well as she could for him, even at this ridiculously early hour.

She could hear him on the stairs now, racing up two or maybe three steps at a time, and she turned just as the maidservant opened the door for him.

"Princess!" His gaze swept the room, a long-barreled pistol in his hand that made Lady Willoughby shriek faintly. "I came as fast as I could when I saw you. What has happened? Has someone tried to attack you here? To have you calling out the window like that—"

"Oh, that is our way in Monteverde. Because our weather is so pleasant, we all call back and forth from our windows, even in the palace. Though there is seldom a need for a weapon, especially so soon after cock's-crow." She smiled, basking in his concern. She hadn't realized he'd carried a gun to defend her; the notion was almost…*exciting*.

Absently she curled one of the ribbons on the front of her dressing gown around her finger. "I have been invited to a ball tomorrow night," she continued, "given by this

Duchess of Avery, and you shall escort me. That is why I needed you, Captain, to tell me which of these gowns will be more proper for the entertainment of an English duchess."

Slowly he lowered the pistol, his expression incredulous. "There is no intruder? No danger?"

"Oh, no," she said blithely. "It is not a ball at the royal court, to be sure, yet it shall do until my invitation from Queen Charlotte arrives, and—"

"You shouted from the window for me to come simply because you couldn't decide which damned *gown* to wear to a party?"

"Forgive me, Captain my lord, but I tried to tell her she shouldn't do it," Mrs. Willoughby said eagerly. "I warned her you'd be displeased, and that—"

"Lady Willoughby." Tom's voice was sharp, his expression black as thunder, as he uncocked the pistol and shoved it back into his belt. "Would you be so kind as to leave us?"

Though the countess looked stricken, she still bowed meekly and scuttled from the room. The maid fled, too, closing the door after, and leaving Isabella and Tom alone.

But Isabella wasn't fazed by Tom's manner. She understood; she didn't care for Lady Willoughby, either. She glanced back to the two gowns on the bed. "So which shall it be, Tomaso? The green, or the—"

"Cover yourself," he ordered curtly, his focus lowering to her untied dressing gown and the gauzy nightgown beneath. "Be a credit to your rank, if you can. It's enough that you've lured me to your bedchamber. At least you can have the decency not to display yourself in your nightclothes."

Isabella gasped with outrage, her fingers shaking as she

tied the front of her dressing gown more closely. "I have not *lured* you anywhere! I called to you, and you came, as was your duty. And—and it is perfectly acceptable for a lady to converse with a gentleman *en déshabillé,* or it would be if you were a gentleman!"

"Not by your lights, no." She could see now he was angry, maybe even angrier than she was herself, but somehow he was managing to keep his temper, which only infuriated her more. "But I am an English gentleman, ma'am, and in this country we respect our ladies, just as our English ladies in turn show us respect."

"Respect!" Isabella snatched a blue-and-white vase from the nearest table, scattering water and rosebuds as she lifted it over her head. "You are *ordered* to respect me!"

"My orders are to keep you safe from harm," he said, his mouth a tight, grim line. "Do not confuse it for more than that."

But she already had, hadn't she? She'd believed he cared for her, the only one in this whole wretched country who did. Now, because she'd foolishly underestimated his pride, his face was closed against her, all the warmth gone. Now he was saying she'd been wrong, that he'd only done it because he'd been told to, and with a little sob of despair, her fingers tightened around the neck of the vase.

"You throw that," he warned, "and so help me, you shall regret it."

She fell back on the old instincts to protect her. No one could know more about pride—and its consequences—than she did herself. "You would not dare! No one speaks to any Fortunaro like that!"

"Then it's high time I did, ma'am," he said. "Watching

over you is difficult enough without you trying to trip me at every step. I've already exceeded my orders for your sake, yet you insist on treating me like the lowest lackey in your whole infernal palace."

"I do not," she said defensively. She felt pushed into a corner of her own making, trapped by her own ways, and she'd not the faintest idea how to get out. "I do *not!*"

"Aye, you do," he insisted, relentless, "and you're doing it again now. So help me, ma'am, orders or no orders, if you fling that crockery at me, I will walk from that door and never come back."

"No!" she cried, shocked he'd dare her like that. "You would not! You *will* not!"

"Try me, ma'am," he said, folding his arms over his chest. "Every man who's ever sailed with me knows I'm a man of my word, and no matter how you might wish otherwise, I'm not going to change now."

"No one sails with you now," she said bitterly, the vase forgotten in her hand. "You're a sea captain without a ship, and what is more worthless than that?"

"I cannot say, ma'am." His face had become the emotionless mask that military men always hid behind. "Unless it's a princess without a country."

She gasped, for once too shocked to speak. She lowered her hand with the vase, unconsciously hugging it against her chest as if it were an infant. Swiftly she turned away to the window, not wanting him to see the pain he'd caused her. But by speaking the truth, she'd hurt him, too, hadn't she? She'd just never expected that truth—or the hurt—to ricochet back to her.

She stood there, her eyes squeezed shut as she struggled

to control her emotions. He'd only said what she didn't want to accept. He couldn't possibly know the rest: how there'd been no word from anyone in Monteverde since she'd left, not from her mother or father or anyone else. She'd told herself that letters were often lost in times of war, that her mother wouldn't forget her, that she'd be home again before the summer was done, and everything would again be as it once was.

Yet he'd been able to voice her darkest fear, there in a single sentence: that she was the only one left, the only one alive, the only Fortunaro to escape the French.

What if she truly were a princess without a country?

Like a captain without a ship....

She'd said it on impulse, without considering what she said, beyond that it was true. She'd never wondered why a man who had earned such praise from Admiral Cranford didn't have a command, especially with England at war, or why he'd been assigned to watch over her instead. He was still a young man, very much in his prime, yet for some reason he was being kept from the life he'd chosen. He was unhappy, and he was bitter. She'd only to recall how he'd practically spat out those last words at her.

Could he be, in his way, as much a castaway as she was herself?

She swallowed hard, unsure of what to say or ask next to try to mend the rift she'd caused. She'd hardly any experience to guide her. Usually others were trying to win back her favor, not the other way around.

"Everyone says you're a—that you're a hero," she began. She kept facing the window, not wanting to see his face if she said the wrong thing once again. "Even before yesterday they called you that. What did you do to earn that praise?"

He did not answer for what seemed like forever, so long that she wondered forlornly if he had in fact left the room, and she'd simply been too preoccupied with her own thoughts to notice.

"Not even in England would a gentleman be called a hero without grounds," she began again, hoping—if he were there—that he wouldn't notice the desperation in her voice. "Tell me what you did."

She took a big breath for courage, and whispered the most unprincesslike word she knew. "Please."

He made a grumbly sound in his chest, almost as if fighting with himself. But at least she knew he was there, and that he'd stayed. She realized now that most other men would have left even a princess, and she appreciated it. No, she appreciated *him*.

"I'm not a hero," he said at last. "I only did what any good captain would. I acted for the good of my ship and my people, nothing more."

"I do not believe you." She looked down at the vase in her hands, at the damp little ovals of nervousness that her fingers were leaving on the porcelain. "If what you say were so, then every one of your English captains would be heroes, yes?"

"No." He took a deep, restless sigh, and she realized he'd stepped closer to her. "If only because other captains aren't so unfortunate as to have a first lieutenant given to hyperbole and overpraise."

"Please," she said softly, not exactly sure what she was asking for. No one confided in princesses, or confessed, or even told them secrets; princesses were supposed to be beyond the concerns of others. "Please. For me."

"It's a sorry enough tale." He gulped, almost as if he were filling his lungs before plunging into the surf. "I was captain of the frigate *Aspire,* twenty-six guns. We had chased a French sloop, much our superior in size and strength. After a heated engagement and heavy losses by the French, their captain finally decided to spare the lives of his few remaining crew, and surrendered his sword and his ship to me."

"To capture a ship of the enemy is indeed heroic," she said, even though she felt oddly disappointed by his dry, formal telling. "Surely you must agree that such an accomplishment is uncommon, even for an English captain."

"If that were all, then aye, I would agree. But it was that damned fool boy and his damned fool stupidity and—and—oh, *blast.*" He sucked in his breath again, struggling with his emotions. "Forgive me, ma'am, I beg you. I did not mean—"

"Go on," whispered Isabella. "Don't stop. Tell me of the boy."

"The boy—he was a green midshipman, as great a fool as any boy of thirteen can be, and I'd only taken him on the list as a favor to his father. What little sense he'd had was flung away by the fighting, and by finding himself living while his mates had died around him. The French captain handed me his sword, and Caruthers—that's the boy's name, the idiot—Caruthers lost his head and jumped forward with his dirk, and I saw the Frenchman's gun flash, and I knocked Caruthers aside and—and that was all."

"All?" repeated Isabella, the vase clutched so tightly in her hands she marveled that it hadn't shattered. "All?"

"All." His voice was hollow and rough, the earlier emotion gone. "I was meant to die then, Isabella. The surgeons said so, and so did my men. I don't even remember the pain of the shot, or lying on the surgeon's table as he labored to save me. Even the chaplain had given me up for dead, and dead I should have been. Clean, neat, with the pistol's ball in my heart instead of beside it, so that I would—"

"You were *not* meant to die!" she cried, hating the chilly doom of these English words. "You were meant to live, and to come here to London, and to meet me, and—and—oh, Tomaso, you could *not* have died!"

She turned and hurled herself at him in one impetuous motion, letting the vase crash to the floor as she flung her arms around his neck to pull his face down to hers. He grunted with surprise but caught her around the waist, steadying her even as he pulled her close to him. He welcomed her, and he wanted her, and she felt the power of that want sweeping her along with it. His arm was like a band of iron around her waist, her breasts crushing against his chest and the brass buttons of his coat.

And this time, when she longed for him to kiss her, he did.

Chapter Six

Tom had spent most of last night and this morning thinking of what it would be like to kiss Isabella. In all that time, he hadn't come close to getting it right, not by half. The reality of her in his arms was that far beyond his imagining.

She'd caught him by surprise, rushing at him like that, and letting his body act on instinct instead of listening to the rational if feeble warnings of his head. But there was nothing rational about holding Isabella, wearing little more than a few lengths of sheer linen and silk. Her small, round body was soft and yielding, filling his hands with the warmth of her flesh and her skin in a way he'd never thought possible in a woman, or at least not in any of the Englishwomen he'd known. Was there any better way to choose life over death, or to be reminded of the boundless joys of one over the grim finality of the other?

Her long curling hair fell down her back and tickled and teased his wrists, and her orange-blossom scent filled his nose. Somehow she managed to arch against him and curve into him in one sinuous motion, and turned her parted lips up to him with such fervor he'd almost no choice but to kiss her.

No choice, and no will to resist. Her lips were soft and eager, her mouth so wet and hot he could quite happily forget everything else except having her in his arms. Well, not precisely all: his body was reminding him of what else he wanted to do with her, of how her unmade bed was waiting only a few steps away, of how even if she was a princess, she still must want this as much as he did, didn't she?

A princess, aye, but his responsibility first, and a duty that he was shamelessly abusing.

Yet she was the one who finally broke the kiss, leaning back in the crook of his arm. Her eyes were half-closed, her expression dreamy.

"Ahh," she whispered. "That was very nice, Tomaso, even if it was very, very wrong."

"Yes," he croaked, struggling to make his body believe anything that felt so good was wrong. "Yes."

She smiled crookedly, her lips red and swollen from the kiss. "Yes, it was very nice, or yes, it was very, very wrong?"

"Both." He eased her arms from around his neck, gently setting her back down and apart from him. "Forgive me, ma'am, for taking advantage of—"

"Oh, hush, you took nothing that I didn't give," she scolded. "You are already my guardian. I do not need you to be my conscience as well."

"But my own conscience is—"

"Hush," she said again, as soft as a sigh as she covered his mouth with her hand to silence him. "If no one else knows, then it's not wrong, is it?"

Manfully he lifted her hand from his mouth. "I'll know, and I'll know it's wrong."

"And so shall I," she said, wriggling her hand free so she could rest it on his cheek. "That is, we *will* both know it was wrong, and we shall be quite racked with guilt, but we can pretend we don't know it yet. I refuse to know it. Did you guess that you're the first gentleman I've ever kissed?"

He hadn't, not at all, but that guileless confession that he'd been the first to kiss her kept him painfully hard. What the devil else was she not telling him, anyway?

"Ma'am," he said, not able to muster much else whether pretending or otherwise. "Isabella."

"Captain," she said, stretching up to reach his mouth with hers. "Tomaso."

May all the lords of the admiralty forgive him, he was kissing her again, and it was even better this time. She parted her lips freely for him, exploring him as much as he was her. His hands slid down along the silk of her dressing gown, gathering up great bunches of the slippery fabric as he caressed the soft flesh of her hips, pulling her against the hard proof of his own arousal. If this were only her second kiss, then she learned fast, and the heady realization ratcheted his own desire another notch. He slid his hands along the narrowing curve of her waist, inside her dressing gown so there was nothing but the gossamer-weight linen between him and the quivering fullness of her breasts and *this had to stop*.

He released her and forced himself to step back, away from temptation. Her hair was mussed and tousled, her nightclothes askew, her cheeks flushed and her lips still parted, and damnation, he'd never wanted any woman more than he wanted this one whom he'd no right to have.

"Oh, my," she murmured, her breath coming in short, rapid gulps. "That was not pretending, was it?"

"No." The blood was still thumping through his body, demanding to be obeyed. "That's as damned real as it gets."

Her smile was shaky as she purposefully retied the front of her dressing gown. "Next you shall warn me of the ill that can come from playing with fire."

"I could, aye." He clasped his hands behind his waist, and remembered the admiral's warning. He wasn't just playing with fire; he was dancing in the very flames. "What happened to that folderol about keeping yourself pure for a royal husband?"

"I do not know." Her smile turned wistful and unexpectedly shy. "I suppose you made me forget."

"Well, you made me forget, too, Bella, if that's any comfort to you."

"Then that is what I wished," she said. "When you spoke of how you wished to die—I did not like that, just as you did not like to hear me speak of that woman who wished to kill me. I wanted you to understand how much better it is to live."

"By kissing me?" he asked, incredulous. He would have to recommend that to the surgeons at Greenwich, for it certainly had worked. "That is how we've both cheated death?"

"Yes." She tossed back her hair, letting her expression soften with concern as she stepped around the shards of the broken vase. "But is that why you do not have a ship? Because you were wounded?"

"Because of the uncertainty of the wound." How in blazes had they circled back to this? "The surgeons swear the ball is still lodged inside my chest, beside my heart, though I would never know it if they hadn't told me. A hazardous case, they call me."

"I cannot believe it." She frowned, appraising him. "You do not look weak or poorly. You look…fine."

"I am," he said, striking his chest with his fist to prove it, "and I find it difficult to believe myself. But the admiralty listens to the surgeons. They will not entrust another ship and crew to my care, from fear that I could die without warning."

"But how much more likely at sea that you would be washed away and drown, or perish from scurvy, or—or a score of other sudden ways."

"And a princess is far more likely to die from smallpox or consumption than any assassin's knife." He wanted to hold her again, just hold her, to reassure them both about a future that neither could control. "But you were right before. A captain without a ship is a worthless creature."

"A princess without a country is not worth much more," she answered sadly. "What a sorry price we would bring together at the market, wouldn't we?"

Her smile faltered but did not fail. She was strong that way, steel beneath the silk; perhaps all princesses were. With a little shake of her head, she swept her arm toward the two gowns on the bed.

"So which shall it be, Captain? You must help me decide. That is why I summoned you here, you know. The green muslin, or the plum Genoa velvet?"

He didn't give a damn about the gowns, and she knew it. But she'd asked him to pretend, hadn't she? And if she could be brave and pretend that everything was fine and right between them and the rest of the world, then so could he.

"The plum velvet," he said at last. "Wear that tomorrow night with me, and I promise you'll make every other lady in the house vanish."

"Thank you, Captain." Her nod of acknowledgment was regal, part of the pretending, part of being her. "You know you are the only gentleman in London whose word I trust."

He bowed gallantly and smiled, and wished to hell he was worthy of that trust.

The line of carriages waiting outside of Avery House snaked slowly through the nighttime streets, each driver waiting his turn to send his passengers up the steps and into the duchess's party. Candlelight streamed from the windows of the house, like a giant lantern glowing there on the corner.

Her heart racing with anticipation, Isabella leaned forward on the seat to look from the window. Their carriage was nearly at the doorway, and already she could hear laughter and conversation and scraps of music drifting from the open windows. With a muffled mutter of anxiety, she flopped back against the seat, her folded fan clutched tightly in her gloved fingers.

"Oh, Tom, what if I make a fool of myself?" she asked. "I do not know these English people, and they do not know me. They will judge me as peculiar and foreign."

Across from her, Tom smiled. *He* could smile, she thought grudgingly. These people would be *his* people, and they wouldn't whisper behind their hands when he walked into the room, or have any difficulty understanding how he spoke.

"They will judge you to be charming and beautiful,"

he said. "You know they will. But if you do not wish to go on, I can have the driver return us to Berkeley Square, and you—"

"No!" She swallowed her fear, for in her mind there was no question of going back. "I am not a coward, Tom. I must go, and do what I can to promote the welfare of my country."

He shook his head. "I don't know how much of that you'll be able to do here. The Duchess of Avery and her set aren't exactly politically minded. They're what we call fast."

That made Isabella smile in spite of her worries. He could be so wonderfully protective, her Tomaso! "You mean they drink and gamble and become amorous, the gentlemen and ladies both."

"In so many words, aye." He leaned forward, his expression endearingly English. "I'll keep close to you tonight, Bella. I won't ever be far, if you ever feel out of your depth, or if some blade becomes too, ah, too amorous for your tastes."

"What if this blade becomes too amorous for *your* tastes?" she asked, unable to resist. "Will you run him through with your sword, or must I ask you first?"

"I'd rather not," he said sternly, "though I'll do what I must."

"I believe you," she said, and she did. He was wearing his full dress uniform—the very model of a brave English warrior!—complete with glittering gold epaulets and medals on his breast, and a presentation sword with a brilliant-studded hilt as a gift from the thankful merchants whose ships he'd saved from French privateers. His dark blue superfine coat had been tailored to display his broad shoulders to best advantage, while the snowy linen of his shirt made his face look more weathered and manly by comparison. He was the perfect image of a hero, and she thought again about how he had risked his life to save the boy on his ship, and then done the same for her. If he was concerned about amorous blades paying too much attention to her, then she was equally worried about these amorous ladies, once they spotted *him*.

"I am serious, Bella," he said, and she believed that, too. "I don't know what kind of mischief we'll find in this house, but together we'll face it. Trust me. That's all I'll ask of you. Don't try to cross me, or set me upon another course, or show me false colors for your own amusement. Just trust me tonight, and all will be well."

She liked this notion of facing mischief together, as if he might actually need her assistance, and she liked the way he'd taken to calling her Bella, without any orders or prompting from her.

But the trust he expected from her—that was more difficult. In some ways, she could and would trust him with her life, but there were other confidences that she'd never be able to share, no matter how much she longed to, and with a shiver she thought again of the jewels hidden above her bed. She'd never left the house—and the jewels—for so long, and uneasily she pictured Lady Willoughby once again searching through her room....

"Bella?" He looked worried more than suspicious, making her wonder how long she'd been lost in her own thoughts.

She forced herself smile. "How could I not trust you, Tomaso? How could you ever think otherwise?"

The carriage door swung open with a bowing footman and polished marble steps rising up to the house. This time Isabella had sense enough to wait until the footman flipped down the carriage step, and to wait further for Tom to hand her out.

She took extra care to make sure the train of her gown draped behind her, free of the heels of her slippers, and that her cashmere shawl was anchored in the crooks of her elbows. Tripping once was an accident, but to fall again would brand her forever as a clumsy, graceless ninny, and her mother would never forgive her. She lifted her head high, tipping it to one side just enough so the sapphires in her tiara would catch the light from the lanterns at the door.

As she tucked her fingers into Tom's arm, he gave her a grin lopsided with admiration and resignation. "You're going to make my life hell tonight, Bella. You know that, don't you? The way you're looking now, fine as any queen, you'll have men around you thick as bees at honey."

"Only a princess." She tapped her shoulder restlessly with her fan. "If you saw my mother, you'd never make such a mistake again. Oh, I wish this were over, Tom! I hate this first part, going into a great room full of people like this and knowing they'll all be gaping at me, wanting me to be *special.*"

"You, Bella?" he asked with surprise. "I thought you'd devour such an opportunity."

She shook her head, feeling the sapphires in her long earrings tap against her cheeks. "Not among so many English. However should I guess what these people will expect of me?"

"Give us no thought, and act like yourself," he said. "That'll be more than enough."

She sighed, her fingers tightening on his arm as they climbed the stone steps. She could hardly argue with his advice. But since she'd come to England, it had become harder and harder to know exactly how Princess Isabella of Monteverde *should* act, and that—that frightened her.

"It's the same for a captain," he continued. "No matter what happens on a ship, good or bad, every other man on-board looks to the captain to know instantly what to do next to make things better. The first time I had to stand on my quarterdeck and address the crew, I thought I'd pitch my dinner over the rail first, I was that terrified."

She laughed with delight, unable to picture his confident self in such turmoil. "You? You would never do that!"

"I nearly did, but I didn't, just as you will forget your doubts and succeed tonight." They were passing through the door now, past another pair of bowing footmen, and yet he dared to wink at her. "Here we go now, lass, and mind from this moment onward, you keep to English."

Despite his wink, she nodded solemnly, appalled that she hadn't realized they'd been speaking Italian. They fell into it so easily now, without a thought, as if it were a secret language for just the two of them, and she'd have to be careful not to lapse again tonight. What gossip would be able to resist such a delicious sign of intimacy between a princess and the officer meant to guard her?

She was so on edge that the next minutes were no more than a blur of flushed faces and loud voices and bright music. They mounted a carved, curving staircase so crowded that it took Tom's broad shoulders to help make their way to the assembly room at the top. As much as she wished to keep his arm for support, she released it, composing herself to stand alone, her fan half-opened in her right hand and her left arm in a slight, graceful arc at her side, as was proper. Tom said her name to the footman at the door, his coat more lavished with gold braid than Tom's dress uniform, and suddenly everything came into focus, as sharp as a winter morning.

"Her Royal Highness the Princess Isabella di Fortunaro of Monteverde. Captain His Lordship Thomas Greaves."

She lifted her head and smiled serenely, the way Mama had taught her to do whenever entering a great assembly: "Smile as if all the world is yours."

And in that moment, it was.

Every head in the room turned to face her, with bows and curtsies. Though the musicians continued to play, the dozen dancers came awkwardly to a halt as they, too, bent and dipped their respect to her title, her family, and her country. This was why she was here; this was why she'd come all the way from London, to make sure Monteverde wasn't forgotten. As she nodded in return, freeing the other guests from the spell her name had cast, she realized she had succeeded, just as Tom had said she would.

But as she turned to tell him so, a tall woman with a pouf of dusty-red hair and a long strand of pearls wrapped around her throat swept between them. Her voice was loud, accustomed to speaking over crowds of people, but because of that, it seemed to Isabella to be very close to an ill-bred bray. She also should not be addressing a princess first, either, but then these English did seem to have difficulty remembering such niceties.

"I am so honored that you have joined us, Your Royal Highness," the woman said, enunciating each word with extra emphasis, as if Isabella were deaf, and not simply from another country, "and more honored to meet you at last. I am Lady Allen, ma'am."

Isabella nodded again, desperately wishing Tom would reappear. He'd promised he'd always be near, but now all she could see was Lady Allen's hair. "You have a handsome home, Lady Allen."

"You are too, too kind!" The duchess clasped her hands over her breasts with a perfect show of gratitude. "We have all read of your fortunate escape at Copperthwaite's. What a dreadful experience that must have been for you, ma'am!"

"You have read of it, Lady Allen?"

Lady Allen smiled brightly. "Oh, yes, the newspapers have been quite full of nothing else. You have not seen them for yourself, ma'am?"

"I do not read the English newspapers, Lady Allen," Isabella hoped she spoke with suitably solemn disdain. The truth was that while her spoken English was much improved, she found the long, gray columns of the London newspapers to be daunting and dull. "Though if the English newswriters can be persuaded to champion Monteverde's cause against the French villains, then perhaps I shall begin to read their gazettes."

"Brava, brava, Your Royal Highness, well spoke!" The gentleman had deftly made his way to Lady Allen's side, and now clapped his hands in appreciation of Isabella's words. He was handsome enough, pale and fair like so many English with a neat little cleft in his chin, and not much older than Isabella herself. He'd been drinking, too, enough to flavor his speech—and breath—with brandy. "Make the rascals serve you, I say."

But what the gentleman said and how it smelled didn't matter, because all Isabella saw was Tom behind him.

"You *are* here, Captain!" She barely remembered to use *captain* instead of his given name, she was so relieved to see him once again. "I feared I'd lost you."

"Oh, ma'am, you never lose a sailor, especially one as stolid and salty as Greaves here," the other gentleman said, thumping Tom familiarly on the shoulder. "Once he sets his course, he'll never go astray, aye, aye, ain't that right, Neptune?"

"Time has not improved your wit, Darden." Tom glowered, and made a rumbling growl that told Isabella that, as familiar as this man might seem, he was no friend—something she'd already decided for herself.

"Nor your humor, Greaves." The gentleman smiled confidently at Isabella. Dressed all in black except for a bright silk scarf tied around the open collar of his shirt, his curling blond hair long around his ears, he was clearly accustomed to having women sigh over him. "But I'll forget your sour temper if you'll but introduce me to the fair princess."

Isabella's glance darted back to Tom, his expression stony. "Princess, may I present My Lord Darden, Marquis of Banleigh? Darden, Her Royal Highness the Princess Isabella."

Darden took her hand and raised it to his lips, kissing the air over the back of it. "Your Royal Highness, I'm devoutly, eternally honored. Please honor me further, and grant me this next dance—unless you do not idly squander your time in dancing, just as you do not read the scandal sheets?"

Pulling her hand free of his, she opened her mouth to refuse, but the duchess answered for her first.

"Oh, certainly the princess shall dance with you, Darden," she said, jabbing him in the arm with the folded blades of her fan.

She smiled at Isabella, whispering as if they shared a great secret between them. "It's no hardship, ma'am, I assure you. All the ladies are quite mad for Darden, and besides, I do believe he's the lord of highest rank in the company this evening."

Now Isabella didn't dare look at Tom. To refuse to dance would be remarked as extraordinary and peculiar in a way that not reading would not. But the duchess was right: if Isabella did dance, protocol dictated that she must first do so with the gentleman closest to her rank, which meant the Marquis of Darden. The fourth son of the Earl of Lechmere would be so far below her, she'd have little chance of dancing with him at all, no matter how much she wished otherwise.

"Ma'am?" Darden was holding his hand out to her, his expression quizzical yet expectant, too, as if no woman in her right mind would even consider refusing him.

A pox on his impudence, she thought irritably. She might have no choice except to dance with him, she didn't have to be agreeable about it. And this one dance, that was all. No more. She would be as loyal to Tom as she could.

At last she accepted Darden's hand, though she pointedly didn't meet his eyes as she let him lead her on to the floor. To her dismay, the dance was an old-fashioned one, slow and stately, with actual conversation expected between partners. After growing accustomed to Tom's height and breadth, she felt off balance beside the marquis. He was nearly as tall as Tom, but thinner, leaner, more lithe and more restless: exactly the kind of man who tended to be good with a sword, and quick to find cause to use one, too. She'd seen enough men like him at her father's court— duels were as common as insults to honor in Monteverde— to recognize another.

"You are a most graceful dancer, ma'am," the marquis said as they moved through the elaborate pattern of the steps. "You are perfection."

"And you, Lord Darden—what are you?" she asked. "By your dress and manner, you would wish me to guess you are a poet of darkling romantic verse, yet by your birth and title, you must be an English aristocrat."

He winced, exaggerating, as if he'd been shot. "That is Greaves speaking, ma'am, and not you. I do write the occasional verse, and I'll admit to some modest success in that arena. But I also sit in the House when the occasional spirit moves me, which I suppose proves I am indubitably a peer of the realm."

"So you are both poet and lord, and likewise, you are neither."

"Perhaps." He smiled again, working to charm her. "Has Greaves told you that we are from the same county, or that our fathers were great friends?"

"No, Lord Darden, he has not," she said, glancing past the marquis's shoulder as she searched vainly for Tom's face among the crowd watching them. She didn't like this black-clad marquis or the way he'd mocked Tom, and she didn't trust him, either. "In truth, he has not spoken of you at all."

"Another wound, ma'am!" He sighed, deftly turning her through the steps to show her to best advantage. Like most gentlemen, he held his liquor well; she'd grant him that much. "We are not close now, I will admit. Being the earl's youngest son, without prospects, he was banished from the polite world and sent away to sea. You've only to hear him speak to see how the low company of the navy and his lack of education have ruined whatever benefits of breeding he once could claim."

Isabella bristled on Tom's behalf. "There are other advantages to be gained beyond the aristocratic world, beyond the cloistered seclusion of scholars and other tedious bores, particularly for a man."

"For a man, yes, but a gentleman is quite another matter." He made an extra flourish with his hand to coincide with the music, the white ruffles falling back from his wrist. "You must not judge all English gentlemen by Greaves's dour, weather-beaten face, you know. Some of us can be quite agreeable, given half a chance."

"But you see, Lord Darden, I *do* find Captain Lord Greaves agreeable." For the first time, Isabella smiled at him, albeit with more triumph than charm. "He is not only a gentleman, but also an officer of great resourcefulness and honor. And he is a true hero, not simply a poet who writes of other's heroics."

"What, ma'am, you are impressed because he saved your life?" He rolled his eyes and again sighed dramatically. "Ladies today are so easily impressed."

"I am impressed when it is *my* life in question, yes."

"But I contend that poets are necessary, too, ma'am," he countered. "Can Greaves conceive a paean to your homeland? Can a common sailor appreciate the subtle differences between the lush greenery in the mountains of Monteverde and the nodding palms of the coast? Can he see the dusky rose of the setting sun as it gilds the walls of the Fortunaro *palazzo?*"

"You like the sound of your own words too much, Lord Darden." Yet against her will, he'd caught her interest, and she was intrigued. "You have journeyed to Monteverde, then?"

"I have," he said, "and a most enjoyable journey it was, too. I stayed in a small villa that seemed wedged between the rocks of the cliffs, with walls painted yellow and shutters of green, all beneath a roof of crimson tiles. One window of my chambers overlooked the glorious sea, while from the other I had a perfect view of *il palazzo Fortunaro*."

"Most likely your little villa is in ruins now," she said, not trying to hide her bitterness. "The French took great amusement in using any buildings along our cliffs for their artillery drills."

"But they would not dare touch your great palace," he said, soothing, realizing he'd misstepped. "Surely those fierce Roman lions at the gates would keep away any lowly Frenchmen."

"Those lions *were* Roman, Lord Darden." It was no surprise that he'd admired the lions. Every visitor did. The huge snarling beasts were carved from stone and pitted by time, and on saints' days the local women would put garlands of flowers around the lions' manes, as if to placate their snarls. "They're Fortunaro lions now. They were taken as tribute from the Forum itself, ages and ages ago."

He smiled indulgently, as if he'd known the history of the lions already, but wouldn't embarrass her by saying so. "Of course they now belong to your family, ma'am. How would I have guessed then that someday I'd be dancing with the fair Fortunaro princess those lions once guarded?"

The dance separated them before Isabella had to answer, but it also gave her the few moments to look beyond her first impressions and think, *think*. Her mother had sent her here to London to garner support for Monteverde's cause. But she'd already discovered that most Englishmen had never heard of her little country, let alone wished it well against the French.

Yet what if she could persuade Darden to frame his memories of Monteverde into verse, to be published and shared? It wouldn't have to be *good* verse—and given the sampling Isabella had heard this evening, her expectations were not high—but any work by a handsome young peer would be sure to find some audience. She might even grant permission for him to dedicate such a work to her. As the dance brought him back before her, she was smiling at the prospect, and therefore at him as well.

"You are enjoying yourself, ma'am," he said as he took her hand again. "I am pleased to see it."

But Isabella shook her head impatiently as they turned together. "I would make a request of you, Lord Darden."

His own smile widened, uncomfortably close to a leer as he let his focus wander lower, to the low-cut front of her bodice. "I will oblige you in any manner you please, ma'am, and in any place that you desire."

Such appalling familiarity should never be tolerated, but for the sake of Monteverde, she somehow held her temper in check. She would have to persuade him to cooperate, though she wasn't exactly sure how. Ordinarily all she'd have to do is *ask,* and the person obeyed.

"You have an empathy for my country, Lord Darden,"

she began, "and you say you have a gift for verse. Now if you could only—"

But too soon the dance came to an end, the music stopping and the partners separating.

"Wait, Lord Darden, I am not done," Isabella said impatiently as he bowed to her. "I have not dismissed you. You must stay, and listen."

"I'd no intention of leaving you, ma'am," he said, making no move to release her hand. "But I believe the next dance is a country jig, and hardly conducive to conversation. Might I suggest a retreat to a quieter place?"

She nodded but pulled her hand free. "For conversation, Lord Darden. Only conversation."

"Oh, yes, by all means." He was leading her quickly across the room, threading through the other guests and dodging footmen with trays of food and drink, and finally through a side door and down a shallow run of steps into the garden behind the house. He walked out onto the terrace and into the moonlight, pausing to turn when Isabella didn't follow.

"Should I add the evening air to your list of dislikes, ma'am?" he asked, the moon silvering his fair hair above the black clothes. "Does that not agree with you any more than our newspapers?"

"You presume, Lord Darden." Tom had warned her of the perils lurking for her in shadowy gardens, but she also recognized the danger of walking alone in the dark with a man like the marquis, especially since he'd been drinking. "We shall converse here."

He shook his head, his frown showing his displeasure. "We might converse, ma'am, but it will not be a conversation of any warmth with you perched so far above me on that step, like the rarest bird of paradise."

"Most rare, and most proper." She did in fact feel a bit like a bird on a perch, here with the toes of her slippers balanced on the edge of the last step, with him the glossy black cat ready to pounce if she fell. And where, she wondered with growing uneasiness, was her loyal watchdog Tom? "Now to our conversation, Lord Darden."

"Indeed, ma'am." He came to stand directly before her, a model of respect with his hands at his sides. At least he would have been had not the step raised Isabella the exact height to place his eyes level with her décolletage. "You had a request for me, ma'am?"

Uneasily she snapped her fan open, using it to shield her breasts. She hoped he showed more originality in his verse. "A suggestion, Lord Darden."

He shook his hair back from his forehead and smiled up at her, his voice now low and purposefully seductive. "I am always ready to oblige a lady's...*suggestions,* ma'am."

Before she'd realized it, he'd circled around and climbed onto the higher step behind her. She gasped with indignant surprise, and hopped backward, off the last step and away from him.

"You forget yourself, Lord Darden!" He followed her off the steps, tracking her, forcing her to keep backing away along the patio, and she thought again of that sleek, predatory cat as she fought the panic that reduced her voice to a squeaking yelp. "You forget your—your place!"

He lowered his chin, his eyes now lost in the shadows. "I remember that you'd something to ask of me, ma'am, and that I was willing to do whatever I could to please you. A favor, an obligation—"

"*Santo cielo*—that is, yes. *Yes.*" She had to stand her ground and stop backing away before she found herself with him beneath the trees, and what Fortunaro ever retreated with such cowardly ease, anyway? "Write me a tribute to my country in your finest verse, Lord Darden, and publish it for all England to read. Yes, that is what I wish from you. That is what I *want.*"

Then she stopped backing away, her chin raised with defiance and her open fan pressed across her chest like a painted ivory shield, so abruptly that Darden stumbled off balance and tripped. Swearing, he jerked his hands outward to catch himself and caught Isabella instead. With a shriek of outrage she swung her elbow up and struck the cleft in his chin as they fell together in a tangle of arms and legs.

"Let me go free, Lord Darden!" Frantically she tried to wriggle clear of him, the silk of her gown catching on the rough stone beneath her. If anyone found her in this shameful position, she'd be ruined, in a way that only a princess could be. All she could see was the black of the marquis's coat, his chest pressed over her face in a smother of superfine wool. He was bigger than she'd first thought, heavier and stronger, too, and pox him, he was *laughing*. "Let me go at once!"

She heard the scrape of metal to her left, the unmistakable sound of a sword being drawn. With a final shove to Darden's chest, she managed to push herself free.

The first thing she saw was the tip of the sword pointed at her and the marquis. The second, when she looked up, was Tom's face, his expression as black as the night sky behind him and every bit as menacing as the sword in his hand.

"Go ahead, Darden." Tom lowered the blade of the sword to rest on the other man's sleeve. "Oblige the princess and let her go free, else I shall have to remove you for her."

Chapter Seven

Three minutes, thought Tom furiously. Three minutes ago he'd left the princess safely dancing while he'd been waylaid by Lady Allen, three agonizing minutes while Isabella had been out of his sight, and this—this was what had come of it.

"I'm not known as a patient man, Darden." He pressed the tip of his sword against the other man's sleeve, not enough to pierce it, but enough to give his warning teeth. "Let her go, Darden."

"I'm not exactly holding her, am I?" With the flat of his palm, Darden carefully pushed the sword aside and disentangled himself from Isabella's skirts. "You can run in your guns now, Captain, or haul down your flag, or whatever it is you old sea dogs do."

"What he did was defend *me* against *you,* Lord Darden." Isabella scrambled to her feet, twitching her skirts away from him and muttering more to herself in Italian. "That has nothing to do with being a sea dog, or whatever other ridiculous insult you choose."

With a final sniff she came to stand beside Tom—not precisely at his side, which would show too much dependence, but near enough to show that she'd rather be with him than Darden.

Of course, that was only because she hadn't realized how angry Tom was with her, too, now that he knew she was safe. What in blazes had she been doing, wandering off with a dishonorable bastard like Ralph Darden? Hadn't her mama the queen taught her to avoid scoundrels with too much lace on their shirts?

Tom had known Darden all his life, and he hadn't improved with time. The marquis drank heavily, fought trumped-up duels, lost vast sums at cards, chased petticoats of every rank, and got himself up like a macaroni so he could pretend to write bad verse. Darden was, in short, everything that disgusted Tom about being an English aristocrat, yet in three short minutes Darden had managed to carry off the princess like a prize, while honest, honorable Tom was left foundering in his wake.

"You are unhurt, ma'am?" He sounded like some damned trained parrot, asking Isabella this yet one more time. "Unharmed?"

She sniffed again, straightening her tiara as she glanced back in the direction of the party. In a way, she should be thankful that Darden had taken her out a side door, where none of the other guests inside had witnessed her indiscretion. She wanted people to speak of her and her country, true, but the last thing she needed was to have her name linked with Darden's.

"Thank you, Captain. I am quite fine." She turned back to him, her voice still breathy with excitement, her hair tousled, things he damned well should not be noticing. She narrowed her dark eyes, slanting her gaze at him with a conspirator's finesse. "Which has everything to do with you being a gentleman."

But Darden only chuckled derisively.

"Pray, what is that 'everything' worth, ma'am, if the gentleman does not behave like a gentleman?" Still mindful of Tom's sword, Darden slowly stood, dusting his arms and legs with fastidious attention. "You can defend Greaves's actions all you wish, ma'am, but the sorry truth is that no English gentleman would willfully draw his sword whilst the other gentleman is unarmed."

Isabella gasped. "He did so in my defense!"

"He did so without provocation, ma'am, and without any need." Darden bowed curtly. "You were never in any danger from me, ma'am, none at all."

Purposefully Tom sheathed the sword and stepped back. "I won't let you lead me off course, Darden, and I won't let you twist this into some wretched affair of honor. My orders are to protect the princess against all dangers. You were that danger, and I protected her. Now come, ma'am, I'll take you to rejoin the others."

But as he took Isabella's arm to lead her away, Darden blocked their path, his chin down and a peculiar half smile on his face. "So you would walk away from me, Greaves? You would pretend that this is no different from scrapes in the orchard when we were boys?"

"I don't have to pretend one damned thing to you, Darden, and if you are still mired in your boyhood, wanting to race all comers to the top of an apple tree—well, that is none of my affair, is it?" Any idiot could see that he was spoiling for a fight, the signs as sure as the bristling fur on a mongrel's neck, and Tom had no intention of obliging him. "Now if you will excuse me, the princess must—"

"No, Greaves, I shall not excuse you." Again the marquis blocked their way. "Not until you admit your game."

"There is no game, Darden." Tom could sense Isabella's anxiety beside him, and he worked to keep his voice steady and firm. "You said yourself I've no humor in me."

Darden rippled the fingers on one hand through the air between them. "But this isn't about your humors. This is about how once again you've arranged things to let you play the hero for the princess, without any real risk to yourself."

"That's not true, not at all!" the princess exclaimed. "However can you say such a lie?"

"But is it a lie, ma'am?" The marquis shook his hair back from his forehead. "All my life it seems I've heard how brave, how daring, how glorious, our Captain Lord Greaves is. But if he were such a great hero, then why is he here in the Duchess of Avery's drawing room, hiding behind your petticoats? Why isn't he off at sea, firing his cannons and fighting the French, the way any good respectable hero should?"

"Damnation, Darden, that's enough!" exploded Tom, finally pushed too far. He hadn't heard the whispers himself, but if Darden was saying it, then there must be others with the same opinion, the same questions about his courage and integrity. "If what you want from me is satisfaction, then—"

"You will *not* fight a duel over this!" ordered Isabella fiercely, pushing between them. "I will not allow it!"

But Darden only smiled, his gaze locked with Tom's. "Alas, ma'am, we are not in Monteverde. What a pity."

"This has nothing to do with you, Bella." Tom shifted her to one side, shielding her from Darden. If only he'd been able to do that earlier, then none of this would be happening now. "This is between us."

But Isabella shoved back. "I will *not* be pushed aside, and I will not let you—what is that music? What is happening?"

Quickly she faced the door, standing on her toes as she craned her neck to see what could merit the crashing fanfare of horns that had interrupted the dancers.

But Tom didn't have to turn. Fanfares like this one were a well-known feature of Lady Allen's entertainments, and he knew exactly what the horns signified—or rather, who. "It's the prince, ma'am. The Prince of Wales."

"He is an English prince? He is here?" She caught her breath with excitement. Her whole body seemed to vibrate with excitement, the possibility of a duel forgotten, or at least shoved aside. "A son of your king?"

"The eldest, and heir to the throne. But that doesn't signify that—"

"You must take me to him at once, Captain." She didn't wait for him to agree, but was already hurrying through the doors.

Tom had no choice but to follow; he couldn't let Isabella go off on her own again, especially not in search of the prince. Who could guess what kind of trouble she'd find next?

He nodded curtly at the marquis. "We shall finish this later."

"By all means, Captain." Darden bowed low over his leg with a mocking flourish. "Don't let the game escape, eh?"

"To hell with you, Darden," Tom snarled, turning away before he blundered any further.

How in blazes had he let himself be goaded so far like that? He swore to himself with disgust. The admiralty frowned on dueling as a sign of impulsive judgment, as well as a selfish waste of manpower. If word of how close he'd come to challenging Darden ever made its way back to Whitehall, he could forget that new ship forever. Nor would he deserve another command, letting a worm like Darden needle him with such ease.

But for now the princess was the key to his future, and as quickly as he could, he cut through the excited crowd to reach her. She'd already been gathered up by Lady Allen, who clearly was in raptures at having two royal persons under her roof at once. Yet though Tom now stood on the edge of the circle around them, he could not speak to get Isabella's attention. Especially here with the prince, Tom had to remember that one never addressed royalty directly, but waited to be addressed first. Alone together, she might be his Bella, but here—here he'd no claims to her at all.

"So we must be cousins, Isabella," the prince was saying, his thick fingers spread over the front of his embroidered waistcoat. "How vastly fine to discover such a charming relation in this way! You must come to Carlton House, my dear. We shall quite embrace you."

Isabella smiled warmly in return, and tipped her head to one side so she had to look up through her lashes. Tom recognized that head-tipping as something she only did when she was pleased or happy—something he now glumly wished he did not know.

"Yes, yes," she was saying, effortlessly raising her voice

so others could hear her, as well. Not even Lady Allen could draw and hold attention like Isabella, or be so lovely while she did it. "What a comfort it will be to know you are here in London during this troubling time for me, gallantly there if I should need to call upon you."

The prince's already abundant chest seemed to swell with pleasure, his ruddy face beaming under her attention. What man wouldn't, thought Tom, whether prince, commoner or navy captain?

"You've but to say the word, my dear." The prince leaned closer to Isabella, as if every other person in the room weren't listening as well. "I've visited your country myself, you know. Seeing you here puts me to mind of your mother. A beautiful woman, the queen."

"Indeed, she is." For a moment, Isabella's smile faltered, distracted by the mention of her mother. Tom wasn't surprised, considering the uncertainty surrounding her family's fate, and he longed to be able to reach out and comfort her.

But then with a deep breath, Isabella's smile returned brighter, even more winning, more charming than before, and Tom's admiration for her persistence rose. This was precisely what she'd come to England to do, and damnation, she'd found a way to do it.

"But you would scarcely know my country now," she was saying. "The French have treated Monteverde most barbarously, swallowing us up in their greedy conquest. We fought with all our hearts and might, but we are a small country, and without the help of our stronger friends, Monteverde will become nothing more than a corner of France."

But despite the emotion that thrummed through her plea, the prince heard—or only chose to hear—part of it. "Your dear mother is unharmed, I trust? And your father?"

She nodded, saying nothing more of her family as she tried to turn the conversation back to where it had been. "If the English ships and army would only—"

"I have the most splendid image of your mother in my mind from that visit." Deliberately the prince let his eyes go hazy and unfocused, savoring the memory as he avoided Isabella's appeal. "She is standing at the top of a long golden staircase, with some wonderful pagan painting of Oriental splendor on the wall behind her."

"That's the staircase to the ballroom in the palace, and the painting is by Tintoretto, a scene of Queen Cleopatra and her followers. But you see, if the French are not made to leave, why—"

"She was wearing the most fantastic jewels, rubies such as I'd never seen before or since. She showed them to me later, so I might see the cunning little lions etched between the facets. Remarkable, even for crown jewels."

The change in her expression was subtle—her mouth tightening a fraction, uneasiness flickering through her eyes—but it didn't escape Tom. Was it the prince's determined lack of interest in her appeal that caused the change, he wondered, or the way His Highness spoke more fondly of the jewels than of Isabella's mother?

"The Fortunaro rubies are remarkable," she said with unusual care. "There are no other jewels like them, not in all the world."

The prince nodded solemnly. "Those rubies are beyond any value the world could put upon them. They are your *country.* Wouldn't do to let those fall into Buonaparte's grubby fingers, would it?"

"Her Royal Highness very nearly fell into those fingers herself, sir." Lady Allen couldn't bear being silent any longer, thrusting herself into the conversation with her usual eagerness. "Surely you have heard what befell her yesterday?"

The prince's sandy brows rose with interest. "Buonaparte's fingers here in London?"

"In a way." Lady Allen smiled with the triumph of a new story for the prince. "Her Royal Highness was in a shop, admiring the ribbons such as any lady might, when a monstrous creature spewing Buonaparte's venom leaped from behind a curtain with a knife as long as my arm, determined to plunge it deep into her royal breast!"

The other guests gasped and exclaimed, even if they'd already read of the attack in the newspapers. But only Tom—and Isabella—knew how far Lady Allen's version ranged from the truth. He couldn't wait to hear her ending to the story, either.

"How terrified you must have been, my dear." The prince patted her on the arm. "But you did escape without harm? Someone came to your aid?"

Lady Allen could not resist. "Oh yes, sir! It was a most thrilling and dramatic rescue! It was—"

"Captain Lord Thomas Greaves." Isabella turned to him, making a graceful little arc with her body that was scandalously close to a curtsy. But it was her smile that captured Tom and singled him out from the scores of others. It was a smile meant only for him, and one that made everything else seem false as pinchbeck. "It was Captain Greaves who saved my life."

"Ah, Captain," the prince said. "Now I recall your name. You're Lord Lerchmere's youngest son, and you've already served your king and country with great distinction, have you not?"

Tom bowed, wishing he'd stayed comfortably unnoticed. "I thank you, Your Highness, though your praise is undeserved. All I did was follow my orders, the same as any other man in the king's service."

"You sailors are a modest lot." The prince managed to make that modesty sound vaguely distasteful. "But I can still praise you for your quick action to save my fair cousin's life. Wouldn't have done to have lost her before I found her, would it?"

Everyone laughed, the kind of duty that courtiers must follow. But Tom wasn't laughing, and neither was Isabella.

Damnation, Bella, don't look at me like this, he thought with growing frustration, as if thinking alone could make it so. Be tart, be sharp, be full of fire and spice, the way you usually are. Don't let them see that you feel anything but indifferent toward me, else they'll tear us both apart for the sport.

He made himself break the lock of her gaze, returning his attention to the prince. "My orders are to guard the princess, sir, whatever the cost. I always strive to do my best, and watching over Her Royal Highness is no different."

"Well, yes, very good, very good." With obvious relief, the prince turned back to Isabella. "Would you like to join me at the faro table, my dear?"

"Alas, not tonight." Isabella's smile was wan as she touched her fingertips to her temples. "My head has begun to ache abominably, and I fear I'd better retire instead."

"Oh, poor lamb." Lady Allen cooed with sympathy. "You've had far too much intrigue and menace for any lady to bear."

"I'll send for the carriage, my lady." Tom beckoned to one of the footmen, then stepped forward to offer his arm to Isabella. Now it was proper, and no one would take any notice. Now he was simply following orders by tending to her welfare. But Lady Allen was right: there *had* been too much intrigue and menace for her tonight, thanks to Darden, and the sooner he could take her away, the better.

The prince waved his bejeweled hand to send them off, his thoughts already on the faro table. "Be a gallant equerry to my cousin, Greaves, that's a good man, but be sure to bring her to Carlton House soon."

Isabella smiled and nodded and murmured all the right things as she made her way from the room, but as soon as she was alone with Tom, waiting in the hall, she sagged forlornly against his arm.

"What a miserable mess I have made of tonight, Tomaso! I have failed, I have failed, and no one, not even you, could say otherwise."

He switched to Italian, lessening the risk of an indiscretion. "I wouldn't call it exactly a failure, Bella. His Royal Highness now knows who you are, and has invited you to call at Carlton House."

"But he didn't want to listen to me speak of Monteverde, let alone help me." She frowned, checking the door for the footman. "Oh, praise the saints, here is the carriage at last."

She climbed into the carriage without any help from Tom or the footman, and slumped in the far corner of the seat without bothering to arrange her skirts with her usual precision. Instead she tugged the tiara from her hair, wincing as she wrestled the pins free, then tossed the little half crown onto the seat beside her, the sapphires and diamonds winking back at her in the carriage's twilight.

"I hate wearing that," she said. "*They* say that every little girl wishes she were a princess, but I would say that is because *they* have never had their neck ache from holding their heads high with a weight of gold prickles and stones nailed into their skulls."

She gave the tiara an extra shove with the back of her hand. "Do you know, Tomaso, that I have written to your King George every day since I've come to London, yet he has never replied? He has ignored me and dishonored me as if I were nothing, worthless, instead of the Princess di Fortunaro."

Tom did not know that, though from what he'd heard from Cranford, he wasn't surprised. "His Majesty is not a well man, Bella. Likely his health keeps him from his duties."

She shot him a withering glance. "Then his attendants and secretaries would answer his correspondence, yes? That is how it would be with my father. Or are the English secretaries sickly, too?"

"How in blazes should I know, Bella?"

"Oh, very well, you shouldn't, not about that. You're absolved." Irritably she poked one of her hairpins at the seat cushion, over and over, no doubt imagining it to be some part of the king's anatomy. "But still, all you English wish to recall your pleasant days in Monteverde, the sunshine, the lions, my beautiful mother the queen, la, la, *la,* but when we would ask for your help, then you only look the other way and pretend not to hear."

"The graybeards in Whitehall claim diplomacy takes time."

"But I do not have *time!*" She smacked her hand hard against the side of the carriage. "I was sent here for a reason. Who knows what has happened to my home since I left? Who knows what has become of my family? No one does, or no one is telling me if they do. All my country and my family has is me, and tonight I did nothing—*nothing!*—to help them."

"You *did* do something, Bella," he insisted. "You made the prince notice you, which is no minor feat for a man so easily distracted as His Royal Highness."

She sniffed. "My mother would have had him eating crumbs from her palm like a pigeon."

He let that pass without comment. "But you gave Monteverde a face and a name, and by tomorrow morning, every person in the *ton* and most of Parliament besides will know you, too."

"But that's not enough, not by half." She sighed with frustration, once again pressing her hand to her forehead. "Is it any wonder my head aches so?"

"Tomorrow will be better. Sleep will clear your head, and then you can chart your next course." That sounded empty and foolish, the kind of meaningless advice offered by spinster aunts, but Tom didn't know what else to say. Though he'd intended on lecturing her about the evils of the Marquis of Banleigh here in the carriage, Darden now seemed the least of her worries, and Tom decided his lecture would keep better until the morning. Besides, Darden was more his problem than hers, anyway. "The world always seems a cheerier place once the sun rises."

"You do not need to placate me, Tomaso." She smiled wearily, closing her eyes. "I need to be strong, not coddled. I am a Fortunaro, and I can bear it. You, of anyone in London, can understand that, yes?"

With her face relaxing, her lashes feathered down across her cheeks and her lips slightly parted, she looked much younger—far too young for all the burdens life had thrust upon her, Fortunaro princess or not.

"Yes," he said softly. "I understand."

But she was already asleep.

With his hat pulled low to mask his face, Lord Ralph Darden hurried through the black shadows of the narrow street. He had left his carriage to wait, not wanting even his driver for a witness, and come the rest of the way on foot. He knew he didn't belong in this neighborhood at this hour, and he touched the hilt of his sword beneath his cloak, just for reassurance.

The comforting haze of the brandy was fading to a dull ache in his forehead, but he hadn't allowed himself the solace of the bottle nestled waiting in the carriage. Later, later, after his work here was done. He might have lost deeply—again—this night at Lady Allen's house, yet still he sensed his luck might be beginning to change.

Behind the shuttered windows he heard a baby crying, then the sounds of its mother singing it softly back to sleep in words that weren't English. The smells that lingered in this narrow street weren't entirely English, either, the usual London coal smoke and river tang overlaid with the fragrances of dark spices and onions and garlic cooked in yellow oil.

Carefully Darden counted the doorways from the corner, stopping at the fifth house, the one with the windows shuttered and padlocked to protect the treasures inside. He hadn't been here for months, but then, he hadn't had anything left of value in his mortgaged houses to sell, either. Yet he was certain the man behind those padlocked shutters would welcome him, even at this hour, once he heard what Darden had to say.

His knock echoed in the empty street, the sound bouncing off the brick walls and cobblestones. He knocked again on the door, harder, and at last it cracked open.

"Maestro Pesci." Darden leaned close to the door, showing his face so the single eye peering at him would make no mistake. "It's Lord Darden. Pray open that door, so we might talk."

The door opened no further. "It's past midnight, my lord. Come back at a seemly hour."

"Hold." Darden thrust his shoulder into the crack, knowing the old man on the other side was too frail to shut the door against him. "Would now be more seemly if I told you I met the Principessa di Fortunaro here, tonight, in London?"

"You are mad, my lord!" The old man struggled to shut the door, but Darden held firm.

"She *is* here, Pesci. She escaped. I danced with her. She is very beautiful, your fair princess, and she dances with the grace of an angel."

Pesci opened the door another fraction, just widely enough to spit on the step beside Darden's foot. "Bah, she is a Fortunaro, with rot in her heart and evil in her soul!"

"What matters is that she is in London." Darden glanced disdainfully at the glob of spittle, far too close to his well-polished toe. "She's that close to you, Pesci, waiting for you to settle the score."

The man laughed bitterly, a painful wheeze. "What of it, my lord? I am too old and sick for such wickedness."

"But you must know many others in London who are neither."

"I know more than I should, my lord." At last he opened the door for Darden to slip inside. "This city can count them by the dozen."

Darden had never been in the dealer's shop by night, nor, after this, did he ever wish to return. A score of blank-eyed statues of ancient gods and goddesses filled this front room like a crowd of pressing ghosts, the flickering light of Pesci's single candle granting the cold marble an unsettling life. Darden would have given his last coin for a drink now, and who would blame him?

Instead he turned his back on the statues, focusing instead on this hunched old man in the striped stocking cap. He'd wound an ancient scarf around his throat against imagined chills, and beneath that was the queer talisman he always wore, a triangle made from twigs, that Darden guessed had powers against the evil eye or other of his superstitious mumbo jumbo.

"You've always claimed the Fortunaro family made you suffer. You said you'd do anything to make them pay for your pain. You said they—"

"I know what they did." Pesci shoved back the grimy sleeve of his dressing gown and held out his trembling arm. Wispy white hairs curled across the shriveled skin, yet still the scar remained sharp and clear: the letter *L,* seared into the flesh forever by an iron brand.

"They said I was a thief, my lord, and they marked me as one: *L* for *ladro,* for thief." Pesci's voice shook with an outrage twenty years old. "They said I'd stolen their antiquities, when I was the one who'd sweated and dug to free the past from the soil. They said what I found was theirs, and made me pay. They were the true thieves, but because they were the Fortunari, I was the one who was branded, and banished forever from Monteverde."

"Then the gods have given you a gift, Pesci." Darden kept his face impassive. He was a gambler to the marrow of his bones; he could not help it, any more than he could forget the look that had flitted across the girl's face when the prince had mentioned her mother's jewels. It was a guess, a gamble, but the chill that had raced down his spine had told him otherwise.

What he was beginning tonight could cost the princess her life if it failed, and maybe his own, as well. He was a peer; he'd never done anything like this before. Yet he couldn't help himself, not with the stakes in the balance almost too great for him to imagine.

"Your revenge, maestro," he continued. "Your *vendetta.* I will tell you when and where the princess will be, and you can arrange the rest."

Pesci ran his tongue across his toothless gum, considering. "She is alone? She is unprotected?"

"She has only one man appointed to guard her, an English navy captain."

"One Englishman." Pesci shrugged elaborately. "That is nothing. But her suffering must last, as did mine. Her fear must be built, step by step."

Darden swallowed his excitement. "Then you will do it?"

"No, my lord." The old man's eyes glittered shrewdly. "Not until you tell me the truth."

"The truth?" Darden was stalling. He had never felt at ease with the truth, and thought it much overrated.

"The truth, my lord." Pesci would not let it pass. "You are one of the wicked ones, my lord. You have lost your patrimony on the turn of a card, and you have squandered the treasures of your mother's heart with each throw of your dice. So how will you profit from this, my lord? What is your prize?"

What is your prize? A beautiful young princess to be his muse? A way to make the rest of the world grovel at his feet when he had a princess on his arm? A chance to play the grandest hero that could make a princess sigh and swoon, and forget that righteous prig Greaves and his foolish histrionics?

Or a dowry so fantastically rich it would outshine the combined wealth of a dozen factory heiresses, a fortune so vast not even he could consume it?

"So, my lord." Pesci's voice shrank to a feathery whisper. "Tell me. What is your stake in my *vendetta?*"

"My stake?" Darden smiled slowly, the smile of a gambler graced with the winning hand. "My stake will be the Fortunaro rubies."

Chapter Eight

"These are for you, ma'am." The maid stood in the doorway to Isabella's bedchamber, her arms filled with a large silver vase of nodding white roses. "They just come, an' Her Ladyship said to bring them up directly."

Eagerly Isabella stood, dusting away the crumbs from her breakfast toast from her palms. Perhaps the flowers were from the prince, a welcome after meeting her last night at Lady Allen's house. "Set them there. You have shown them to Captain Lord Greaves first? He has found no dangers hidden away inside?"

"No, ma'am. Captain His Lordship is taking his morning walk, and is not at home." With great care—and relief—the maid placed the vase in the center of the table. "But Her Ladyship says since they came from the Marquis o' Banleigh, by the hands o' his own footman in his own livery, then they must be safe for you to accept."

"The Marquis of Banleigh?" Her curiosity piqued, Isabella pulled out the card that had been tucked inside the branches. After the disastrous way she and the marquis had parted last night—or rather, how Tom had arrived just in time to part them—she'd doubted she'd ever have a civil exchange with the man again, let alone receive roses from him. Briskly she waved away the maid and unfolded the note.

You know me now, most grievously chasten'd,
By the princess fair,
With these blooms, my regard shall hasten,
To beg her forgiveness from there.

> Yr. Ob't. Svt.,
> Darden

Isabella read it again, out loud this time, hoping that the verse would improve if she better understood the English words. It did not, and she shook her head sadly. If the marquis's work was ever published, it was clearly because of his title, not his talent.

At least he had not kept away. If he were willing to compose and sign his name to this dreadful plea for her forgiveness, then the possibility for a grander verse honoring Monteverde might still remain.

But making such a request of the marquis would require considerable care. Darden might be useful, but he was also untrustworthy and impulsive. She must never again allow herself to be left alone with him, of course. She did not like to repeat such foolish mistakes. But she must also keep *him* apart from Tom, which would be infinitely more difficult.

With a little frown, she bent to sniff the nearest rose, cradling the blossom in her fingers as she lifted it up. The English did know how to grow roses in their chilly climate;

the ones in Monteverde's hot sun never flourished to this size or fragrance.

"You're awake." Tom knocked on the frame of the door that the maid had left ajar, then pushed it open the rest of the way. "After last night, I didn't expect to see you before noon."

"You promised things would be better in the morning, and I wished to see if they were." She twirled the rose's stem between her fingers.

"For once you took my advice, Bella." He grinned, marveling. "Was I right?"

"Well, yes." Thoughtfully she let the rose slip back into the vase. She hadn't really considered this as taking his advice, advice-taking not being a princessly quality. Still, she supposed she had, and no ill seemed to have resulted. "You said when dawn came, my head would be clear and I'd be better able to chart my course, and I was."

She smiled, glad he'd returned. While she couldn't begin to understand his unholy need to rise early and go racing about the city at an hour when most gentlemen were blissfully asleep, she couldn't deny that the practice favored him.

His skin had a ruddy glow and his blue eyes were keen and alert and ready, she supposed, to scan the horizon for enemy sails. It made her feel safe, that alertness, but it also made her acutely aware of how *male* he was.

And yes, she liked that, too. Very much.

"That's a handsome lot of roses." He set his hat on the table and bent to smell them. "Generous of Lady Allen to have them brought in from the country for you."

"She didn't." Isabella hesitated, not wanting to ruin this lovely morning. But sooner or later Tom would learn that the flowers were a gift from the marquis, and in the long run it would be better if it were sooner, and from her. "They were sent to me by Lord Darden as an apology for his behavior last night."

"Darden sent them?" He recoiled from the flowers as if they'd turned to snakes. "Why the devil did he do that?"

"I suppose because he wished to."

He frowned. "And I suppose you were pleased?"

"Yes." She let the word hang there between them, as cold as any icicle. She'd intended to tell Tom about having the marquis write a poem about Monteverde, but not if he was going to be so belligerently narrow-minded. "There is certainly no harm or evil to be found in a bunch of flowers."

"There is when they come from Darden." He turned so his back was against the table, blocking the flowers from her sight as if they were the marquis himself. "I'd hoped you'd learned last night what manner of man he is."

"I learned you do not care for him, any more than he cares for you. Is there more beyond that?"

"Damnation, Bella, don't be stubborn!" He shook his head again, as if he didn't know where to begin. "I have known Ralph Darden all my life. He is a wastrel and a scoundrel. He has lost his inheritance through gaming, and the properties that came to him when his father died have been mortgaged to the hilt. He lies and cheats and drinks and charms his way through a life of pure hellacious idleness. He's not fit to be on this earth with you, Bella, and that's the truth."

"Does he drown kittens in a bucket? Does he steal sugarplums from children?"

"Bella, I am serious."

"He also would have challenged you to a duel, if you'd let him." She folded her arms over her chest and raised her chin so her eyes would meet his. "You did forget that."

"I haven't forgotten." His frown grew darker, and she realized too late that mentioning the risk of a duel had perhaps gone a step too far with him. "Why in blazes are you defending him anyway? Because he sent you these blasted flowers?"

"I am not defending him. I am defending *myself*." She hated being lectured like this, as if she were no more than a naughty, ignorant child. "How foolish do you believe me to be?"

"If I had come after you two minutes later—"

"What *would* you have found, eh?" She stepped closer, challenging him the same way she felt he was challenging her. "Could you come down from your pulpit long enough to tell me?"

"Damnation, Bella, I'm not preaching," he growled. "I'm warning you against a man who is beneath you."

"'*Beneath me*'?" She spread her fingers and swept her hands through the air with scornful disdain.

"Yes." He took a step forward, so close now that she had to fight the instinctive urge to back away. "Because I don't believe you can tell the difference between a good man and a bad."

"But of course *you* can." She didn't like having to look up at him this way, and that was enough to make her taunt him now. "To be warned against an *English* marquis by the younger son of an *English* earl—oh, yes, as a Monteverdian princess I must be especially careful not to—*oh!*"

As much more as she had to say, she couldn't continue,

because he'd seized her by the shoulders and was kissing her, kissing her hard, kissing her as if he'd no intention of ever stopping. She thrashed about indignantly, trying to pull away, but he folded her flapping arms at her sides and kissed her mumbled protests into silence. It was shameful for him to treat her with such freedom. It was *outrageous,* and if she'd been within reach of some bric-a-brac, she would have cracked it over his head.

But at the same time there was something extraordinary happening to her. The more she struggled against him, the more exciting the kiss seemed to become, as the heat of their anger changed into the heat of longing and desire. They were still too angry to be cautious or reverential, too angry, really, for anything but unthinking sensation.

She could taste his morning coffee in his mouth, and smell the warmth of the outdoors on his skin, and feel the raw strength of his chest and arms as they embraced her. Her breath was coming faster and her heart was racing as she twisted against him, and to her chagrin she realized she'd stopped fighting and he'd stopped holding her hands, and all that was left was the kiss, deep and hot and making her so deliciously dizzy she was swaying against him to keep from toppling over.

Until she remembered the undeniable fact that she, a royal princess, had *surrendered.*

She struck his cheek as hard as she could, enough to make him swear and to make her palm sting so badly she gasped as she recoiled.

"Was that meant to show a good man from a bad?" she demanded, her breathing still ragged as she pushed her hair back from her forehead.

His expression didn't change, the red print of her hand glowing on his cheek. "You tell me, Bella. Or would you rather tell me how to find a good woman instead?"

She raised her hand to hit him again, and he caught her wrist, holding her hand frozen over her head.

"If we were in Monteverde—"

"But we're not, are we?" He held her hand still with infuriating ease. "We're in London. The rules are different here."

"You would be in irons in Monteverde!"

"For kissing you, or for letting you kiss me?" He smiled, but there was no amusement in his eyes. "Mark what I say, Bella, and mark it well. You cannot rely on your rank alone. It's not enough, not in London, nor the rest of this world."

"I thought you were done preaching, *Captain.*" She was still angry, but now she was also confused. How had things gone so wrong so fast between them?

"Not quite," he said. "You have to use your wits, Bella. God knows you're clever enough. But you'll never accomplish one damned thing for your country or your family unless you start judging men for what they are, and not how they've been born."

He released her hand and she jerked it away, rubbing her wrist where he'd held it. "I'm a Fortunaro. I don't need anyone to tell me what to do."

"That's good," he said, taking his hat from the table to leave, "because I'm done with telling. I'll guard you, Bella, and put your life before mine, but I can't stop you from being a fool."

Once again she folded her arms over her chest, but now it was more a kind of hug to reassure herself than to challenge him. It would take precious little now for her to cry, the hot tears of confusion and frustration waiting to spill over. But she refused to let them come, just as she refused to give him that kind of satisfaction, no matter how much it cost her.

"I thought you were different, Captain," she said. "I thought I could always trust you."

"You can." He paused at the door. "That hasn't changed, and it won't. But the question for me, Bella, is whether I can trust you."

And as he quietly closed the door between them, Isabella made the one reply she'd always relied upon. With a low howl of frustration, she swept her arm across the top of the table, and the vase with Darden's roses crashed to the floor.

"I am very sorry, Captain my lord." Once again the clerk studied the leather-bound book of appointments open on the desk before him. "But there is no record here of an appointment for this hour between you and Admiral Cranford."

Tom drummed his fingers on the edge of the desk. This day had already taken a dismal turn when he'd lost his temper with Isabella and she'd lost hers with him. Now he'd rushed here to Whitehall at the admiral's own summons, only to be told now that the admiral was not expected in his offices for the remainder of the day—what in blazes could happen next?

"The message was quite specific," he said, wishing now he'd brought the note as proof instead of leaving it on the table beside his bed. "Admiral Cranford wished me to meet him here at two o'clock on urgent business."

It was that mention of "urgent business" that had

brought Tom so swiftly. The only business between him and the admiral would involve the princess. Had news of her family's fate finally come through the official channels? Or had His Royal Highness taken steps toward offering Monteverde more English assistance after meeting the princess last night at Lady Allen's house?

Or perhaps he was being too optimistic. Perhaps instead the admiral had learned of some new threat to the princess's welfare that Tom needed to know.

He leaned over the desk toward the clerk, his grim-faced reflection glittering back at him in the glass of the man's spectacles. "Exactly where is the admiral at present?"

The clerk drew back, pursing his mouth. "I told you, Captain my lord. Admiral Cranford has joined several other gentlemen for a supper down the river, and will not return to Whitehall this day. Might I ask, Captain my lord, if the note you received was in the admiral's own hand?"

Tom frowned, and shook his head. "I do not believe it was. I thought it written by some scrivener here at Whitehall, at his request."

"Well, then, Captain my lord, there is the end to your mystery." The clerk's pursed lips arched in the tiniest of smug smiles, as much as he'd dare. "Because I am the sole individual entrusted with Admiral Cranford's correspondence, and because neither the admiral nor myself did write a note for you, then it is safe to venture that no such appointed meeting as you mention was ever intended."

"And so you are claiming my summons was a forgery?" Tom had intended that to be a preposterous suggestion to the clerk, yet as soon as he'd said it aloud, he realized it wasn't so farfetched.

The clerk bowed, his arms stiff at his sides. "I would not presume to make any such claim to an officer such as yourself, Captain my lord, nor could I dare to suggest a reason why anyone would wish you here at this time."

The clerk might not presume or dare, but then Tom's imagination didn't need the help. While bringing him here to Whitehall on a fool's errand might seem to have no purpose, it also meant he was not at the house in Berkeley Square, and not with the princess. For the wrong person with the wrong reasons, that would be purpose enough.

And in no time at all, the day had plunged from bad to worse to straight to hell.

"Forgive me for interrupting you, Your Royal Highness." Anxiously Lady Willoughby twisted her wedding ring around her finger, her way of wringing her hands. "But Lord Darden is downstairs for you. Whatever shall I tell him, ma'am? What am I to *do?*"

"You will tell Lord Darden that I shall be down directly." At once Isabella lowered the book she'd been attempting to read. Here she'd been wondering how to contact the marquis about her idea for the Monteverdian verse, and now he'd conveniently brought himself to her. "Offer him tea, or whatever else you offer your guests. He is not different from any other, is he?"

Yet Lady Willoughby didn't move. "What of Captain Lord Greaves, ma'am?"

"What *of* him?" Isabella tried to look imperious, untroubled by such a piddling concern, even though she shared the same worry.

"He disapproves most vigorously of His Lordship,

ma'am." The countess's hands twisted again. "He feels the marquis is a danger to you, ma'am, and he was most unhappy that we'd even admitted the flowers to the house without showing them first to him for inspection."

Lady Willoughby gave a nervous little smile, clearly not wishing to speak further of the waterlogged mess of broken flowers and porcelain that had recently been cleaned from the floor of Isabella's bedchamber.

"Then tell the captain that the marquis is here." Isabella glanced at her reflection in the looking glass, smoothing the folds from her gown. At least her eyes had cleared; the last thing she wished was for the marquis to see that she'd been crying, and over Tom Greaves at that. "Tell him to join us in the drawing room, so that he might inspect the marquis's person for danger."

"But the captain is not here, ma'am," said the countess with a pitiful shrug.

"He's not?" What if she'd made him so angry that he'd forsaken his famous orders and abandoned her? What if that were the last she'd ever see of him, telling her how he couldn't trust her? "When did he leave? Where has he gone?"

"He has gone to Whitehall, called there by my brother. He left a quarter hour ago, with no word on when he would return. Oh, what am I to *do?*"

"You will come with me to the drawing room and sit with Lord Darden and myself," Isabella said as firmly as she could. One of them had to think clearly, and it wasn't going to be the countess. *Why* had the English saddled her with this quaking ninny of a woman? "You will act as my lady-in-waiting. You will make sure that Lord Darden says or does nothing that is improper or offensive to me, and summon one of the footmen to remove him if he does. *That,* Lady Willoughby, is what you will do."

She was already on the stairs before Lady Willoughby's quavering voice came echoing after her. "Lord Darden does not wish to be received in the drawing room. He wishes you to go driving with him."

"True, true, every last word. Good day to you, Your Royal Highness. I trust you are well?"

Isabella stopped on the stairs, holding on to the railing as she peered down to the floor below. There in the front hall stood Darden, smiling as he somehow managed to bow upward to her, and elegantly, too, with his soft-brimmed black hat in his hand.

Again he was dressed all in black with a white shirt, and while he'd wished that she was well, it was clear that he was not. In the sun that streamed through the fan light, his newly shaven face was ashen, his eyes ringed with shadows, and a sheen of sweat beaded his upper lip above his smile: all the sorry, sour products of too much drink at Lady Allen's. Isabella was not surprised; the marquis had already been halfway along that shaky path when she'd left with Tom.

"A good day to you, too, Lord Darden," she called over the rail, "especially since it seems you are not quite ready to meet it."

He waved away her observation, dabbing his upper lip with his handkerchief. How much more harmless he seemed this morning! "It is nothing that I haven't survived a thousand times before, ma'am. But you will, I trust, understand my preference for a bracing ride in the open air as opposed to a perilous seat in a close drawing room."

"Of course," she said hastily. All too often in the palace she'd witnessed the morning results of excessive reveling the night before, and she wouldn't wish for such a scene, not even in the countess's drawing room.

"Then you will join me, ma'am?" He offered his hand up to her like a drowning man might, his pale face lighting with a greenish hope. "I would beg the chance to make amends for last night, and to grovel suitably for your forgiveness for my unforgivable behavior."

She had not agreed, but as she began to chide him for twisting her words to please himself, Lady Willoughby came to stand behind her on the stairs.

"Oh, ma'am, you know Captain Lord Greaves will not like this," the countess warned in an anxious whisper. "You are not to leave this house without his company, ma'am, and with him at Whitehall—"

"Greaves isn't here?" asked Darden. "How splendid for me."

"No, Lord Darden, he is not," the countess said before she plunged on with more reminders for Isabella. "You know those are his orders for us both, ma'am, to help keep you safe. You know that as well as I do, and after the flowers this morning, why—"

"Did you like the roses, then?" the marquis asked disingenuously. "They did arrive, ma'am?"

"Yes, and they were lovely." Isabella smiled as she began down the stairs to join the marquis, her decision made. If Tom had abandoned her, then she saw no reason to respect his orders. His *orders:* why should she be taking orders from anyone, anyway? "I shall be happy to join you for a short drive, Lord Darden. About this neighborhood, that is all."

She ignored Lady Willoughby's protests as she skipped down the stairs, pausing only for a maid to fetch her hat and gloves.

"I cannot tell you how honored I am, ma'am." Darden offered her his arm, which she pretended not to see. He was poorly, yes, but she saw no reason to test her luck. Instead she frowned down at the sword that jutted out from the skirts of his coat.

"Do you believe that is necessary by day?" she asked as the footman opened the front door. "Everyone keeps telling me London is so civilized, but perhaps they are wrong. Or do you mean to try to challenge another gentleman like you did Captain Lord Greaves last night?"

"You are observant, ma'am." He placed one hand over his heart and the other on the hilt of the sword. "But you see, I feel quite naked without my dear blade, my most loyal companion, and as for Greaves, we are ancient acquaintants, and—"

"Your carriage is open." The elegant landau before them had bright yellow wheels and Darden's arms painted on the door, but with the top folded back, passengers on those cushioned leather seats would be as exposed as if they were sitting on a pianoforte bench in the middle of the street.

Tom had warned her against being as vulnerable as she'd be in such a carriage, how she'd be a perfect target for every window in every house that they passed, and for once she decided to agree.

"I believe I have changed my mind, Lord Darden," she said. "I believe I must decline your offer after all."

Surprised, Darden tried to look contrite. "Ah, ma'am,

how have I sinned again, and so soon? What have I done or said to offend you?"

"It's not you. It's your carriage. I don't believe it's wise for me to show myself so—so boldly."

Darden shook his head. "And here I'd chosen the landau because I thought you'd judge it safer to your reputation, not to be closed away with my wicked old self."

"That, too, must be considered." She caught herself wondering what Tom would advise, as if she were unable to think for herself.

"I promise we shall keep only to streets in the best neighborhoods," he said, "and if at any time you wish to retreat, why, I give you my word that we shall turn about the horses directly."

"I believe you gave me your word last night before we went into the garden, and look at what happened then."

He winced. "I'm guilty of many foolish actions by night, ma'am. But in the bright light of day, I'm as meek as a kitten, and my word is as reliable as Sheffield steel."

Still she hesitated on the doorstep, though she took the parasol the maid offered her against the sun.

Seeing her reluctance, Darden sighed. "You know, ma'am, Greaves is not the only gentleman capable of looking after you as you deserve."

That *was* true. She'd managed most of her life without Tom at her side, hadn't she? And she did need to discuss the verse. "Only a brief drive, Lord Darden. And be sure your driver keeps only to the safest streets."

She gave her hand to one of the countess's footmen to help her to her seat in the carriage. She caught how Darden ducked to one side to gulp surreptitiously from the flask he'd pulled from his coat. Some men could not exist without their drink; she was sorry to see that Darden was one of them, just as Tom had said.

She was glad that Darden chose to seat himself respectfully across from her, avoiding the tussle of too-familiar side-by-side. She was glad, too, that he seemed determined to be vigilant for her sake, keeping his hand on the hilt of his sword while he purposefully glanced around the street in much the same way that Tom himself did. Yet still she doubted he'd have Tom's reflexes in the face of any genuine threats, and uneasily she snapped open her parasol, wishing it would shield her from danger as well as the sun.

Yet as the carriage rolled through the streets, the sun warm on her shoulders, she finally began to relax and look about at the houses and terraces and parks that they were passing.

"This city seems to be endless," she said, craning her neck to look to the golden top of a church spire. "How long it would take to see everything!"

"It would take weeks, ma'am. Maybe months. But I would gladly be your guide, if you'd but ask."

"Years," she said, "if you English continue your building at such a pace. Everywhere I look there is industry, scaffolding and carpenters and donkey carts full of lumber and stone."

"That's because everything in London must be improved, ma'am," he answered, clearly savoring his role as her instructor. Not that he'd gaze up at church spires and pediments the way she was doing; instead he'd pulled his floppy-brimmed hat low over his forehead to keep the bright sun from his eyes. "Little stays the same from one season to the next. The grandest houses from our fathers' day are torn down to make way for grander ones in their place. London gobbles land like a child with sweets."

"The common people in Monteverde do not look to the future like that," she said, remembering how scornful her father could be about the average Monteverdian's lack of ambition. How curious it was that the English didn't seem to be like that, too. "They are by nature lazy and idle, and content to let things remain as they are."

"Then I'm afraid we don't share your country's veneration for the old times." He sighed dramatically, a romantic's lament for the lost past. "Our heritage is Roman, too, you know, but we have no handsome stone lions to show for it. If we had, they likely would have been tossed into the river generations ago with a bridge built on top."

"Then you understand what will be lost if the French triumph." She tipped the parasol back over her shoulder and leaned closer to him, her voice low with urgency. "You have not only regard for Monteverde, but respect, as well. This is good."

"Of course I have respect and regard for Monteverde, ma'am," he said easily. "Just as I have respect and regard for that country's beautiful princess."

Impatiently Isabella waved aside the compliment. "Have you considered my request from last night, Lord Darden?"

Instantly the marquis's expression turned wary. "We said many things between us last night, ma'am."

"Yes, yes, but only one of real importance." She must keep her temper; artists and poets were notorious for being oblivious to details, and this poet drank, too. "I asked you to write me a tribute to Monteverde in verse. A great poem to be published, and help garner sympathy for my country's plight."

"You would trust me with such a task, ma'am?" It wasn't just that he'd forgotten her first request, or maybe hadn't heard it; he was so stunned that she wondered uneasily if the favor she'd asked was too much for him. "You would ask so much of me?"

She nodded. "I would, Lord Darden. I *did.*"

He leaned back against his seat and laughed softly up at the sky before he looked back at her. "Ah, ma'am, nothing—nothing—would give me greater pleasure. You cannot know how you honor me and my humble talent."

"I should hope they are not so very humble," she said uneasily. "They will be required to produce a work of the utmost importance to the future of my country."

But his smile only grew, more like the cocksure Darden she'd danced with last night. His color was coming back to his face as well, though Isabella wasn't sure if that was due to the fresh air or the furtive swig from the flask beneath his coat.

"So, ma'am," he said. "You can tell me. Is Greaves's jealousy perhaps more founded in truth than I realized?"

"There is nothing to tell." Isabella frowned, remembering the sour way that she and Tom had last parted. "The captain is not by nature a jealous man, Lord Darden, or at least he is not jealous where I am concerned. He has no special fondness for me, nor should he. You have misinterpreted his attentions. He is simply following his orders where I am concerned, nothing more."

"Then you misread him, ma'am. I've known Tom

Greaves all my life, and as much as he loves his orders—aye-aye, anchors aweigh!—his reaction last night had more to do with your lovely royal self than with any words from a mere admiral."

"You forget yourself, Lord Darden," she said tartly. She supposed this was his manner of flirtation, or perhaps the effect of those furtive gulps from the flask, but she didn't care for it, whatever it was. She regretted now that she'd asked him to write the poem for her and Monteverde, inviting this intimacy and obligation. Who knew what he'd write, or what favors he'd expect in return? "I find I must rescind my request to you regarding the poem. I find you are not suitable for such a gallant task."

He winked broadly, shocking her. "Since when does a muse take back her divine inspiration?"

"I am not your muse, Darden." She'd lost track of how far they'd driven from Berkeley Square by now, but if he continued in this vein, she'd have no compunction about ordering the footmen to put Darden out on the nearest street corner and then having the driver take her home alone. "You grow too familiar."

"Perhaps I do," he admitted, without an iota of remorse. "But then I'll wager Greaves has, too, hasn't he? He never was one to chase the skirts for sport, not even when we were rammy young lads. But when he found one he favored, he'd never want to let her from his sight. You're the lady he wants now."

"He does not!" Yet her conscience wasn't entirely at ease, not when she couldn't help remembering how they'd kissed this morning, and the excitement that had rippled between them. And her regret, too, that things had ended so badly when he'd left. If he—and she—didn't care, then it wouldn't have hurt, would it?

"Aye-aye, and ahoy to you." Once again he winked and pulled the brim back over his face. "I saw it at once, ma'am, writ bold all over his weathered old salt's face. He fancies you, admires you, worships you—we poets can count a hundred ways to say the same thing. Surely you, too, must recognize the signs. Why else do you think I could push him as far as I did last night?"

She didn't know which was upsetting her more: the marquis addressing her with so little respect, or his suggestion that Tom's feelings ran deeper than his orders. "Lord Darden, you misspeak."

"Why ever is that? Because for once I speak the truth?"

"Because you don't." For the marquis to concoct such tales of Tom and her—no. *No.* She leaned past him, addressing the driver. "You will take us back to Berkeley Square at once. At *once.*"

"Ah, ma'am, you give me hope, indeed you do." With a lazy grin, Darden suddenly recalled his role as protector. He shoved his hat back and peered out at the street, belatedly trying to look vigilant. "Where in blazes are we, anyway? We haven't crossed Oxford Street again, have we?"

"No, my lord," the driver said. "Once we turn about, we'll—"

"Follow the route we planned back to Berkeley Square." The marquis's grin remained, hardly the look of a scorned admirer. "If Her Royal Highness has had enough of my company and wishes to return home, I've no intention of keeping her against her will."

Pointedly Isabella looked away, concentrating on the

elaborate scaffolding that covered the face of yet another new house being built, instead of the marquis. Lady Allen had sworn that all the London ladies loved Lord Darden, for which Isabella could only feel monstrous pity for the London ladies who had so little taste or feeling.

The carriage slowed, preparing to turn the corner, and as it did a small wagon full of bricks cut in front of it. The driver shouted and swore at the wagon while he struggled to control the carriage's pair, the horses balking skittishly at the dray now blocking their way. Others on the street began to gawk and add their own suggestions, blocking the street even further.

"Bumbling ass." Darden had turned around in his seat to watch, too. "Letting his nag go lumbering out before us like that."

"In Monteverde, he could be put in gaol for such an insult to a nobleman." Isabella sighed impatiently, twirling the handle on her parasol. "Such affronts are not—oh, *santo cielo!* Darden, look! *Darden!*"

Two men with scarves tied over their faces were rushing across the scaffolding, bounding over the narrow boards, running as the sunlight caught the bright sheen of a blade and there was nothing, *nothing,* to stop the first man from jumping into the carriage beside her....

Chapter Nine

Though she had only a fraction of a second to decide, Isabella knew she had two choices when the man dropped into the carriage beside her. She could tremble with terror and shriek piteously for help like a proper English lady, or she could be a true Fortunaro princess, and fight back.

It wasn't really a choice at all.

The man was large, heavyset enough to make the carriage pitch and buck, and in his hand he held a long-bladed knife. She could see his muffled mouth smile beneath the grimy scarf, and the confidence in his eyes proved he'd already decided she was his for the taking.

He was wrong.

As he reached out to grab her, she smacked the parasol as hard as she could up into his chin. The bamboo handle cracked across his jaw, shattering in a tangle of painted silk and bent spokes across his face that made him topple back against the seat.

Furiously he threw it aside, swearing at her in Italian— *Italian?*—but Isabella had already hiked up her skirts and scrambled out of the carriage, running to the pavement beneath the shelter of the scaffolding. If only she could reach the crowd gathered around the horses, if only she could join the safety of the others!

But then the second man dropped down in front of her, jerking from side to side like a tattered crab to block her path as she tried to dodge around him. With each step he was forcing her back, until she bumped against the rough brick of the unfinished wall. No one would see her now; she was trapped in this corner, hidden by the stacks of lumber and brick. Fighting her panic, she groped blindly behind her, searching for a way out.

"Lost something?" The man wiggled his fingers, taunting her. "Something dear?"

"You let me go!" she ordered, her voice shaking. "You cannot keep me here!"

"Oh, yes, I can," he said, laughing at her. "I'm doing it now, ain't I?"

"You do not laugh!" cried Isabella furiously. She grabbed a short board from the pile left by the carpenters. "No one laughs at *me!*"

Using both hands, she swung the board with all her force, striking the man squarely in the chest. He grunted and staggered a step, giving her time to look back over her shoulder toward the carriage. She had a swift glimpse of Darden crashing swords with the third man, both of them struggling to stay upright in the rocking landau with the crowd now watching them instead of the horses—and instead of her.

But Darden had defended her after all, she thought with guilty surprise, and he was doing it with considerable skill, too. She could only pray he wouldn't have to pay for his chivalry on her account.

Not that she had time now even to pray for herself, not when the man in front of her was finished laughing.

"You're no better than the rest of your litter." He tore away his mask, not caring that she'd see his face now. His eyes were wild, outraged that she'd dare fight back. "Foolish royal bitch."

"You're from Monteverde," she said, holding the board like a sword between them. "I hear it in your Italian. You should feel nothing but shame for what you are doing!"

"A Fortunaro can speak of shame? The daughter of a tyrant?" He spit at her feet. "You think you can cross me, eh?"

"I can, and I will!" Breathing hard, she swung the board again, but this time he grabbed the far end of the board before she could strike him. She struggled to wretch it free from his hands, digging the heels of her slippers into the sandy soil. "A pox upon you, I *will!*"

"Not so, my royal whore." He jerked the plank, making Isabella stumble forward, then abruptly flipped it up, knocking her back against the brick wall. Waves of pain burst from her shoulder, sharp enough to make her cry out. She sank to her knees, and he yanked the plank from her hands.

"Begging for it now, are you?" He leered, smacking the board against the palm of his open hand. "Not so proud now, are you?"

"I *am* proud, because—because I am a Fortunaro!" She forced herself to stand and raise her chin, willing her unsteady legs not to give way beneath her. "I beg for nothing!"

He raised the board over her. "Then I'll give you this for nothing, you—"

His eyes bulged out with shock and his mouth gaped open as he lurched away at a crazy angle, clasping his side. Blood oozed through his fingers and spread over the cuff of his shirt to drip to the ground. He nodded once, twice, then pitched forward in a heavy heap at Isabella's feet. Only then did she see the yawning hole the bullet had torn through his coat and into his back.

"Bella!"

She hadn't realized she was crying until she saw how blurry Tom's face was as he rushed to her. In one hand he held the pistol that had killed the man between them, the acrid scent of gunpowder still ripe in the air. In the other hand was his drawn sword, and that, too, had blood on it, bright red on the silvery steel.

"Tomaso." She felt the tears now, sliding down her cheeks. "You came."

"I heard you. Tell me you're not hurt," he demanded, still breathing hard from whatever he'd had to do to save her. "Tell me this bastard didn't harm you."

She shook her head and took a deep breath, then another, laboring to calm herself and stop the tears. That was what she needed to do to ease the tension of a difficult situation, and to behave the way a Fortunaro should. But still she longed for him to take her into his arms and hold her, just hold her, and be only a woman, not a princess.

But of course that was impossible, especially with all the world seemingly here to watch. The narrow space seemed filled with people now, an audience of marveling, curious faces swirling behind Tom's shoulder.

"You are sure?" He was searching her face, confirming that she was telling the truth.

She nodded again. She felt as fragile as spun glass, and her shoulder was aching where it had struck the wall, but she would be fine. She *would* be fine. "I—I hit him back."

"You did what?" He frowned, not quite comprehending as he hooked the pistol back on his belt, then wiped off his sword and sheathed it. "You hit *him?*"

"I hit him. With that board, there." Remembering made fresh tears start in her eyes, thinking how close she herself had come to being another lifeless body lying on the cobbles. "I—I hit him as hard as I could with the board, directly upon his chest. It hurt him, too, enough to make him swear."

Tom whistled low. "Then you're more fortunate than you know. A man like that wouldn't like to be shown up by a lady."

"I struck the other man, also. He jumped in the carriage, and—and I hit him in the jaw with my parasol."

"You did that, too?" He glanced back at the carriage, as if looking for the parasol weapon.

"Yes." She sniffed in quick little jerks. "My parasol was carved ivory and painted silk from Florence, most lovely, and now it is broken beyond repair, but it was quite—quite worth the sacrifice."

"I'll buy you another." He handed her his handkerchief. "I'd say it died a noble death."

That reminded her. "Have you seen Darden? Is he—?"

"Darden is perfectly well." Tom's voice told her he'd just as soon Darden weren't well at all, but gone straight to the devil.

"Then where—"

"By his carriage. He fell, and struck his head, and I had

to finish things for him, which did not please him. He is…restoring himself with a flask."

She didn't have to ask more after that. She understood too much already. Poor Darden, to have his one chance at real heroics end so badly!

But Tom's attention had returned to the dead men. "Not much to be said for these two." He prodded a corpse's leg with his toe. "I wish we'd taken at least one of them alive, so we could thrash some answers out of him."

She took a deep breath and glanced again at the body at her feet. She'd never realized that the dead still bled once they'd died, or exactly what a huge amount of blood that could be. A sudden wave of nausea rolled over her, and she pressed Tom's handkerchief over her mouth. However wrong it was for a princess to cry in public, it would be infinitely—and ignominiously—worse to be sick to her stomach.

"Don't look," he ordered quickly. He stepped over the dead man, trying to shield Isabella as he took her arm to guide her away. "Here, let's find a way to get you back to Lady Willoughby."

But she insisted, steeling herself as another man rolled the body over to show the dead man's face, now frozen into an uneven mask of eternal surprise. "I must see, Captain. I need to know who they were, and what they wanted."

He frowned. "With vagabonds like these, we may never know."

"It—it's more complicated than that, Captain." Conscious of the others around them, she lowered her voice and switched to Italian. "At least two of the men were from Monteverde. I could hear it in their speech, and what they said to me. They knew who I was, and they knew my family, and—and they were hunting for me, Tomaso. I am sure of it."

"I thought as much." Tom's expression hardened. "Someone forged a note to send me on a damned fool's errand, else I would have been here to protect you."

"Again." She tried to smile. "If I hadn't been the damned fool myself, you wouldn't have had to."

"I'm not going to quarrel with you, Bella," he said, not smiling in return. "It was my duty to watch you, and my fault that I didn't, and that's an end to it. Besides, no princess should have to admit to being a damned fool about anything. Now tell me. You didn't know this man, did you?"

She made herself look at the body one last time to be sure, then shook her head. "Take me to see the others."

"Be certain," he warned. "It's not a pleasing sight for a lady."

"I don't expect it to be," she said. "But I need to know my enemies."

Reluctantly he led her through the milling crowd toward the carriage. Sword fights and gunshots, murder and mayhem in the broadest of daylight: Isabella doubted that such things were common on the tidy new streets of London. She shouldn't be surprised by the numbers of the curious still hurrying to gape, as many children and women as men. Dusty tarpaulins from the construction had been tossed over the other two bodies, and several bricklayers stood with outstretched arms to keep the bystanders from coming too close. A constable in a greatcoat and an old-fashioned wig stood beside one of the bodies and dictated his observations to his clerk.

"Ah, Captain my lord," said the constable. "A sorry business, this. But I can assure you that there'll be no charges pressed. I have a score of witnesses who've told me what happened, and all say you're the hero of the day, not the villain. I'm told there's a third body?"

"Behind the wall," Isabella said, striving to sound composed and calm, as if she faced such events every day of her life. "I wish to view the others."

"This is Her Royal Highness the Princess di Fortunaro," Tom said, and an excited murmur rippled through the bystanders. "She was the target of the attack, and she believes she might know the dead men."

The constable touched the front of his hat to her, then bent down and flicked back the tarpaulin from the body. Isabella recognized this man as the one who'd jumped first into the carriage. His wide face bore a crisscross of scratches and light bruises where she'd broken her parasol, but what drew her eye immediately was the long slash of a sword wound deep into his chest. She remembered the blood on the blade of Tom's sword and wondered uneasily if he'd killed this man, too. The front of his coat and shirt was stained dark with blood, as were the cobblestones on which he lay, and once again Isabella had to swallow hard not to be sick.

"This one was the leader," she said softly, "but I do not know his name."

"Nothing on him to tell us, either," the constable said. "Not that I'd expect to find it. This lot's too clever for that. I'll wager no one will claim any of the bodies, either. A pauper's grave and a dose of quicklime will be all the blessing they'll have, or deserve, either."

But Isabella had to ask one more question, though she dreaded the answer. "Is there anything about his neck? A pendant?"

"A necklace, y'mean?" With none of Isabella's own squeamishness, the constable roughly shoved the dead man's head to one side and ripped open the front of his worn shirt. A narrow cord was tied around his throat, and the constable snapped it free.

"Don't know what this is about." He studied the crude pendant looped through the cord. "Must be the sign of one of their gangs or cabals. Is this what you sought, ma'am?"

He held his palm out to Isabella. There was the same triangle of twigs, tied with red thread, that she'd seen first around old Anna's neck, and also worn by the murderous seamstress at Copperthwaite's. All three were from Monteverde, and all had wished her harm.

Yet not once before in her homeland had she seen such a necklace or symbol, or overheard anyone in the palace discuss it. Why had no one warned her of this group, whatever it might be, or the grim power it held? How had her family and their advisers been so oblivious?

For the last years she'd been taught that the French, first with the republicans and then under Buonaparte, were her country's worst enemy. But what if there were another, more terrifying threat, eating away at Monteverde from the inside? What if the same anarchist madness that had destroyed the royal Bourbons of France was now growing beneath the noses of those famous Roman lions, eager to devour the Fortunari in one vicious bite?

What if, except for her, it already had?

"Bella." Lightly Tom touched her arm, drawing her back to the present. "Have you seen such an emblem before?"

She nodded, a tiny jerk of her chin. She didn't wish to tell him more here, not before so many others, and he understood.

"Do you know its meaning, or what group would wear a charm like this one?"

"No." She must be strong, stronger now that she'd ever been in her life. "Not yet."

"With your leave, Constable, I'll take this to White-hall," Tom said. "The navy has experts there who might decipher its meaning, or at least give us more clues."

"Then good luck to them, I say." The constable handed the triangle to Tom, who slipped it carefully into his pocket. "The sooner we can rid London's streets of such foreign vermin, the better."

"Praise the gods, ma'am, you are safe." The marquis was ashy pale, leaning heavily on the arm of his driver. Although a makeshift bandage, patched with blood, was tied around his head, his hand still purposefully clasped the hilt of his sword as if eager to fight again. "To think that this should happen while you were with me."

"Oh, Darden!" Isabella gasped. "They said you'd not been wounded!"

"I wasn't, at least not by these rascals." He uneasily glanced at Tom, the tension between the two men palpable. "I was on the verge of delivering the final blow to one of them—that fellow, there—when he played me most barbarously false, kicking out my knees so I fell out here and struck my head."

"Yes." Tom smiled faintly. "What a pity the fellow didn't play fair as you tried to kill him."

At once Darden shoved himself clear of his driver. "Forgive me if I haven't had your advantages, Greaves, mastering the art of common brawling in His Majesty's navy."

Swiftly Isabella stepped between them. "Be mindful of how you behave, both of you. You have each done me a great service, and I thank you for it." Impatiently she shoved away the lock of hair that had slipped down into her eyes. "But do not spoil things now by strutting about like bantam cockerels to impress me, because it does *not.*"

She faced the constable. "I have seen enough. You need not show me the third man."

"My carriage is ready, ma'am." Somehow the marquis managed to bow with his usual flourish, even as his knees obviously threatened to buckle beneath him. "I'll have you back in Berkeley Square directly."

Tom bowed, too, but with the brisk efficiency of a sailor, not a courtier. "I have a hired carriage waiting. A *closed* carriage."

"You need to recover after this ordeal, ma'am," the marquis urged. "You've suffered more than any lady should have to bear."

"But you see, Lord Darden, I'm not a lady." She raised her head as grandly as if she'd been wearing one of her hated, heavy crowns instead of just her bedraggled hair. This wasn't for the two men alone, but for her larger audience, there on the pavement, and she raised her voice so they'd be sure to hear her. "I am the Principessa Isabella di Fortunaro of Monteverde, and I will not be cowed by a pack of low ruffians, no matter how far they have come to find me!"

To her disappointment, no one cheered or really even

seemed to notice. A few scraps of disinterested conversation, that was all, and as the constable's men began to cart away the bodies, the bystanders began drifting away, too. True, most of them likely had never heard of Monteverde, but she'd thought at least they would champion *her,* after what they'd just witnessed.

"You're not one of them, Bella," Tom said gently, reading her confusion. Sometimes she felt she'd soon have no secrets left, he understood her so well already. "These are regular English folk, not the grand ones you met last night."

"They're ignorant swine," muttered the marquis with contempt. "They should be made to show more respect to their betters."

"They're free Englishmen, Darden," Tom said, "and they'll show respect when it's earned. I've learned *that* in His Majesty's navy, along with the common brawling."

"Dangerous ideas, Greaves," Darden warned. "Republican ideas. Or is Robespierre now included in the Articles of War?"

But Tom only smiled, refusing to be baited again. "Any bully can keep order on a ship through fear and force, but in battle he'd better watch his back against his own men. I would imagine the same holds true for kings and countries."

And even, thought Isabella, for the daughter of a tyrant.

"Take me home, Captain," she said, her voice no more than an exhausted whisper. Her shoulder hurt, but the ache inside that had come with this unwanted knowledge was so much worse she didn't know how she'd bear it. "Please, please. Take me home now."

* * *

Tom stood before the looking glass in his bedchamber with his sword in his hand, critically studying his bare chest. He sliced the sword through the air, watching how the muscles worked. He could feel how they protested, too, after the brief skirmish in the street this afternoon. Yes, he'd won, and he lived while the three Italian men had died, but he'd been fortunate his opponents had relied more on untrained bluster than finesse, or things might have ended differently.

He scowled, lifting the sword over his head. Being on shore for so long had cost him his fighting edge. All the practice in the world couldn't replace that. By the candle-light, his skin looked too pale, or maybe it was the contrast with the jagged scar that cut across his ribs. Even after so many months, the flesh remained still puckered and red, twisting the dark hair on his chest into an odd asymmetrical pattern.

Yet the scars didn't trouble him. He knew precious few sailors who didn't have more gruesome souvenirs than these, and there was a certain kind of honor attached to scars, anyway. What worried him lay beneath the bones and flesh, to the grim predictions that the surgeons had made about his heart.

Today he'd tested that heart without a thought except to save Isabella—running, jumping, fighting, feeling the familiar heady rush of battle for the first time since he'd been wounded. He hadn't hesitated or held back.

With the sword still raised, he touched his other hand over the scar, over his heart, feeling the steady beat of his life. He'd done what he'd had to for Isabella, and his heart had followed. As straightforward and practical as he was, not even he could miss that irony. But exactly how much more could he risk for her? How much more could his heart withstand?

He heard the quick, light footsteps in the hall outside before the knock came on his door. One of the servants, he guessed, though he couldn't guess why any of them would come to his room now unless there were some emergency. Not taking the time to replace his shirt, he swiftly opened the door.

"Ah, Captain Greaves." Raising one brow, Isabella looked down at the sword still in his hand. "You have been fighting hobgoblins, yes?"

"Yes." He took her by the hand and drew her quickly into the room, closing the door after her. "Is there anything wrong, Bella?"

She raised her chin. "No more than before."

Yet even as he sighed with relief, he couldn't miss the agitation that seemed to vibrate from her small figure. "Does anyone else know you're here?"

"No one saw me come to your bedchamber at this shameful hour, if that is what you mean."

"It is," he said, trying to remind himself as well.

"How very gallant of you." She glided into the center of the room, her bare feet tucked into heeled mules. She wore the same light silk dressing gown that he'd remembered—how the devil would he ever forget?—from the first time he'd kissed her. This time, though, she'd pulled it tightly around her like a shroud, with her hands wrapped in the sleeves and tucked beneath her arms. "Gallant, but unnecessary. The household is all asleep by now, or pretending to be, leaving no witnesses either to Lord Willoughby's roaming, or my own."

"Lord Willoughby's roaming?" He was thankful for any distraction. She could dismiss his objections if she wished, but there was no mistaking the instant intimacy of having her here in his bedchamber. The covers had already been turned back invitingly on his bed for the night, and the single candlestick made for more shadows than light. "The earl sleepwalks?"

"After a fashion." She gave her shoulders a little shrug of indifference, the heavy loose braid of her hair shimmying down her back. "Each night the earl is in the habit of warming the beds and the bottoms of the parlor maids. I listen, for there is naught else to do. I hear. The countess retires to her rooms directly after dining, and drinks herself into the exact state of unconsciousness that will allow her to ignore the obvious. Is that scar the one that nearly killed you?"

"A pretty bit of cutwork and stitchery, isn't it?" He slipped his sword back into the scabbard on the table and belatedly reached for his shirt from where he'd tossed it over the back of a chair.

"Don't," she said softly, her attention lingering on his bare chest. "Please. You and I are beyond such petty English modesties, aren't we?"

"Are we?" he echoed, but still he left his shirt on the chair.

"We're past a good many things, I suppose." Restlessly she smoothed the tiny curls that had sprung free from her braid. "Besides, soiling your good name is not the reason I've come."

She fumbled in the deep sleeve of her dressing gown,

finally pulling free a thick cream-colored card. "This came for me earlier. The prince remembered his promise after all. He's invited me to an evening ball at Carlton House."

"Has he now?" Tom glanced over the elegantly penned invitation with mixed feelings. He knew this was where she belonged, among royalty like herself, yet he couldn't help wanting to protect her from the disappointment that he felt certain was sure to come with such an invitation. "You wish to accept?"

She looked up at him, her dark eyes solemn and oddly expectant. "Should I?"

"That's for you to decide." He looked at her curiously. "You've never asked my opinion before this. Why should you begin now?"

She flushed and plucked the card from his hand. "Because you are supposed to recognize danger and threats that may come to me. Because you are supposed to advise me in such matters. Because—because I did not wish to be alone tonight, and I needed a reason to come to you."

Abruptly she pivoted away, her head still high and her shoulders rigid. "Nothing in my life is how it should be, or how it was, or, more than likely, how it will ever be again. The whole wretched mess of it is turned upside down and inside out, without any rightful place for me to *be*."

"You're doing well enough in London," he said, that stiff, straight, little back adding a special poignancy to her words. He should have expected this from her. She'd been too calm, too collected, after all she'd been through earlier this day. "Mind, London's where your mama sent you. For now, you belong here."

"But why?" she cried forlornly. "As much as I try, I cannot begin to do what is right. No one wants to listen to me, or to help my country."

"Oh, Bella." He wanted to comfort her, but the words he needed wouldn't come. "Perhaps the prince's invitation will begin to change things."

"I am not so foolish as to believe that, Tom, not even from you." She sighed deeply, her shoulders shuddering. "He has invited me because I am young and pretty and amusing. He doesn't care a fig about Monteverde's future, or my own, for that matter, except that I might be a kind of talisman to protect him from sharing my family's fate."

"Then the prince is an ass, and blind in the bargain."

"And so, perhaps, am I." At last she turned back around to face him, her mouth twisting as she fought her tears. She flung her arms out to either side, the sleeves of her dressing gown slithering down her bare arms. "Look at me, Tom. Judge me. You said you have no trust in me, but by all the saints in heaven, I still do trust you."

"Now hold there, Bella, please," he murmured as he reached for her. He hated having his own words about trust, spoken in anger and frustration, tossed back at him, and he'd have given much to be able to take them back, or at least to make her forget them. "You're upset, that is all."

"Tell me more than that, Tom." She scuttled away, out of his reach, her breathing uneven and her voice rasping with misery. "Tell me *more!* Tell me why I am hated, despised, scorned by the same people who two years ago cheered and tossed flowers in my path."

"Bella, don't—"

"No, tell me, because I wish to hear it!" she cried, her arms still outstretched and beseeching. "Tell me how a wretched triangle of twigs now means more than the golden lions at our palazzo's gates. Tell me why I've become an evil creature to be—to be *killed* and ground into the dirt like some loathsome beetle."

"It's not you, Bella, I swear." He was moving slowly closer to her now, scarcely moving at all from fear of how she'd react. "It's the Bastille and Marie Antoinette and Buonaparte, and a thousand other things that have nothing to do with you."

"But it *is* me." She drew her hands in, hugging herself, and her eyes filled with fresh sorrow. "It's all because I am what I've always been proudest to be, and what I am above everything else—a Fortunaro princess."

"No," he said softly. Now he knew what to say. He'd tell her the truth. "No. Forgive me, Your Royal Highness, but you're wrong about that."

"Wrong?" Fat tears had begun to squeeze free of her eyes, sliding down her cheeks before she furiously dashed them away with the heel of her hand. "How can that be wrong?"

He lowered his voice to calm her and capture her attention. "Because when I look at you, I no longer see the Princess di Fortunaro of Monteverde. What I see first is just Bella."

Her face seemed to melt beneath the weight of her emotions. "Oh, Tom," she whispered. "Why am I so scared?"

"Oh, sweetheart," he said. "You'd be daft if you weren't scared after what you have survived."

"But I'm supposed to be brave and strong."

"To me you are, and always will be," he said, and he realized as he spoke that he'd never meant anything more. "But for this night, just be Bella, and I'll be brave for us both."

He held his arms open to her, a sanctuary if only she'd take it. For a handful of moments she hesitated, and in that endless few seconds Tom felt his own kind of despair and doubt, wondering if he'd gambled too much of himself.

But then with a broken sob, she flung herself at him in a tangle of tears and Genoa silk, her arms tight around his waist and her cheek pressed to his bare chest, over the scar that had, in a way, been the reason they'd met.

"Don't make me leave, Tomaso," she whispered hoarsely. "Let me stay here with you, where I know I will be safe. If you force me to go back to my room alone, I'll not last the night, I know it!"

"Hush now, hush," he said, brushing back the damp hair from her face. How could she imagine he'd ask her to leave? There were few things that had seemed more *right* in his life than having her in his arms, the glide of light silk and linen only a feather-light barrier between them. He could feel the warmth of her skin and every resilient curve of her body where it pressed against his. It was more temptation than any honorable man should have to face, and far, far more than he'd be likely to withstand after what they'd shared today. "I'm not about to cast you off now. I told you I have courage enough for the two of us, didn't I?"

"More than enough!" Her words tumbled out in giddy gulps as she pulled back to search his face, the anxiety and fear still bright in her eyes. "But how many times can we outlast death together, Tomaso? How many times will we be the ones who live, while others die in our place?"

"You cannot think that way," he said firmly, unable to imagine anything more vibrantly alive than this woman who had come to mean so much to him. "If you do, you might as well surrender outright. You have to start each day believing you'll live to see its end."

"Then make me think only of life, and forget the rest," she whispered, and before he realized it, she'd pulled his face down to hers and was kissing him.

Chapter Ten

Isabella sank into the kiss, losing whatever resistance she might have had and not caring, either.

She hadn't come to Tom's rooms intending to kiss him like this. She hadn't intended much beyond sharing the prince's invitation with him, and then spinning their conversation out as long as she could, keeping him awake to provide her with company. She didn't mean to admit to more than boredom and sleeplessness, and she certainly hadn't planned to confess that she *had* to stay awake because every dream became a nightmare that made her wake gasping with terror and soaked with sweat.

But once she'd seen the scar that slashed jaggedly across Tom's chest, tidy little resolves had melted away. The scar reminded her again of death and life, and how tenuous the line between them could be, not just for him, but for her as well. Over and over he'd risked his life to save hers, and each time they'd had luck on their side. But luck was fickle, luck was changeable as the wind, and again she wrestled with the awful consequences.

How easily she could have been killed today, her head cracked open by a swinging board. How easily Tom, too, could have ended his life in the street, lying in a congealing puddle of his blood.

And how easily it would have all ended without her telling him, showing him, that she couldn't fathom her own life continuing without him in it.

She parted her lips and hungrily drew him deeper, slipping her arms around his shoulders to hold herself steady against him. His fingers spread possessively to cover as much of her hips as he could as he drew her closer, and he kissed her more possessively, too, harder and deeper. She could feel how her heart was racing with desire and anticipation, melding together with the last scraps of her fear.

Without his shirt, she was newly aware of his scent, of the difference between the wiry dark hair of his chest and the smoothness of his skin, as well as the intensity of the heat that simmered between them, burning everywhere they touched. She could feel the hard ridge of his erection through his breeches, pressing there against her hip, and realized with heady joy that he wanted her—no, *needed* her—as much as she needed him.

She slid her lips from his mouth to his cheek, feathering little kisses across the length of his jaw. She loved the rough-smooth texture of his stubbled beard against her lower lip, his beard darkening his cheeks by this hour. She dipped lower, to the place on the side of his neck where his heart beat, and kissed that, too, her own heart quickening to match his.

"Damnation, Bella," he said raggedly, even as he slid his

hand up the length of her spine. "You're playing with tinder, lass."

"*We* are, Tomaso," she said, urgency making her voice husky. The sash of her dressing gown had come unfastened, and with a little shrug of her shoulders, she let it slide down her arms. Only the thin white holland of her night shift covered her now, no real covering at all. "Together."

He groaned deep in his chest as he realized how little she now wore. "You're making it precious hard for me to remember who you are."

"For tonight I'm just Bella," she whispered, kissing the salty little hollow at the base of his throat. "You said so yourself."

He turned her face up to kiss her again. "But in the morning you'll once again be Princess di Fortunaro."

"Oh, yes, for all that may be worth," she said, unable to hide her unhappiness. "Only a glorious past that may get me killed, and not much of a future."

"It's still worth a great deal. At least an invitation to Carlton House."

She sniffed. "The Fortunari were already great princes when the Hanovers were still barbarians, living along the Palatine in huts made of straw and mud."

"There, now, you make my point." He'd continued to stroke her back, down her spine to the curve of her bottom and up again, enough to make her arch like a cat. "You're a Fortunaro through and through."

"But I'll be Bella to you, as long as you wish it." She looked up at him through her lashes. "That is, *if* you wish it."

"How in blazes could I not?" he asked. "Bella, you'd tempt a saint to sin."

He hooked his thumb through the narrow strap of her night shift and eased it over her shoulder. The front of her shift slipped lower, and his thumb followed, tracing and teasing the swell of her breast until she shivered. She could feel her nipple pucker and harden, begging to be touched next. She flushed and didn't dare look down, sure the crest must show through the thin linen to betray her.

"Oh, my," she breathed. "That—that feels quite fine, Tom."

"It's supposed to, lass. There's no other reason to do it," he said gruffly, then paused. "Damnation, Bella. Did that bastard do this to your shoulder today?"

"Yes," she admitted with a quick gasp, forcing herself not to flinch as he traced the livid outline of the bruise with infinite care. "But it doesn't signify."

"It does, because it's you." His concern touched her almost as much as his caress. "You said I was the first man to kiss you. Does that mean you haven't—"

"I've never done any of this," she confessed quickly, blushing again. "Princesses don't. But I'm not one of your silly ignorant English virgins. We are much less prudish in Monteverde, and what my mother didn't explain, her ladies-in-waiting did. Oh, and my friends and my cousins. I was the only one who hadn't been married yet, on account of Buonaparte causing so much mischief among the other royal houses. But they told me everything about their wedding nights."

"I'll wager they did." He swallowed so hard it was more of a gulp, and he was unable to look away from her breasts. "But you *are* a virgin."

"I told you that already. I was being saved for the proper royal husband, who may now never appear. Exiled princesses are of little political value, you know, because my poor father had no power left to make me useful except for producing heirs with an ancient lineage."

"They should value you for yourself. You're not a broodmare."

"That's exactly what a princess is. The Queen of Naples has at least sixteen children, and is much praised for her fecundity." Because she was nervous, she knew she was talking too fast, babbling and saying too much, until she truly *was* like one of those foolish English virgins. To make things worse, Tom was sliding his finger back and forth just inside her shift, grazing the side of her breast at the same time in a way that was exceptionally distracting. "I don't have any yet, of course."

"Because you're a virgin."

"Yes." She smiled uncertainly. She'd always heard that gentlemen liked being the first love in a woman's life. Why else were there so many songs and stories whose entire point seemed to be deflowering maidens? "But I do not see this as a hindrance to you."

"A virgin, and a princess whose purpose in life is to be fertile. Oh, blast. Blast and *hell*." He took a deep breath and carefully pulled the lace-trimmed strap back over her shoulder. "I'm sorry, lass, more sorry than you'll ever know. But my orders are to keep you safe. Taking you to my bed wouldn't qualify."

"I suppose it would not." She sighed with unhappy frustration, and fidgeted with the strap he'd just replaced. "But I don't answer to your admiralty, do I? And you would not 'take' me to your bed. I would go because *I* wished to be there. Because you are the only rock left in my life, and because—because I do not want to *die* a virgin."

"Bella, I never said—"

"Stop, Captain, I am not done yet." She was making him angry now, testing his precious self-control, and she didn't care. "I will tell you what I have never told another man, Captain Greaves, not anywhere under heaven. I love you. *I love you.* There, I have said it, and now if you die or I am killed by my enemies, then at least I—"

"Damnation, Bella, I will not let them take you from me!" He seized her by the shoulders and kissed her again, his mouth hot and demanding and leaving no space for her to protest. She twisted against him, pushing back, and felt herself swaying off balance. She clung to him to keep from falling, but instead he crooked his arm beneath the back of her knees and swept her backward onto the bed.

With a gasp of surprise, she sank deep into the feather bed, and then sank further still as Tom stretched out over her. He was holding most of his weight on his arms, but she was still acutely aware of how much larger and stronger he was than she, of his body against hers and all the places they touched, especially since so many of them now were skin against skin. Her bruised shoulder hurt, too, but if she told him, he'd stop.

"Don't talk to me of death and love together, Bella," he whispered hoarsely, his breath hot on her cheek. "Not for us."

"Not love?" she whispered fiercely, daring him, refusing to back down, even if she was already lying beneath him. "Or not death?"

"Didn't I tell you to believe in life?" He bent to kiss her, his mouth pulling such dizzying pleasure from her that she whimpered, a sound lost between their mouths. But he heard it, tasted it, retreating just far enough to nip at the lobe of her ear, making sure she listened in return. "This is life, lass. This is for you."

"Then this *is* love." Her heart was racing with excitement and anticipation of what would happen next. She wriggled beneath him, struggling to pull her shift back down over her bare thighs, but all the wriggling seemed to do was settle him more intimately between her legs, making him groan. "Even I can tell that."

"Can you now?" He pushed aside the fragile bodice of her shift, and his hand closed over her bared breast. Gently he cupped the soft flesh and rubbed his thumb over her nipple until it began to harden and peak. She gasped at the unfamiliar sensation, stunned by how instantly her body reacted to his touch.

Her own hands were sliding up and down his back, her fingers moving almost convulsively over the knotted muscles and smooth skin. She loved touching him as much as she loved being touched, and she doubted she'd ever tire of either. She was hot inside and out, her breath so tight that she felt as if she had hot coals in her chest, and her limbs seemed at once both languorous and restless with a yearning that she still didn't quite understand.

Knowing what to expect was one thing, but she was fast realizing that experience—and its lack—was quite another.

"Ah, Tom!" She dug her fingers into the dark silk of his hair as she turned his mouth back to hers. "This is passion, too, yes?"

"*Yes,*" he growled, and she tasted the single word on his lips as he kissed her again. Yet it wasn't the same as when he'd kissed her before, because now he was reaching down to raise the hem of her night shift, his hands seeking her nakedness beneath. He slid his palm along the inside of her thigh, higher, higher, until he reached the softest place of all.

Instinctively she tried to close her legs over his hand, partly because she knew he'd discover exactly how ready she was for him, and she wasn't sure how he'd react to such wanton enthusiasm.

"Don't turn shy, sweetheart," he murmured, rubbing her taut muscles to make her relax. "You've never been shy with me before."

"I'm not—not shy," she answered automatically, her thoughts too fragmented by what he was *doing* to frame a better retort, "and I—oh, Tom. *Tom!*"

He'd found a place between her legs that she hadn't realized existed, at least not like this, and the way he was touching it, stroking it, teasing it, was making her sigh and shake and long for more. Vaguely she could remember what the other women had whispered about pleasure and passion and blinding joy, and now, at last, she was beginning to understand what they'd meant.

"I knew you weren't shy," said Tom, feathering hot kisses along her jaw that only served to build the fire within her as his fingers worked their magic. "You're brave and bold and hot as sin itself."

Whatever might have been left of her modesty evaporated. She arched and twisted, helping him free her body of the damp linen, and relishing this new feeling of his hot skin across hers. Almost, almost: he was still wearing his breeches, and impatiently she slipped her hands inside the waistband and over the muscled curves of his buttocks.

Blindly she tried to push the waistband lower over his hips, only succeeding in making him groan.

"You're a wicked creature, Bella," he said hoarsely, breathing hard. He pushed himself up on his knees, tearing at the buttons on the fall of his breeches. "I thought you'd never done this before."

"By all the saints, I haven't," she said, desire turning her voice into a panting, husky purr. She reached up to touch his leg, unwilling to be separated from him even for these past few moments it took for him to undress. "It's you, Tom. You—you *inspire* me."

"Ah, Bella," he said hoarsely, coming back to lie beside her. "You can see what you do to me."

She could see it by the candlelight, and she could feel it, too, as he pulled her close. She couldn't help trembling as he parted her, feeling him there at the very edge.

"Don't be frightened," he whispered, his breath hot beneath her ear.

"I'm not." She lifted her legs higher, drawing him closer as she circled his waist, as much invitation as she knew. "Besides, you said you'd courage for us both, didn't you?"

Yet as ready as she was for him, she still cried out with surprise when he entered her. She hadn't expected him to be so large, or so hot, and she hadn't expected him to plunge so deeply into her. The pleasure vanished, scattered, disappointing her even as she clung to him.

Somehow he kept himself still at first, letting her grow accustomed to him. "I'm sorry, sweetheart," he said raggedly. "Blast, I did not want to hurt you."

"It—it's not so very painful," she whispered, keeping back the tears so she wouldn't shame herself. "Truly."

"Brave lass," he murmured, kissing her. "It will get better, I promise." Slowly he began to move, another kind of stroking that echoed the touch of his fingers, and slowly, too, she began to move with him. She felt awkward and unskilled and not very brave at all.

Yet with each rocking motion it became easier, better, just as he'd promised, and as it did, the pleasure returned with it. She realized she couldn't keep still even if she'd wanted to, not with the sensations simmering and coiling inside her, pulling her tighter and tighter with delicious agony that she never wanted to end, until suddenly it all seemed to burst, exploding in a brilliant rush of release that made her gasp with delight. Almost at once Tom followed, collapsing with her in a tangle of arms and legs, ragged breathing and sweat-sheened skin.

"Come here, lass." Tom rolled onto his back, bringing her with him.

"Oh, Captain, not another order," she said, chuckling as she propped herself up on his chest.

He smiled, his eyes half-closed as he smoothed her damp hair back from her face. "Aye, another order, and for your own good, too."

"And yours, too, I'd wager." She bent to kiss him, a long, lazy, contented kiss that ended only because she had more to tell him. "Oh, Tom, what you've shown me, what you've given me, was perfection."

He grunted. "Not perfection, not by half, but I warrant we made a decent start."

"Decent, ha," she scoffed, tapping his bare chest for emphasis. "There was nothing decent about it, and a good thing, too. But I did mean what I said, Tomaso. I love you. I love you, and that only made the rest of it all the better."

"And I love you, too," he said with such gruff tenderness that she felt tears sting her eyes. "How could I not?"

"I will not answer that," she whispered, "because I don't think I *could* love any other man, not like this."

"I doubt there could be another woman after you, either, lass," he said, his expression endearingly solemn. He took her fingers and lifted them to his lips to kiss. "Though I've picked a devil of a way to show it, haven't I, tumbling a royal princess as if she were—"

"As if she were the woman you loved." She sighed, rubbing her cheek against the back of his hand. "That's enough, isn't it?"

He pushed himself up higher against the pillows. "What if there are consequences, Bella? Or didn't those fine friends of your mother's explain that as well?"

"Of course they did," she said softly, curling up against him. "Infant princes and princesses don't sprout beneath cabbage leaves any more than common babes do. But you know better than anyone else how—how unsure my future is. Why else would I have asked you to make me forget?"

"I will not forget," he said, as honorable as any man could be. "You have my word of honor. I'll be there for you, no matter what happens."

She smiled sadly, doubting he realized how little weight his promise would carry if there ever were any "consequences." There would be no question of marriage, not with his rank so far below hers, and no question of acknowledging the child, either. If she were still in Monteverde, she would be whisked away to a distant, discreet nunnery in the mountains before her belly began to show. Once born, the child would simply be made to disappear. The Fortunaro name would remain untainted, and with a suitable increase in her dowry, her virtue would, too.

Not that she'd spoil this moment by explaining any of it to Tom.

"I know it is a gamble," she said, "and I know the risks. But as much as I might wish it otherwise, I cannot consider my life beyond this day, this night with you, and not to-morrow until it comes."

"You'll always be a princess," he said, the regret and res-ignation in his voice unmistakable. "Even naked as you are, here in my bed, you're still Her Royal Highness. It's in your blood, and all the love in the world can't change that."

Perhaps he did understand after all. "And won't you al-ways be Captain Lord Thomas Greaves no matter what I do or say, with seawater in your veins instead of blood?"

He sighed, yet he smiled, too. "What a sorry pair to plot a course together, eh?"

"A most splendid pair," she whispered, turning her mouth up toward him, "because we'll plot it together."

"Together," he said, gathering her in his arms to kiss her. *"Together."*

Though the room was still dark with night, Tom woke at once. It took him only a second to realize where he was, and another second after that to remember that the woman curled sleeping in the bed beside him was Bella. But that was all the time he had to spare before he heard the scream again, echoing through the darkened house, and then he was out of the bed and pulling on his breeches.

"What is it, love?" Bella rolled over, her voice thick with sleep. "Where are you going?"

"I'm not sure." He buttoned the fall on the breeches, then took one of the pistols he kept loaded, quickly checking the powder. The woman's scream had turned into a long, quavering wail, and now there were other voices and doors slamming and running feet on wooden floors. "I must go find out."

Now Bella heard it, too. She flung back the covers, and scrambled to retrieve her dressing gown from the floor. "I'll come with you."

"No, sweetheart." He bent to kiss her swiftly. "I want you to stay here, where I know you'll be safe."

"You know nothing of the sort!"

"I promise I'll be back as soon as I can," he said, already halfway out the door. "Lock this after me, and mind you don't open it for anyone else. Understand?"

"Oh, yes, I understand," she said, thrusting her arms into the sleeves of her dressing gown. "You're giving orders again, Captain."

"Exactly." He paused, wishing for all the world he could stay here with her. "I love you, Bella. Always remember that."

She let the sleeves of the dressing gown flop down over her hands, and sighed. "I love you, too. But take care, Tomaso, please. For me."

He nodded, shut the door and ran down the hall toward the clamor of voices.

"Captain Lord Greaves!" Roused from his bed, without his powdered dress wig or livery, the butler hurried forward with a candlestick in his hand to light the fear in his face.

"Thank God you are here! There has been a terrible, terrible crime! Down here, quickly, in Her Royal Highness's bedchamber. I've instructed everything to be left as Rachel found it."

"Oh, Captain Lord Greaves, I am so glad you've come!" cried Lady Willoughby forlornly, looking faded and confused. "You will know what to do, won't you?"

"I shall try, my lady." A small crowd of frightened servants was gathered around the doorway to Isabella's rooms. They parted for Tom, and with the pistol in his hand, he stepped warily into the candlelight and swore.

The room was a shambles. Shattered glass from the forced window glittered across the window seat, with the casement still gaping open to mark the path of the intruders' hasty escape. Gowns and shoes had been torn from the wardrobe, stockings and ribbons and shifts dumped from the drawers of the chest and dresser. Feathers drifted like clumps of snow from pillows that had been ruthlessly slashed open, and even the vases of flowers had been dumped and smashed onto the carpet.

"Should I send a footman for the constable, Captain my lord?" asked the countess anxiously. "Should I summon the watch?"

"Not yet," said Tom curtly. "There's time enough."

Whoever had done this had been both thorough and brutally efficient, and a chill ran through Tom as he thought of what could have happened if Isabella had been sleeping here instead of with him. They must have known this was her room, though she'd been so free with calling out the windows that anyone watching the house would have figured it out.

But had they come here only for her, or was there something else they'd sought? The slashed pillows seemed too deliberate to be only frustrated vandalism. What could they have been hunting for? Her jewels? Though Tom wouldn't consider himself an expert, the jewels that Isabella wore—including the hated tiaras—surely would be enough to tempt thieves.

Yet he still couldn't shake the feeling that the intruders had come with another purpose, something darker and more complicated than simple thievery, and uneasily he glanced around the disheveled room again, expecting to spot the triangle of twigs that was becoming all too familiar.

"They—the men—they were still in the room when I came, Captain my lord," stammered the terrified young servant, tears streaming down her cheeks. "I came to build up the princess's fire, same as I always do at this hour, for she does like it precious warm when she rises, like she was still in Italy."

"Surely you must have heard them in here, Rachel," coaxed Tom. "It would have been impossible to cause so much mischief in silence."

The girl nodded. "'Course I heard the racket, but I thought nothing of it, on account of the princess breaking things so regular. But, oh, Captain my lord, I'd never thought it all would come to this!"

She began to weep again, and the cook slipped a comforting arm around the girl's shoulders.

"Did you see them, Rachel?" asked Tom gently. "Did you open the door before they'd left?"

The girl nodded and snuffled back her tears. "They must've heard me knocking, my lord. I opened the door, and they was fleeing out that window, there. I must've started them. I only saw the back o' the last one, climbing out like a thieving weasel."

"A thieving weasel's what he is, Rachel, stealing the poor princess away like that from her very bed!" The cook looked up at Tom, her eyes pleading for reassurance. "But you'll fetch her back, won't you, my lord? Even if it takes the whole royal navy, you'll rescue her, won't you?"

"Of course the captain shall rescue her," answered the butler sternly. "Kidnapping's a hanging offense, Bess. Captain Lord Greaves will see that Her Royal Highness is recovered and justice is done."

Stunned, Tom found himself lost for words. No wonder they thought he'd been wasting time, not calling for the constable. They believed Isabella had been kidnapped, when the only rogue she'd met with this evening was already standing before them. How in blazes was he going to explain *this?*

"I don't mean to doubt," said the cook contritely, "but when a royal princess is snatched away from our safekeeping, why—"

"Did you have a particular royal princess in mind?" Isabella sauntered down the hall, a half-eaten apple in her hand. "If this lazy chit had not been idle, but had come to my room at the usual hour, then she would have answered my wish, and I would not have been forced to go hunt for this apple for myself."

The servants stared, openmouthed with shocked surprise, while Tom felt nothing but relief. Was this part of being in love, he wondered, caring so much about another person? He fought to keep the grin from his face, and fought, too, against the urge to sweep her into his arms. She'd disobeyed him by following him, true, yet he didn't care. At least she'd shown the sense to invent an alibi to explain her absence from the room, however farfetched it might be. But much had changed since he'd left her in his room, and having her here was the only indisputable proof that she was safe.

"You are unharmed, Your Royal Highness?" asked the countess tentatively. "There is no further reason for alarm, ma'am?"

"Alarm? Because your staff is lazy, or because I am hungry?" She took another bite from the apple with crunching relish, and tossed back her braid back against her shoulder blades for good measure. "Neither would seem to me to be worthy of alarm, but then, I am not English, am I?"

She glanced impishly at Tom as if sharing some wicked joke. In a way she was. Her hair was once again smoothed back from her temples and her dressing gown tied neatly over her night shift, but all Tom saw was the unmistakable glow of satisfaction that radiated from her. Damnation, how could the others not notice it, too? She was swaggering with happiness, she was in love, and she'd just joyfully lost her maidenhead. And now, of course, he was going to ruin it all.

"I am sorry, ma'am," he said as gently as he could, "but there unfortunately is reason. While you were, ah, away from your room, several thieves forced their way in through the window and ransacked your belongings."

She gasped, her eyes wide with horror. "Thieves? In my room? Oh, *santo cielo,* no, *no!*"

She dropped the apple and pushed past Tom. With her

hand pressed tight over her mouth, she raced to the center of the room and stopped abruptly before the bed. Overwhelmed, her eyes filled with tears as she looked up to the heavens for solace, babbling to herself in Italian.

"Look, ma'am, there be your one of your jewel cases!" The countess's lady's maid darted forward, pulling the leather case free from the pelisse that had covered it. She unfastened the clasps and flipped open the lid, holding it up for Isabella to see. "Look, ma'am! They didn't touch your sapphires! Safe and sound, they are."

Yet to Tom's surprise, Isabella didn't seem relieved, or even particularly interested as the maid uncovered another shaped-leather jewel box, and then another.

"And here, ma'am, here's the case with your gold-and-coral tiara, and the one with the diamond roses and gold leaves, too." The maid opened and turned each case to display the contents to Isabella, almost as if they were in a jeweler's shop. "Rachel must have scared those nasty thieves away before they could rob you. But we'll have this tidied up for you in no time, ma'am, indeed we shall."

"Yes," murmured Isabella at last. "Yes, that is true."

She dropped onto the edge of the bed, clutching the bedpost with one hand to support herself. Yet as Tom hurried forward she drew whatever steeliness she needed from inside, and took a deep, shuddering breath to compose herself.

"They didn't steal the jewels, Tomaso," she said in Italian. "I thought they'd been taken, but they're not."

"A small blessing, yes. But I don't believe that's what they came for, and I don't believe they were ordinary thieves."

"No." She nearly faltered again. "Most likely they wanted me instead."

"I'm sorry, Bella," he said, hating how useless and empty the words sounded. This morning he'd go to the admiralty and raise hell. He would give his life to save hers—especially after tonight—but he'd reached the point where he couldn't do it alone.

"There is no reason for you to be sorry." She tried to smile. "I'm safe, and I'm here. Let those villains be content with empty pockets."

But Tom couldn't afford to be so optimistic. It had to be the same group of discontented Monteverdians that had attacked her before, and clearly nothing else would satisfy them except seizing—or murdering—Isabella herself. Tomorrow he'd give orders that all the house's windows be shuttered and barred at night, and he'd ask the admiral for a sentry to stand guard before the house. Her enemies were becoming more daring, and he'd no intention of letting them win. "They'll try again, Bella. They'll be back."

"So I must be sure to always stay with you, yes?" She nodded, as if everything were solved, and her resolution grew as she smiled again. "We'll be brave, and we will triumph together, Tomaso. *Together.*"

It was, decided Darden, the best thing he'd ever written.

For once his inspiration was a bottomless well, the words flowing so fast his pen could hardly keep pace, scratching feverishly across page after page. He'd almost forgotten the bump on his head, and he hadn't stopped for sleep or food, only pausing to refill his glass from the decanter that always sat on the corner of his desk.

This is what came of having a muse, and he couldn't imagine a better, finer one to have than Princess Isabella di Fortunaro. His first schemes for her fortune now seemed hopelessly shallow and petty, a shame he hated to admit to himself. And he'd tried to forget that she'd told him she'd changed her mind, that she hadn't wanted him to create for her after all.

None of that would matter now. Love would redeem him, and make everything right. Yes, love: for he was certain now that he loved her, with the pure, honorable love that a gentleman could only have for such a woman. She had the beauty of the goddess, the spirit of an Amazon warrior, and the rare genius to be his muse. To be sure, she would still have the great fortune in jewels that had first attracted him, but now he could grandly regard that as a pleasing incidental. Surely destiny had sent her to him for the express purpose of salvaging his life, his talent and his soul.

He had never seriously considered marriage. No suitable lady had ever held his interest long enough, and besides, no suitable lady would in turn consider him a likely prospect, not with all the debts and mortgages that would come with him.

But the princess was different. He would woo her with all his charm, save her from Pesci and the others, rescue her from the bumbling attentions of that philistine sailor man Greaves. He wouldn't always be able to fob the man off with a false note from his admiral. Perhaps he'd send Pesci after Greaves. And then, at last, he would make the princess his wife and his marquise.

He finished the last line of his poem, adding an inky slash of his pen to underscore the final brilliant irony, and sank back in his chair, exhausted. The first grimy light of a London dawn was creeping over the city's rooftops and chimney pots and through his windows. He couldn't recall working through the night like this before, as fired for writing as he ordinarily was for cards or faro. But then, he'd never had a muse before, had he?

He smiled, remembering how his fair Isabella's face had glowed with pleasure when she'd sat with him in the carriage. Surely she'd beam that way again when she read what he'd written for her and Monteverde, and purposefully he began stacking and squaring the pages, readying them to be sent to the printer. He would push the man to publish the work as soon as he possibly could. He wanted to declare his love proudly for all the world to see, and there wasn't a moment to be lost.

With a sigh of satisfaction, he patted the manuscript, then raised his glass in the general direction of Berkeley Square.

"To my own muse, my own love," he said. "To you, my darling Isabella, and to our future together!"

Chapter Eleven

"You know, Tomaso, it has been days and days since the admiral has called upon me." Isabella sighed, resting her head against Tom's shoulder as she stared out the carriage window. "Do you think he will be cordial, or has he quite forgotten who I am?"

"He's not forgotten you," said Tom. "I can guarantee that. No man who has a breath of life left in his body could forget you, Bella."

It should have been a compliment, a flirtatious, silly bit of exaggeration for fun, but instead Isabella heard something in his voice—an edginess, perhaps, a distance—that kept the words from being as light as they should have been. Not enough to protest, but enough to make worry flutter in Isabella's breast, even as she smiled up at him as brilliantly as she could from beneath her bonnet's curving brim.

"Still, he has reduced *me* to calling on him to make my inquiries, which is barbarously rude of him," she said, striving to keep her own manner light. "Royalty never makes calls upon anyone, or at least we never did in Monteverde. But it is still most kind of you, Tomaso, to take me with you to Whitehall like this!"

"I could hardly leave you behind after last night, sweetheart." He shifted his shoulder, not exactly shrugging her away, but making her feel as if her head was not entirely welcome there. "As you said yourself, the only way I'll know you're safe is if I keep you in sight. Besides, I want you to tell Cranford whatever you can, too."

Her smile faded, and she turned away, pretending to straighten her bonnet. What he said was true enough. But how she wished he'd said he'd wanted her there because after last night he couldn't keep away from her, that he was dizzy with passion, that he was half-mad with love for her!

That was what she longed for, and that was not at all what she'd gotten. The magic of their lovemaking—and it had been magic—had been scattered by the thieves who'd invaded her bedchamber.

Instantly Tom had become the ever-efficient Captain Greaves with a problem to solve, asking questions, taking notes, curtly ordering the servants about as if they were his own crewmen. Even the way he'd sought to comfort her had felt vaguely like a duty. Though it was barely dawn, he'd gone ahead and shaved and dressed in his uniform and gulped his coffee while writing letters, while she would have much preferred to escape from what had happened and return with him to the cozy sanctuary of his bed. But her wonderful, gallant lover had turned back into her brusque bodyguard, and nothing she'd tried seemed able to undo the change.

Why had all that detailed advice about finding pleasure in bed with a man never included what happened once you rose the next morning?

But she was honest enough to realize it wasn't entirely his fault. No: she'd claim a good measure of the blame for herself, or rather for the Fortunaro jewels still safely hidden away in the canopy of her bed.

She didn't know which had been worse: that awful moment when she'd been sure the jewels had been stolen, or the one afterward, when she'd realized they hadn't. She'd come horribly close to telling him, to breaking down and confessing to him and the servants—ha, to all of London!—what a priceless fortune she'd squirreled away above her bed.

She'd given herself to Tom, body and heart, but she couldn't break her vows to her family and share with him this last secret. Though she hated herself for lying to him, hated how that lie would destroy the trust between them, she still couldn't turn her back on what those jewels had represented to more generations of Fortunaro than she could count. What was her pitiful little life and love compared to tradition like that?

And she was certain now that Tom knew. Not about the crown jewels—not even he could guess such a secret—but that she was keeping some truth from him. Why else would he be so intent on whatever was happening in the street outside the carriage window instead of on her?

"We're almost at the gate," he said. "There's some sort of wagon blocking the road, but I expect we'll be there soon enough."

He frowned and self-consciously patted her hand in a way that made Isabella instantly wary.

"You do realize, Bella," he began, "that you're going to cause something of a stir at Whitehall."

She smiled, relieved. She had chosen the same wine-colored velvet gown with the gold embroidery, the necklace and earrings of rubies and pearls, that she'd worn the day they'd met, not only as a reminder to Tom, but also because it *would* attract attention in the entirely male halls and offices of Whitehall. She didn't have a uniform with gold lace and swinging epaulets and a chestful of medals to do it, but a gown like this was so thoroughly un-English that it brandished her difference without a word. Her dress announced her rank as a royal princess—even if that rank were losing value by the day.

"I should be vastly disappointed if I weren't noticed, there among all those sailors," she said. "I recall the 'stir' of being onboard the wretched ship that brought me here. A hundred men, all gaping at me as if I were the greatest curiosity imaginable."

"Exactly." He cleared his throat again, his fingers curling into hers. "You see my challenge, Bella. This morning I'd be inclined to thrash all hundred of those bastards—I mean men—for gaping."

She squeezed his hand, her rings glittering through the black lace of her gloves. "That would be very gallant of you, Tomaso, but also very foolhardy."

"I'd have my head handed to me for my trouble, true," he admitted. "Hell, they'd clap me in irons and have me flogged 'round the fleet, too, considering how most of the gapers at Whitehall will be admirals. But the worst would be that they'd all realize how matters have changed between us."

"Ahh." She wasn't sure how to answer this, and her hand went still. "This change—does it shame you before your superiors?"

"*Shame* me?" He stared at her, incredulous. "Damnation, Bella, what do you take me for? How could I be ashamed of the woman I love?"

She shook her head, not trusting her voice to answer. He loved her, no matter what she'd had to keep from him. *He loved her.*

"No, Bella," he continued firmly. "What I fear is that if the admiral learns we are lovers, then he will relieve me of guarding you, as rightly he should."

She gasped indignantly. "He couldn't! I would not allow it!"

"You would have nothing to say about it, any more than I would." She could hear the despair welling up in his voice, breaking through that gruff wall of naval duty. "The admiral would assign another officer to watch over you, just as I replaced the others. And it would damned well kill me, Bella."

"Then that is but one more reason for us to keep this between us alone," she said fiercely, twisting on the seat to cradle his jaw in her hand. She knew what he wasn't saying, too—that his career would be over, that he'd never again command a ship, that he'd have ruined himself for her sake—and every bit of it as damning as the ruin she could be facing with an illegitimate child. "My dearest Tom! What right does the rest of the world have to know about us?"

"None." He pulled her face to his and kissed her, quickly, possessively, as if daring the rest of the world to try to take her from him. "I won't give you up, Bella."

"Nor I you." She fluttered a rapid line of tiny, breathy kisses along his cheek before her lips returned to his. She curled into him, the better to feel the kiss vibrate through her entire body as his hand circled around her waist. Knowing how near they were to Whitehall's gates, how at any second the carriage's door might be flung open by a footman, how it could be their last kiss if the admiral learned the truth—all only increased their desire.

"Whitehall, Cap'n m'lord!" called the driver, and abruptly Bella realized the carriage had begun to slow. As fast as she could she flew away from Tom, across to the opposite seat, and hurried to smooth her skirts, retying the ribbons of her hat. By the time the footman opened the door to hand her out, she was once again Her Most Impeccable Royal Highness.

"You can clear the decks faster than any woman I've ever known," said Tom as he offered her his arm. "And I'll grant I'd never have expected it from a princess."

"Ha, you should learn to expect everything from me." They were walking beneath a tall arched entryway, crowned with a pair of carved winged sea horses. Before them was the wide, open courtyard before the old palace that housed the admiralty offices, the walkways and steps bustling with clerks and officers intent on navy business. A shutter telegraph blinked its messages from the rooftop, gathering important war information relayed from the Channel and the Continent beyond. The offices were the centerpiece of the English military strength, the intelligence that fueled the effort against the French.

Yet even in this place with so much serious purpose, she was still attracting attention, exactly as she'd wanted, with heads turning and feet slowing to gaze after her in her wine-red velvet and black lace. Any moment now one of the officers was bound to recognize Tom and come to greet them. Once again they'd become the princess and the captain, and this last scrap of time alone together would be done, perhaps forever.

"Steady now, Bella," said Tom softly, sensing her anxiety though he kept his attention straight ahead. "Be brave. You've only to master this day, and not the next. That's how we'll steer through this together, lass. One by one by one, exactly as you said."

"I *am* brave, Tomaso." They passed two officers who frankly appraised her from her toes upward, even as they lifted their hats to her. In return she stared at them with such frosty Fortunaro disdain that the younger flushed, and the other pretended to look past her. "And I am very, very good at keeping secrets."

"Yes," said Tom quietly, almost sadly. "I believe you are, Bella."

She glanced at him sharply, but he was already stepping forward to salute Admiral Cranston, who was hurrying down the steps to greet them.

"Good day, Your Royal Highness," he said, his expression serious and far more preoccupied than when he'd come calling in Berkeley Square. "I'm honored to have you here, though I regret that it's taken such an unfortunate circumstance to bring you."

"You should thank Captain Lord Greaves that it's not even more unfortunate, Admiral," she said, sweeping ahead and through the door with Tom at her side. "He has saved my life once again, you know, though he may have been too modest to tell you so himself."

"I did know that, ma'am." The admiral was huffing a bit

to keep up with her up the staircase. "Captain Lord Greaves is a reliable officer who reports events as they occur, including his own participation in them."

"I should hope so." She didn't dare look at Tom now, who was likely most unhappy with her championing him like this. But he *was* too modest, and she wanted him to take credit and be rewarded for all he'd done—especially if she were the reason he ever fell from favor with his superiors. "If I were you, I should make sure to grant him another fine medal to recognize his heroism."

"Thank you, ma'am." He didn't agree, noted Isabella, but then, he didn't refuse, either. He bowed, ushering them past a row of clerks' desks to his office. "This way, ma'am."

She was surprised by how small and cluttered the office was, with the two chairs waiting for her and Tom obviously brought in from elsewhere. Stacks of letters and dispatches covered the desk, and the detailed maps showing coastlines and currents hung along the walls. Isabella quickly noted that Monteverde's harbor was not among them, but before she could ask why not, she saw the crude little triangle of twigs sitting in the center of the admiral's desk and forgot everything else.

Tom saw it, too. "What have your experts told you of the triangle, sir? Did it make sense to them?"

"Unfortunately, it did." With a sigh, the admiral sat heavily in his chair, prodding at the triangle with the quill of his pen. "Though they seemed stunned to see it reach beyond Monteverde to surface here in London."

"Because of the princess," said Tom, his face grim. "The villains must have followed her here."

"That is possible," admitted the admiral. "Though more

likely it's the princess's arrival that has served as a cata-
lyst for those who are already here in London. Because of
the French, there are a great many foreigners in the city,
and a few more malcontents such as these would scarce be
noticed in such a motley stew."

Isabella's smile was tight. "My family sent me here because they believed I'd be safer than in Monteverde."

"Oh, you are, ma'am, you are." Cranford nodded em-
phatically. "If you were still in Monteverde, you wouldn't
have Greaves here to keep you from harm's way."

"That is true." She couldn't imagine her life now without Tom in it, and without thinking she glanced at him, as
much to reassure herself as to acknowledge his importance. He nodded slightly, encouraging, and just enough
for her. She longed to have her chair closer to his, and to
be able to hold his hand for comfort. Fortunaro or not,
alone she wasn't nearly as brave as she wanted to be. Together, together: that was what she needed now, to be together with Tom.

"Were any of your attackers known to you, ma'am?"
continued the admiral, either ignoring or not noticing the
exchange. "A man who might have worked in the palace
stables or kitchens, or perhaps the woman stitching on
your mother's clothing?"

Isabella shook her head. "I would never have known
such people."

"But surely when you went to the dressmaker, or the
theater, or—"

"Recall who I am, Admiral," she said firmly. "I am a
Fortunaro, not one of your newly minted Hanovers. We are
different. I have lived all my life inside palaces, and the

only time I left one was to travel to another. The world would come to us, not the other way around."

Yet even as she spoke, she could hear the change. Not so long ago, her speech would have been a scathing declaration of Fortunaro superiority, but now—now the same words had become more of an apology than a declaration, an explanation of what her life had lacked, instead of its glories. She couldn't help glancing back at Tom again, to see if he'd heard the difference, too.

The admiral, of course, did not. "You had never seen any of these individuals, ma'am, yet you knew they were from Monteverde."

"Oh, yes," she said. "The Italian spoken in my country is very different from other countries. More pure, more precise, more directly descended from the Latin of the Caesars. I know to your English ears there is no such distinction, but as soon as these—these traitors addressed me, I knew where they had been born."

"There are certain details of dress that marked them, as well," said Tom, leaning forward in his chair. "The men favor a kind of short coat, cut like a fisherman's, except for twin rows of buttons at the waist—almost like a belt."

Isabella nodded eagerly, hoping such details might be useful. "They wear coarse scarves around their throats, too, dyed a purple color from the ink of a shellfish to be found in our bays and nowhere else."

"Most interesting, ma'am," murmured Cranford, scribbling his notes. "Yet you never saw the triangle before you came to London."

"I didn't say that at all," said Isabella defensively. "Do not put words into my mouth. I first saw the triangle hanging from the neck of one of my mother's maidservants, the night I left the palace."

She heard Tom make a little grunt of surprise beside her, enough to make her wince. She should have told Tom about old Anna before this, and she wasn't sure now why she hadn't.

Thoughtfully Cranford tipped the twig triangle on its edge between his fingers. "Was she loyal to your family, this maidservant?"

"Until that night, I believed her to be so, yes." It wasn't a memory Isabella wished to recall—her first indication that her life as she'd always known it was ending—and she looked down at her lap. "She was to travel here with me as my servant, but instead she betrayed me, refusing to come and saying—saying many hateful and disloyal things to me."

Cranford leaned across the desk, not bothering to hide his eagerness. "Exactly what manner of things, ma'am? You must remember. You must tell me. What were the woman's exact words?"

Abruptly Tom stood, his hand on the back of Isabella's chair. "You press too hard, sir."

The admiral rose to his feet, too. "You forget yourself, Greaves."

"What I recall, sir, are my orders to protect this lady from harm, and you, sir, are overstepping your—"

"The admiral is merely doing his duty as well, Captain," interrupted Isabella, determined to hide her racing heart. Here she'd been worrying over revealing too much with a sidelong glance, while Tom might as well be pasting broadsides all over London. "Pray, sit at once, both of you, so I might answer his question."

Tom searched her face. "You are certain, ma'am? You are not too distressed to continue?"

"I can continue," she said to him, more softly than she should have. "I will."

Slowly Tom retook his seat, and the admiral did as well, while Isabella took a deep breath, both from relief and for courage.

"The woman called me a tyrant, a—an evil woman. What you would expect, yes? Then I noticed her necklace—exactly like the one you have there—and asked her if it was some heathen symbol, and unwelcome in the palace. She hid the triangle away in her bodice, and said it was not a heathen symbol, but one special to her family. After that, I gave the necklace no further thought."

"Thank you, ma'am," said Cranford, satisfied. "You have been most helpful."

But Tom's impatience spilled over again. "Her Royal Highness has told you what she knows, sir. She deserves to know what your experts have told you."

"Indeed she does. You both do." Cranford raised the little triangle up in his fingers. "Our scholars were delighted that you sent this to us yesterday, Greaves. They'd only heard of the wretched things, and never seen one firsthand."

"So what *is* it?" Isabella's hands clutched the arms of her chair. "If you know, Admiral, why won't you *tell?*"

"It is the sign of Trinita," said the admiral, so solemnly that at any other time she would have laughed. "An ever-growing group of revolutionaries working from within to overthrow the Monteverdian monarchy."

"Trinita—the *Trinity?*" Isabella gasped, horrified. "To

overthrow my father's kingdom? Oh, Admiral, that is not only evil—it is blasphemous!"

Cranford nodded. "Especially because in this case, it stands for a revolutionary trinity of the people, the army, and the state."

"Traitors, all of them!" Now Isabella was the one on her feet, pacing back and forth across the small carpet while the men stood as awkward witnesses. "What of a king, a leader? Such people can scarcely expect to rule themselves! They are like children, tempted to eat too many sweets. They *need* someone like my father, someone with wisdom and experience to guide them, and decide what is best!"

"They have decided for themselves, ma'am," said the admiral gently, "and they've decided to, ah, do without your family."

Isabella froze, the dread sick in the bottom of her stomach. She tried not to envision the worst: her mother, her father, her brother, slain with the same barbaric efficiency that the French had shown their king and queen. "My family are still alive, aren't they?"

"All our latest dispatches say so, yes." The admiral smiled, intending to reassure, yet there was still something in his smile that rang false to Isabella, and did little to calm the feeling of foreboding. "Be assured, ma'am, that to the best of my knowledge your family is safely removed from danger, though I cannot say precisely where they have found sanctuary."

She did not smile in return. "Are they safe because of their own devices and loyal supporters, or because of English assistance? When the enemy is Buonaparte, you will oblige, but when my father's enemy is from within, you won't?"

Cranford's gaze slid a fraction to the left, just enough to the left to make Isabella question whatever he said. "The navy's resources are stretched most thin in Italy, ma'am."

"Meaning they have not stretched sufficiently to include the Fortunari?"

Cranford's face settled into a ruddy, defensive mask. "We arranged your safe passage from Monteverde to London, ma'am, didn't we? Have not we protected you from these revolutionaries, ma'am, even though you are as much a target as anyone in your family?"

She made a dismissive little flick of her hand. "Considering how many favors the Fortunari have granted your king and his precious navy over the centuries, that is a paltry beginning at best."

She'd known she'd been a target from the night she'd fled from home, especially now that others must suspect she had the Fortunaro jewels. But hearing the admiral say so made it somehow more real, and even as fear shivered through her, she refused to be cowardly and show it. She *would* be brave. She was defending hundreds of years of her family's honor, wasn't she?

"Hasn't Monteverde always been England's ally against your hated French?" she continued. "Hasn't her great harbor always been a haven for your fleet's ships, whether fleeing from storms or enemies?"

"That is true, sir," said Tom beside her. "There's likely not an English captain stationed in the Mediterranean who hasn't thanked God for that lighthouse and the safe harbor behind it."

The admiral's white brows twitched with irritation. "It is not necessary to supply such obvious information, Greaves. I am not so far in my dotage that I've forgotten landfalls."

But Isabella realized that once again Tom had come to her aid, and it gave her fresh confidence. "Then I do not need to remind you, Admiral, that to know one's enemy is half the challenge of defeating him. You know this Trinita. Now all you must do is capture them, yes?"

The admiral's expression darkened. "It is not as simple as that, ma'am."

"For a great power such as your Royal Navy, with all your men and resources? To defeat a ragtag pack of scoundrels with twigs tied around their necks? Why, it should be as easy as that, yes?" She snapped her fingers, the sound muffled by her lace gloves but the emphasis unmistakable.

"It is not, ma'am." The admiral's face was livid from struggling to keep his temper. "It is not."

"Kings and kingdoms should keep together in these times, shouldn't they?" She smiled, daring him. "You are mistaken, Admiral Cranford, if you believe I came to England only to escape the French, running away like a frightened little chick. I have told you this before. I came here to help my country however I can, and I mean to do so."

"Very well, ma'am." The admiral let out a long sigh of concession, like steam rushing from a teakettle. "I will speak with the other admirals here, and we shall see what can be done. But mind you, I cannot promise—what the devil is it, Rogers?"

A hapless clerk had cracked the door. "I am sorry to interrupt, sir, but you did request that you—"

"To blazes with your damned request," said the admiral sharply, rising to his feet. "Tell them I shall be there directly. Forgive me, Your Royal Highness, I must excuse myself for a moment."

He stalked from the room, leaving the clerk to close the door after him, and at once Isabella rushed to Tom to throw her arms around him and steal a quick, fervent kiss.

"Here now, he could come back at any moment," said Tom, even as his hands settled on her waist to pull her closer. "You don't want him catching us like this."

"No," said Isabella breathlessly, slipping into the Italian that had become their lovers' language. "No, that would not be wise. But oh, Tom! Did you hear how vastly brave I was, standing up for Monteverde?"

He smiled crookedly. "You were only being yourself, Bella. Standing up for your country to other people is much of your charm."

"I know, I know, I know," she said quickly, unable to keep from running her hands lightly over his arms and shoulders, "but it needed to be said, just as the admiral needed to listen."

"You didn't leave him much choice, lass." He couldn't keep from touching her, either, and as he brushed his fingers along the side of her arm, he lingered on the curve of her breast, just enough to make her shiver. "You are an impossible woman to ignore."

"Oh, Tom, we shouldn't," she murmured. She stepped away again, out of his reach, but covered the place on her arm where he'd touched her, as if to keep the warmth of the little caress. "We cannot! I will not give him reason to order you away from me, the way you said he would."

He sighed deeply, clasping his hands behind his back with his legs slightly apart in the way that Isabella always associated with him.

"He hasn't yet, anyway. But I expect when he returns, he'll wish to speak to me alone."

"Alone!" she cried, pressing her hands together with dismay. "But I do not wish to be *dismissed!*"

"It will only be for a few minutes, and wherever they put you here in Whitehall, you'll be safe." He worked her hands apart, raising one to his lips to kiss. "Admiral Cranford is my commanding officer, Bella. I must do what he says, and so should you, if you care for me."

"You know I do, Tomaso."

"Then answer me quickly, before he returns. Are there any other, ah, details you should share with me?"

"You mean the old maidservant wearing the Trinita's triangle, don't you?" Guilty despair washed over her. "Oh, Tom, I never intended to keep that from you! It's only that—"

"Don't explain, Bella, because it doesn't matter now," he said gravely. "In difficult times, the mind often forgets things it doesn't want to remember, and God knows you've suffered enough these last months. But if there's anything else that you've just now recalled, any secrets I should know that would help—"

"No." She said it quickly, before she told him the truth that wasn't hers to tell. "No."

"I am glad." He smiled again, almost with relief, and that made her feel worse. "I haven't forgotten your claim to being so clever at keeping secrets."

She smiled back, her mouth dry as ashes and the reality of the Fortunaro rubies pressing down upon her. She pulled her lace-trimmed handkerchief from her reticule, dabbing it nervously at her temples. Oh, saints in heaven, she did not deserve his understanding, his trust, his patience, his love!

He glanced at the still-closed door, expecting the admiral to return through it at any moment.

"I've been thinking since last night, Bella. It's deuced hard to ask this of you, being a princess and all, but for your own welfare, I cannot put it off any longer."

His face was so serious, all captainish and dutiful, that Isabella's heart sank with dread, even as she tried to make a jest of it. "Ahh, Tomaso, you are as solemn as the grave itself! Cannot this horrible subject wait until we've more time?"

But Tom only shook his head. "We have to speak of it, Bella, or rather, them. The jewels, sweetheart. It's time we spoke of the jewels."

Chapter Twelve

"Jewels?" asked Admiral Cranford as he came through the door. "What jewels?"

"The ones belonging to Her Royal Highness, sir," said Tom, acknowledging the other man's return. "While the thieves last night fled before they could take her jewels from their cases, I believe it would be less tempting for her not to wear so many in public here in London, or perhaps to substitute some of the, ah, brighter ones with paste. That, sir, is what we were discussing."

But when he turned back to Isabella, he saw to his surprise that she'd be in no state for discussing anything. She'd turned as pale as the handkerchief in her hand, so white and frozen he feared she'd faint, and swiftly he grabbed her elbow to steady her.

"Here, ma'am, sit," he said, trying to guide her back to her chair.

But Isabella was too rigid to move. "That is what you wished to tell me, Captain Lord Greaves? That my jewels, my rings and other little baubles, were too gaudy for you?"

"Not for me," he said gallantly. "I only wanted you to make less of a show, a target, for those who wished you ill."

"Oh, let the lady keep her gimcracks, Greaves," the admiral said indulgently. "She's a princess. She should make a show when she steps out. Are you feeling better now, ma'am?"

Isabella nodded weakly, but the color was beginning to return to her cheeks. "Thank you, Admiral, I am. The mention of the jewels brought back the memories of those dreadful thieves last night, that was all."

"Good, good," he said, taking on the air of an indulgent host. "You've seen a spate of rough seas for a lady, ma'am, and according to my wife, the best cure for all that ails a lady is a dish of strong tea. How fortunate, ma'am, that Rogers here has just brewed a fresh pot, and if you'll join him in the antechamber—"

"For God's sake, sir, let her recover herself first!" protested Tom, but Isabella waved him aside with her handkerchief clutched tightly in the black lace gloves.

"Thank you for your concern, Captain, but I am recovered enough to oblige the admiral's wish to be alone with you. For this once, I shall be properly obedient, and go sip tea with his lackey." She smiled sweetly, and shifted to Italian that only Tom would understand. "And I wish you joy of that righteous old windbag of an admiral, Tomaso. See that he keeps his word about sending aid to my country, yes?"

She sailed from the room before he could answer, already overwhelming poor Rogers.

"So what's she prattling about now, eh, Greaves?" With a grunt, the admiral sat heavily in his chair, obviously pleased to be rid of the responsibility of female company. "No doubt spewing more venom about me in her foolish lingo. Well, no matter. We'll be done with her soon enough, won't we?"

"Will we, sir?" asked Tom, more sharply than he'd realized. He hadn't let himself think of the future where Isabella was concerned. Day by day, that's what they'd told each other.

"Indeed we will," the admiral said with far too much relish. "Go on, Greaves, sit, sit. I cannot tell you how pleased the admiralty is with you, and how you have handled this most difficult assignment. You have done precisely what we hoped, with verve and resourcefulness."

Though mystifying, that was better than the dressing-down he'd expected. "Thank you, sir, but I do not see how I—"

"Don't be falsely modest, Greaves," the admiral said. "Why, just consider what you did for the service yesterday. A captain in uniform rescuing a princess from a pack of foreign rascals, there in the street for all the world to see. Blood and thunder and courage to spare, swords clashing, a maiden in real distress. No wonder the papers are full of it this morning!"

"Thank you, sir," Tom said again, his discomfort growing. "But I did it from duty, sir. My orders were to save Her Royal Highness."

"Of course, of course." The admiral leaned over the desk. "Be honest, now. The scar—your old wound near the heart—it didn't give you any grief in that skirmish, did it? Not a twinge whilst you fought?"

"No, sir," Tom said, and to his own satisfaction, he *was*

being honest. "Not at all. But if I am to continue guarding the princess, then—"

"You might, and then again you might not." Cranford winked broadly. "The winds are changing, Greaves. I cannot say more than that at present. But I do believe you will be pleased with how you shall be rewarded for how you've acquitted yourself."

Instantly Tom's hopes skyrocketed. The admiral could only mean another command, a new ship and crew at last. For over a year, during his long, lonely convalescence, he'd thought of nothing else. He'd been tested, and he'd proved himself and his heart, and now he'd be rewarded.

And damnation, it wasn't going to be enough. How could it be, when his every thought kept returning to Isabella, to her laughter, her courage, how she'd looked in his bed with her hair tumbled over the pillow and the sheets tangled over the curves of her breasts and hips?

One day at a time was what they had, one day at a time....

"What of the princess, sir?" he asked softly. "What is to become of her?"

"I told you as much as I can, Greaves. Just mark what I said about those winds of change, and that they're blowing toward Her Royal Highness, too."

"Meaning that the princess will soon be able to return to Monteverde, sir?" It was not a question Tom wanted to ask, but for Isabella's sake, he would. As much as he loved her, he could never expect her to give up her homeland for his sake. "Meaning that she'll soon be rejoined with her family?"

Cranford's glance was faintly pitying. "Meaning that she'll no longer be plaguing you, Greaves. I should think you'd be pleased, considering all the princess has put you through. Your concern for her is admirable but soon will be unnecessary."

"Then your offers of assistance to her country weren't empty promises." Tom said it as a statement of fact, not a question, though God knows he didn't trust the admiral to tell him the truth any more than he'd told it to Isabella. "You knew that there were English ships in Monteverde's harbor already."

"Be reasonable, man." The admiral lowered his voice even though there was no one else within hearing. "Monteverde is a small country, of little strategic value to England. It produces nothing that England needs or covets, nor are any of its royal family related to our own king and queen. For generations its main value to us seems to have been to offer a wastrel's paradise to our young gentlemen on their tour. In my opinion that does not make it worth risking so much as one of my sailors' lives, especially not now."

"But what of the princess herself, sir?" Tom could not believe the admiral was speaking of Isabella so callously.

"Her future?" Cranford asked, his disinterest clear. "Oh, I suppose some manner of small pension will be settled upon her if she does not return to Monteverde. She will not continue at my poor sister's home, to be sure, but perhaps she can take rooms somewhere in town if—"

"But why the devil was she brought here to London in the first place?" Tom could barely contain his anger on Isabella's behalf. Why was it that no one else in London seemed to regard her as a person, a woman with feelings instead of just a titled exotic? "Why didn't you just leave her with her family?"

"Because her father the king asked it as a favor, and at that time the princess was believed to be useful." Cranford shrugged, toying idly with the Trinita's triangle. "Surely you must recall that from your original orders. She was to serve as a symbol of resistance to Buonaparte on the Continent—a way to remind the people here in London that we were not fighting the French entirely on our own."

Tom did recall this explanation of Isabella's value. But that had been *before,* before everything had changed. "And now the princess is no longer useful, sir?"

"That is not my decision to make, Greaves." The admiral frowned. "Nor is it yours. You are to continue to look after the princess as you have been doing. Take her about the town. Entertain her as she pleases, and amuse yourself, too."

He slid a folded paper across the desk to Tom. "There's a box secured in your name at Covent Garden for tomorrow night's performance. That should make the princess forget her troubles, eh?"

"Covent Garden, sir?" Tom couldn't keep the disbelief from his voice.

"Yes, Greaves, tomorrow tonight." Cranford had heard that disbelief, and his displeasure showed. "And steer the princess clear of that wretch Banleigh. I know the ladies all dote upon him as a charming scamp, but the marquis is a drunkard and a rogue, and known to keep dangerous company in the bargain."

"Yes, sir." Hell, he'd forgotten about Darden completely, as if the troubles surrounding Isabella weren't complicated enough. "But now that we know of this damned Trinita, surely the princess should not be as—as visible. Consider the risk, sir. She'll be as good as a sitting turtledove in a theater box."

The admiral glanced at him sharply. "I never expected you to be frightened, Greaves."

"I'm not frightened, sir. I am careful, and there's a world of difference between the two."

"And I say you are overreacting. The princess will enjoy the plays and sitting in the box to be admired, same as every other lady does. Hiding her away in cotton wool and wood shavings serves no purpose."

"Except that it might save her life." Damnation, why was it he seemed to be the only one who gave a fig about Isabella's survival? "I propose, sir, to keep her within your sister's house for the next few days, and, with your permission, to post a guard outside the—"

"A sentry in Berkeley Square?" Cranford asked incredulously. "Don't be preposterous. I would never insult my sister and her husband that way, not after the strain of the hospitality they've already had to show such a thankless guest."

"But, sir, the princess—"

"The princess has you, Greaves." The admiral's expression was stern and fixed, putting an unquestionable end to any further protests from Tom. "That's more than she deserves, and if she's fortunate enough, it's all she'll need."

And as Tom rose and bowed, he could only pray the admiral was right.

"You can't possibly know how exciting this is for me, Tom." Isabella leaned over the edge of the box, holding tightly to her fan as she stared down at the swirling crowd below. Even though it was nearly seven, time for the first play to begin, most of the seats in the boxes and benches in the pit were still empty, just as most of the other patrons were much more concerned with calling to their friends and showing off their clothes than in actually finding their places for the performance. "I've never seen anything like it."

"There's nothing much to see so far," said Tom, not nearly as enchanted. He was leaning back in his chair, concentrating more on studying the theatergoers in the boxes around them than on watching the musicians tune their instruments in the orchestra below. "Not until the curtain rises."

"It's all new to me," she said, "and I'll still thank you, whether you are bored or not."

"I'm never bored with you, Bella," he said, so matter-of-factly and with so little gallantry that she laughed aloud. "Now don't take offense. It's the truth, that is all."

"I'm not offended, Tomaso. I'm amused." She laughed again, pressing her fingers over her lips. "Everything amuses me tonight. Oh, dearest, dearest, you see I am *happy,* because you have made me that way."

He still was not at ease with her being so demonstrative, even in Italian, and she could have sworn he blushed now. Her rugged, weathered captain, shifted his shoulders and rubbed the back of his neck, and she loved him all the more for it.

Her smile widened, her joy spilling out. That was what she couldn't help, and why not? Since they'd left Whitehall yesterday, everything seemed to be better between them than she could have imagined. Something must have been said between Tom and the admiral, something that merited this change; she didn't ask, not really wanting to know.

But there had been no men with swords attacking them,

no menacing seamstresses or Trinita to threaten their lives. For these few days, she had made herself stop worrying about the Fortunaro rubies and Monteverde and the fate of her poor family, and he had not asked about them, either. It was almost as if they'd acknowledged how precarious their lives were, and agreed upon a truce, just for these few days.

Instead they'd retreated to his bed, laughing and teasing and eating biscuits and drinking chocolate, and making love in lazy, perfect passion. Day by day together was what he'd promised her—day to night, to day again—and together that was what they'd had. They both understood there wouldn't—couldn't—be more.

"I cannot take credit for the evening, you know," Tom was saying now. "It was Admiral Cranford who suggested it, and who secured the tickets for the theater."

She wrinkled her nose and made a little puff of dismissal. "But it is you who have brought me here, Tomaso, and it is to your bed that I'll go afterward."

"Where I intend to make you even happier," he said in a gruff whisper that made her shiver with delicious anticipation: he could do that to her without even trying. "And where you'll be safer, too. Here now, sit back a bit from that railing. No use in showing your colors to the whole world."

She pushed her chair back, more to be closer to him than to keep away from the rail. "I'm not showing any colors to anyone. Look at me! No one will guess who I am. Because you asked it, I'm drab and dull, without a tiara or any other jewels to speak of. Your Bella dressed as a dry little crow! No other man will notice me now, that is certain."

"No other man should," he said sternly, but the admiration in his eyes told her she'd managed to please him anyway, crow or peacock.

She *was* dressed with daring simplicity by her standards, in a midnight-blue silk gown with only the slightest silver embroidery at the hem and cuffs of the tiny puffed sleeves. No one would guess she was a princess. She wore no tiara, no necklace or bracelets, and only her smallest, most modest, gold earrings. Yet because she was on the arm of the man she loved, she felt more beautiful than if she'd been wearing the grandest court dress with garlands of rubies and pearls draped over her.

"No other man *will* notice me," she declared softly, "because I will not allow it."

"That won't stop them." He indicated two foppish young men in the box diagonally from theirs, both bowing and placing their hands over their hearts and generally trying whatever they could to catch her attention. "There's a pretty pair of fools for you now. But then I expect you've seen much the same in theaters all your life."

She shook her head. "I told you. This is my first time in a proper theater. We Fortunari never went to playhouses. Instead Father would summon the acting companies to come to us, and we'd have our entertainments in the palace. We'd sit on armchairs lined in a row in the ballroom, we children as solemn as could be so we wouldn't be sent to bed early. The actors and musicians would do their best, but without any curtain or scenery or lights, the performances were often not very good. I'm sure this will be much better."

But he wasn't thinking of the play. "You really were like a prisoner in that palace, weren't you?"

"I suppose I was." She smiled, but without the joy she'd felt earlier. "I never thought of it that way, of course, because it was all I knew. But now that I have gone out with you—in a carriage to an entertainment, a playhouse, even a milliner's shop—I realize how much I have missed."

He sighed, covering her hand with his own. "I've felt that way as well. When I would be keeping some endless watch on a ship in dirty winter weather, so cold my breath would freeze on the collar of my coat, I'd curse all the luckier bastards back in London, drinking and dancing with pretty girls."

She glanced at him curiously. "Did you think of Lord Darden then?"

"He would head the list." He smiled, remembering. "Though because you are a lady, I cannot tell you half the torturous punishments I imagined for him at the time."

"Then I shall simply have to imagine them for myself." She grinned, then turned back toward the railing. Finally people were taking their seats, while scraps of an overture were beginning to rise from the orchestra. Two boys were carefully lighting the footlight lanterns on the edge of the stage.

Down on the benches, in the cheapest seats, Isabella spied a young couple so enthralled with each other that she doubted they'd even notice when the play finally did begin. The girl was close to her own age, and from her checkered kerchief and plain linen gown, Isabella guessed she was a milkmaid or a laborer in a factory. Her sweetheart was an able-bodied sailor in his shore-going best—a glossy black straw hat with his ship's name painted on the crown, a new bandanna around his neck, and brass buckles on his shoes—with his long pigtail proudly plaited down his back. He was holding the girl so tightly she might as well be sitting on his lap, while she giggled and tickled his nose with one of the daisies from the bouquet he'd given her.

"Look at them." Isabella pointed with her fan. "Those two, there. That could be us, you know, if fate had put us with different parents."

Tom looked over the rail to where she was pointing, and raised a skeptical brow. "Why can I not picture you living beneath a cottage thatch, rising before dawn to draw water from the well and scatter corn for the hens?"

"I could do it," she declared. "I could, if I knew how."

"There's not much of a skill to learn, pet." He laughed. "But I can't see you being content with such a life, not after having lived in a grand palace with more servants than you can count."

"But I would be free to go where I pleased," she countered. "I could go wherever I wanted, whenever I chose, without worrying over the scandal I might cause. I could be Bella, just Bella, with no wretched Fortunaro name tied around my neck like a great gilded millstone."

His smile faded as he realized she wasn't jesting.

"You are serious, Bella," he said softly, turning her hand so their fingers meshed. "You would prefer such a life?"

"Yes," she said without hesitation. "Because, Tomaso, I would be free to love you forever. Is that so very bad of me to want?"

The curtain rose and the audience whooped and applauded, but neither Isabella nor Tom were looking at the stage, this moment between them stretching on and on while the actors began their speeches.

"No, lass," Tom said at last, his voice raw with longing for what neither of them could have, his fingers tightening around hers. "It's not such a very bad thing at all."

Lord Ralph Darden stepped from the door of the tavern and patted the front of his waistcoat once again, making sure the folded news sheet was still tucked safely inside. Once again fortune was smiling upon him, and he wanted to be sure he smiled back.

For two days the princess had been not at home to him, but this evening the young footman who'd answered the door in Berkeley Square had revealed that Her Royal Highness had gone to Covent Garden with Captain His Lordship Greaves. Darden had waited until the first play was done, and now he would go find their box in the intermission. Greaves wouldn't be able to keep the princess from Darden there, not with so many others around them, and at last Darden could present her—his fair muse!—with his masterpiece in her honor.

No wonder he'd had to pause at this tavern for a drop to settle his nerves. He was acting like a greenhorn boy at the very thought of seeing the princess, his palms sweating and his mind a blank. But then, he'd never had so much invested in a lady, either, and one more time before he crossed the street to the theater, he patted the rustling spot where the printed poem sat in his waistcoat.

"*Buona sera,* my lord Darden." The old man's hand clutched at his sleeve with surprising strength. "Who would have guessed our paths would cross in this humble street, my lord?"

"Maestro Pesci." Darden's voice was purposefully

frosty. He'd no time to squander on the old man now, nor had he any wish to be linked so publicly with a foreigner of such questionable reputation. "You must excuse me, for I have other business."

"But my lord, my business *is* your business." Pesci smiled, his teeth mottled with age and decay. Wrapped in old shawls and scarves as if it were a January evening instead of June, he leaned heavily on the shoulder of a small, silent boy for support. "We must speak, my lord."

Darden pulled his arm free. "I am not in the market for any of your antiquities at present, *maestro,*" he said loudly, in case anyone among the passersby was listening. "Good day."

But Pesci's hand darted out and grabbed Darden's arm again, making it impossible for him to escape. "You are not listening, my lord, and you will want to hear what I say. Unless, having written your little filthy screed defending the Fortunaro tyrants, you have no further use for your whore of a muse?"

Now Darden grabbed Pesci by the shoulder, half-dragging him and the boy into the shadow of one of the square's market stands, now empty for the night. "You have no right to call her that."

Pesci's eyes burned feverishly bright. "Fine words from you, my lord? Who told me the bitch was here in London? Who gave her to me for vengeance?"

"Then I'm taking her back." Darden shoved the old man away from him, watching him stumble unsteadily, clawing at the boy for support. "Keep away from the princess, or I'll send the constable after you."

"Send him, send him, my lord!" Pesci cackled. His fingers trembling, he fumbled through the cocoon of scarves and shawls to find the crude triangular pendant hanging around his throat. Gently he stroked the amulet, calming himself, taking comfort from the three little twigs. "Do you think I would fear a lowly English constable, after I've seen the devil himself? I am an old man, my lord, with one foot already in my grave. Only the hope of retribution keeps me alive, my lord, the wish to make my persecutors suffer as I have."

For the first time Darden realized what he'd set in motion, and the real danger that faced the princess because of him. "The Princess di Fortunaro has done nothing to you!"

"But those of her blood have, my lord, and that will suffice." He coughed, a rattling rasp. "Unless I can know for certain the Fortunari are gone from Monteverde, their filth swept away, I will not stop, and she will be made to pay."

The intensity of the man's hatred horrified Darden. "You've already sent three men to their deaths."

Pesci's smile turned sly, smug. "No thanks to your keen swordsmanship, my lord, no?"

Darden flushed but refused to be sidetracked. "Three Monteverdian men dead," he said doggedly. "How many more will follow you?"

"As many as I need, my lord. London is full of those who have suffered from the Fortunari." The boy made an odd whimpering noise, and Pesci cuffed him hard with the back of his gnarled hand, then wheezed with the exertion. "I ask, and they will follow."

His desperation rising, Darden pulled the newspaper with his poem from his jacket and brandished it before Pesci's face. "Your cause will be ruined when others see this. London will be full of sympathy for the princess and

her family. I've shown the Fortunari for the noble rulers
that they are, descended directly from the ancient leaders
of Rome."

The old man shoved aside the newspaper. "You are
blind, my lord. The honest common Englishmen have no
patience for murderers and tyrants, and your vain, insult-
ing scribbles will only serve to show them the evil of the
Fortunari. 'The fools and rabble in the streets/Are the
wickedest tyrants o'er true nobility.' Ahh, I should be
thanking you for that, my lord, considering how many here
will join our side because of it."

"You're the evil one, Pesci!"

"Evil, evil." The old man squinted, an evil eye indeed.
"Did you know your darling muse has already spread her
legs for another, my lord? She shares the bed of the man
who guards her."

Darden swore. He was shaking from this terrible conversation, his forehead slick with sweat. "You don't
know that!"

"My men went to hunt for her and the jewels, my lord. Her
bed was empty. His was not. I tell you, she is a born whore."
Pesci smiled, clearly relishing Darden's reaction. "And you
lied about the jewels, my lord. If she had such a cache here
in London with her, my men would have found them."

"Maybe she gave the jewels to Greaves," Darden suggested, grasping for a way to shift Pesci's focus from the
princess to the captain. "Maybe he has them hidden in his
rooms, or in his belongings. Maybe he's taken them to
Whitehall for safekeeping!"

"No, my lord. A Fortunaro would never share such a
treasure with another. She will think only of herself, in this

and in everything. Your muse has no soul, my lord, no heart. She is as rotten, as corrupt, as every other in her family."

"But the captain—"

"I have no quarrel with the captain, my lord, nor *will* I."

Darden shook his head, denying everything. Yet still he could see his hopes for marrying the princess crumbling inside him, breaking apart in the place he liked to think held his heart, and with it was faltering the creative spark she'd inspired.

But maybe all he needed was another tumbler of brandy to make him think clearly. Yes, that would help. Brandy always soothed him, didn't it? A quick sip or two, just to make him sort out the truth from Pesci's lies, pure love from false hopes.

"I tell you, old man, you are wrong about the princess," he said, one last bit of defiance. "She is not like you say, not at all."

"Then go to her, my lord, and judge for yourself." Pesci seemed spent, done. Carefully he tucked the little triangle back inside his scarves and shawls. His eyes were heavy lidded, as if he were in danger of falling asleep, and he leaned so heavily on the shoulder of the boy that the child sagged forward, his head hanging from supporting the man. "But know that I will find her, too, my lord, and when I do, she'll be gone from you forever."

Chapter Thirteen

"**Y**ou say there is more to come after this, Tomaso?" Isabella sighed happily as the curtain dropped for the last time. "I'd be content if that one play were all, though I do believe that one player was not right for Apollo. He was far too stout for his costume, and I do think his whiskers were pasted on his cheeks. How sorry for the god of light!"

"It's all trumpery, lass." Tom laughed. He'd thought the play the silliest nonsense imaginable, but Isabella had enjoyed herself so thoroughly that he had, too, sharing her delight. "They say the ancient gods were immortal, but these poor players aren't. Forty years ago or so, when that old bloke first took the role, he was probably as perfect an Apollo as ever you'd wish to find."

"Oh, you are so very *logical,* Tomaso." Isabella scowled fiercely, as if to chase away his logic. "I suppose that is excellent when you are at sea, but you are supposed to be whimsical and impractical when you are watching a play."

"One of us must be practical and logical, lass."

"Meaning you, and not I?" She flipped open her fan and

pouted over the top, teasing. "I can be perfectly practical when I must, yes?"

"Do not make me answer that, Bella," he said gravely, but she only laughed. Yet he wasn't entirely teasing. All the time that the portly Apollo was declaiming on the stage, Tom had been watching the other boxes around them as well as the pit below. It came naturally, this watchfulness, and life at sea had taught him to glean the significance from the smallest ripple of water, or to spot the black pinprick on the horizon that could be the top of an enemy's mast. Now he was searching the well-dressed crowd instead of the water, looking for a pistol barrel, or the glint of a knife blade, searching for anything or anyone that didn't seem to be as it should.

Perhaps the admiral had been right, after all, and Tom had overestimated the danger. Perhaps the three men who'd attacked the princess and Darden were also the leaders of the Trinita here in London, and their plotting had died with them.

Perhaps, but not likely.

Tom had purposely not told the usher or other attendants that the woman on his arm was the Princess di Fortunaro, and they were so well trained in discretion that none had asked. He was sure that most guessed he and Isabella were lovers, and there was no help for that. He could ask her not to wear a tiara, but there was no way he could make her put aside the happy glow on her face.

Again he glanced over the outside of the box. "The ballet should start soon. Would you like me to send for a dish of sweets, or a cup of punch?"

"You see, there you are, practical once more." She snapped her fan shut and held it alongside her face, lightly tapping her cheek. "And being practical myself, Tomaso, I'm considering more than a cup of punch."

"You are," he said, a statement, not a question. She was, of course, planning something, though he wasn't yet sure what.

"Yes, yes, yes," she said. "I'm considering how dark it is in the back of this box, and how, once the ballet begins, everyone will be looking at the stage and not at us. I'm considering that plush-covered bench, back there in the shadows."

"Bella," he said, his mouth turning dry because now he could guess exactly where this was headed. Already she'd discovered that she liked variety, and with her, he'd discovered he liked it, too, no matter how impractical it would be. Damnation, he was hard in his breeches already. "Bella, recall where we are."

"I do." She smiled, a wicked, seductive smile he'd come to recognize. She leaned from her chair closer to him, heedless of how near she came to spilling her breasts from the front of her gown as she rested her little hand on his knee. Her voice was low, husky, just for him. "And I'm considering, Tomaso, how it's been at least four hours since you last made love to me. Is there anything more practical than that?"

"Only if I'd said it first, Bella." He covered her hand with his own, sliding slowly up her bare arm. He'd never have enough of the touch of her skin, as velvety soft as that on a peach. "Though I'll grant that you—what in blazes is that?"

They both turned toward the box's door and whoever was knocking on the other side of it.

"Don't answer it," whispered Isabella breathlessly. "Then they'll go away."

"They won't," said Tom, and the knock came again, more insistently, to prove him right. With a muttered oath of frustration, he lifted his hand from Isabella's arm and eased his knee away from her hand. "And the door's not latched shut anyway. Enter!"

One of the theater's attendants swung the door open, bowing at the same time. "His Lordship the Marquis of Banleigh."

"Darden." Tom didn't bother to hide his feelings as he rose to bow curtly to the marquis. Like it or not, he did have to acknowledge the differences in their rank, even with such a sorry specimen as Darden. "What devil has brought you here?"

"No devil." The marquis made a graceful leg to Isabella, taking her hand to kiss the air over her fingers. "Rather it is Her Royal Highness that has drawn me here—a tiger moth to her fiery flame!—ready to pay her the tribute she deserves. You are enjoying the theater, ma'am?"

"I was." Isabella pulled her hand back, making it into a tight small fist of protest in her lap. "Mind what I say, Darden. I am here tonight not as the princess, but simply as the guest of Captain Lord Greaves. I hope you can respect that, and my privacy with it."

"But you *are* a princess, ma'am," he said, striving to be disarming. "And a most divinely lovely one, too. What could possibly be gained by pretending you are otherwise?"

He placed another chair beside Isabella's, sitting close beside her as if she hadn't spoken at all. Though Darden was, as always, beautifully dressed for evening, the greenish cast to his skin and the dark circles ringing his eyes were at odds with the fine linen and black broadcloth, and he was speaking too quickly, as if speed would mask the slurring.

Tom didn't know which disgusted him more: that Darden had blustered his way into their box, or that he'd needed drink to give him the courage to do it.

"The princess asked you to leave, Darden." Tom stood beside her chair, stopping just short of resting his hand possessively on her shoulder. "She was a sight nicer about it than I'll be, too. Clear off, Darden. Go, now, before I have to toss you out myself."

Darden tipped back his head so he could look down his nose at Tom. "You forget yourself, Greaves," he drawled. "Or rather you forget who *I* am, to address me so."

"I'd say it's you who's forgotten to oblige Her Royal Highness's wish."

"But you see, Greaves, I've done exactly that." He swung around in his chair to face Isabella, placing his open hand dramatically over his heart. "I've obeyed you, ma'am, and I have followed your wishes in a way no other could. You have seen today's *Herald Gazett?*"

Again Isabella drew back, away from Darden. "I do not read the English papers. I find the language oppressively taxing."

"But you should see this particular edition, ma'am. You must!" He drew a newspaper from inside his coat, smoothing the folds lightly between his fingertips before he handed it to her. "See what I have done for you, ma'am, precisely as you wished!"

With obvious reluctance Isabella took the paper, staring down at the page where he was pointing. She wasn't pretending when she claimed she didn't read English.

She'd told Tom much the same thing before, and he'd never seen her willingly do it. But she was reading now, frowning, her lips moving slightly as she struggled with the foreign English words.

"It's exactly as you wished, ma'am," Darden said excitedly, so eager for her approval that he didn't see the shock growing on her face with each word she read. "I do believe I've captured the essence, the very heart, of your family's heroic struggles against the base upstarts trying to wrest your country from you. An epic piece for an epic battle, ma'am, when right and nobility of spirit shall truly triumph!"

"No," she said, her voice shaking as she stared at the paper in her hands. "That is not what you have done, Darden. What you have written, what you have printed for all the world to read—ah, *santo cielo!*"

Darden pursed his lips and frowned, clearly stunned by her reaction. "Perhaps as you say, it is the language you find difficult. Perhaps you are unaware of the subtlety of the meanings I have given the words."

"Subtlety!" She shoved the paper back at him. "There is no subtlety in this, Darden, not in a single word of it!"

He held the paper with the rejected poem cradled in his hands as if it were a wounded bird. "But you could not have read it all, not so swiftly!"

"I have read enough to judge it." Her face was flushed, her eyes so bright with agitation that Tom couldn't tell whether she would strike Darden or burst into tears. "I have read enough to see how you have portrayed me!"

"That's enough, Darden." Tom grabbed the marquis's arm, determined to send him from the box. He didn't have to read any of the poem. The damned thing had wounded Isabella, and that was reason enough for him. "You're leaving now."

Isabella nodded, quick little jerks of her chin that betrayed how upset she was by Darden's offering. "I asked you not to do this, Darden. How right I was not to trust you!"

Darden struggled in Tom's grasp. "I've shown you as you are, ma'am, a princess rising like a phoenix from the ashes of her homeland!"

"You have made me into a hateful, selfish shrew, with no regard for anyone other than myself!" The tears were there in her voice, a tremble of white-hot fury. "You say I would trample the babies of my people and laugh at their suffering, that I might make myself richer by their deaths!"

"That was an allegory, ma'am," protested Darden. "A poetical fancy, no more! How could you not see that?"

"What I *see* is how you have insulted not only me, but all the Fortunari, from ancient times until now." She rose, furiously swinging her skirts around her legs, and snatched the paper back from his hands. With the paper raised high, she ripped it in half, then in half again, letting the pieces flutter like inky ribbons to the floor at the marquis's feet. "What I *see*, Lord Darden, is how much you despise me, to have treated me so callously, and with such cruelty, for your own amusement."

Aghast, Darden stared at the tattered remains of his poem as Tom roughly pulled him back toward the box's door. "I do not despise you, ma'am! That is as far, far from the truth as is possible—"

But his words were drowned out by a trumpet's fanfare from the orchestra, calling attention once again to the stage.

The portly actor who'd played Apollo had shed his false whiskers and buskins, and now, in a flowing purple robe, was holding his hands up for silence. He didn't get it, but the chatter and bustle dulled enough for him to be able to roar over it.

"Fair ladies and kind gentlemen," he began, rolling his *r*'s for extra effect. "We are most honored here in our little playhouse by the presence this night of an esteemed guest. A gallant salute, if you please, for Her Royal Highness the Princess Isabella di Fortunaro of Monteverde!"

He swung his arm up to indicate their box, leaving no question which belonged to the princess. The orchestra began a hearty, if ragged, version of the Monteverdian national anthem, while Isabella—Tom's own dear, darling Bella—stood riveted in place alone at the rail, stunned by the unexpected, unwanted attention.

And the attention was there. As the music rattled on, more and more faces turned to gawk at the princess in the midst, with envy or curiosity, admiration or lust. Yet somehow Isabella faced them all, standing straighter, her small figure more regal, more the perfect image of a Fortunaro princess with every unsteady note of her country's anthem.

She was, decided Tom, absolutely magnificent.

She was also as easy a target as he'd ever seen.

"Damnation, Darden," he said. "That infernal actor, the music—you did this to her, didn't you?"

Darden groaned, pressing his palm to his forehead as he slumped against the wall. "I thought the princess would want to be noticed. She told me she wanted to do what she could for her country by drawing attention to herself. She told me—"

But what Tom was hearing was the first catcalls over the music, a handful of jeers scattered throughout the crowd, all proof that others had read Darden's poem. Tom wouldn't wait for more.

He slipped his arm around Isabella's shoulder, sheltering her. "Come, lass. There's no dishonor in retreating to fight another day."

"I should wait for the end of the music," she protested. "It's not right for me to—"

The apple struck the chair beside her, landing on the seat with a hard thump that sprayed chunks of brown, rotting fruit over her skirt.

"Now, Bella, this way. Now. *Now.*"

This time she didn't argue. Ducking her head against any more apples, she took Tom's hand, her fingers damp with more fear than she'd shown.

"Where's Darden?" she asked breathlessly as they hurried from the box into the hall. "Where has he gone, the wretched coward? You did not read the poem, Tomaso. You don't know what he wrote about me. And now he has just run *away?*"

"He's gone to the devil, if there's any justice." More people were clustered in the hall than Tom would have liked, loitering there before they returned to their seats, and blocking the way to the lobby. "More likely he's gone skulking off to the nearest tavern to—"

"Look, it's that foreign princess!" called a man. "There, with her bullyboy! Another bleedin' Mary-Antoinette, are you, hussy?"

At once Tom turned around, back the way they'd come, pushing a path through the others as fast as he could, before anyone else recognized her. At the end of the hall was a door to a back staircase, and he forced it open and pushed her inside, latching it shut behind them. He didn't know if they'd be followed. He didn't wait to find out.

"Down the stairs?" she asked breathlessly, bunching her skirts in one hand as she began down the narrow, twisting staircase.

He nodded, leading her. He'd only done this once, years before, when he'd come with a friend who'd fancied one of the actresses. "This goes to the stage and dressing rooms. We'll leave by the back door, through the alley."

She nodded, her face tense. "They're following us, Tomaso. I can hear them. Oh, *santo cielo,* why do they *care* so much about me?"

"I don't know, lass." He could hear them now, too, someone pounding on the latched door at the top of the stairs. "This way, here."

He shoved open the door at the bottom of the stairwell, and they were suddenly on the edge of the stage itself. Dancers with rouged cheeks and plumes in their hair hurried past them, ready to take their places for the ballet.

"Here now, you two, you can't be here." The man blocking their path wore a leather apron, his sleeves rolled high over his arms and a dented, pinchbeck crown perched on top of his graying hair. "Manager's orders, Cap'n. No visitors backstage until last curtain. That means gentry, too, no exceptions."

"But we don't *wish* to be here, sir." Somehow Isabella had put aside her fear and now smiled up at the man, beseeching him with a sweetness no male could refuse. "We

were looking for the door to the alley. You see, there's a—
gentleman following us that we do wish to avoid, and—"

"Your husband, eh?" The man nodded sagely, studying
Tom with new regard. "Then down that hall, Cap'n, to
your right, and out you go. And not a step otherwise, mind,
or I'll send your old man after you."

They followed his directions, through the theater and
into the alley. He drew his pistol from inside his coat, and
she caught her breath beside him. He knew she didn't like
the gun, but this was a perfect spot for thieves to lurk. The
narrow space behind the theater was shadowy and dank
with oily puddles, and piles of discarded scenery and other
rubbish made the alley smaller still. Stray cats and dogs
picked through the trash, while two prostitutes were nois-
ily servicing their customers against the wall.

"Don't look, sweetheart," he cautioned as they hurried
by, spotting the light of the street ahead of them. "God
knows they'll pay no attention to us."

Yet once they'd reached the lights, Tom turned away from
the milling crowd at the front of the theater, dodging along
two side streets before he dared flag down a hackney. She
didn't protest, even though she was panting from keeping
pace with him in evening slippers not meant for walking.

He thought back to the first day they'd met, how she'd
belligerently insisted on attracting as much attention as she
could. Now she understood the risks all too well, even
pulling her shawl over her head to mask her face. It was
not a lesson most women in her position ever had to learn.

With a sigh she dropped into the corner of the cab, her
eyes closed as she caught her breath.

"My own brave Bella," he said softly. "Are you all right?"

She nodded, her eyes still closed. "They called me Marie Antoinette. You know what they did to her, don't you?"

"You're in London, lass, not Paris." He took her hand, her fingers icy. "We don't keep a guillotine in Leicester Square."

"I cannot say the same about Monteverde," she said, her misery palpable. "If I go home, who knows how long I'd be allowed to keep my head?"

"Then you had better stay a bit longer with me here in England." He pulled her closer, and with a sigh she nestled beneath his arm. He could not imagine giving her up now. It was a madman's hope, a lunatic's dream, yet he still couldn't picture his future without her in it. "Now we're going to call on Admiral Cranford, and decide what to do next. I'm thinking the country air would do you a world of good."

"Meaning you do not believe London is safe for me any longer." She sighed again, burrowing closer. "I am not a fool, Tomaso. Surely you have learned that of me by now."

He pushed aside her shawl to stroke her hair. "A fool would not have been clever enough to spin that tale backstage. There's nothing more beloved in the playhouse than a sorry cuckold."

She laughed softly. "You would not be so amused if you were my husband instead of my lover."

"The proper husband would always be amused with you as his wife." How much was not being said in this conversation, he wondered, and how much more did she expect? "The challenge will be to find him, won't it?"

She laughed again, warm, intimate, encouraging. "Given the paucity of suitable princes and grand dukes, I should venture that I never shall wed."

"Then perhaps you should venture beyond grand dukes and princes for your choice."

But she didn't answer, holding the silence long enough for him to realize he'd blundered.

"This day, this night," she said at last, her voice unbearably wistful. "Remember? Nothing more beyond that."

"Damnation, Bella, that wasn't what I—"

"This day, this night," she repeated. "That was what we promised one another, Tomaso, yes?"

But he did not answer, and she did not ask again, and the question was left to hang between them as the cab rolled through the London streets.

They sat on stiff little chairs in the admiral's back parlor, discreetly apart for the sake of propriety, but leaving a gulf that yawned as wide as the English Channel. Without his touch she felt adrift, and the single candlestick on the table that the disgruntled butler had left them for light only made the room more gloomy. Isabella tucked her hands into the corners of her shawl, wishing the butler had at least revived the coals banked in the grate for the night, or offered her a dish of hot tea. She was always chilly in London, and on this particular night, she felt as if the entire inhospitable English summer had settled in her marrow.

She wished Tom hadn't teased her about marriage and husbands. What good could ever come of such talk, longing for things that could never be, even in jest?

"I'm cold, Tomaso," she said softly, her shoulders hunched.

"I'm sorry, lass." Jagged shadows from the lone candle danced across Tom's face, hiding his emotions. "Who'd have guessed the entire household would be abed so early?"

"Your admiral keeps farmer's hours."

"Sailor's hours," he corrected. "Though that amounts to much the same thing. Not very hospitable for late guests."

"We're hardly making a social call, are we?" She tried to laugh, but the sound that came out was dry and weary, with no humor anywhere.

"Be brave, my Bella," whispered Tom. "Surely the worst of this night is already done."

Surely, surely he must be right, she told herself, for what more could go wrong?

But before she could answer him, Admiral Cranford himself came bustling into the room, in a florid brocade dressing gown with a tasseled nightcap to match.

"Ah, Greaves, prompt as ever," he said. "I'm glad you appreciated the severity of the situation from my note, for this is not—ah, Your Royal Highness!"

He stopped short, perplexed and frowning at her without any further greeting, and she felt that English chill spreading through her with fresh foreboding.

"I received no message, sir," Tom was saying. "The princess and I have been at Covent Garden this evening. You recall, sir. The box at the playhouse was your gift, sir."

"So it was, so it was." Fingering the sash on his dressing gown, Cranford frowned down at the floor, as if he couldn't quite bring himself to meet either Tom's gaze, or hers. "Well, now, this is deuced awkward, isn't it?"

"Not as awkward as what happened to Her Royal Highness tonight at Covent Garden," began Tom, but the admiral held his hands up to make him stop.

"Will you excuse us, ma'am?" He reached for the bell-pull to summon a servant. "This is tedious navy business, ma'am, and I'm sure you'd rather—"

"It is *my* business, Admiral, whether tedious or not," she said, sitting ramrod-straight in the uncomfortable chair. "I will not excuse you or myself, or oblige you, or otherwise leave. I will stay, and I will listen."

Cranford shook his head. "I do not believe that is wise, ma'am. What I must say to Captain Lord Greaves is not quite, ah, quite proper for you to hear."

"The princess stays, as she wishes," Tom said quietly. "She is a strong woman, sir, and since whatever you say will affect her life, she deserves to hear it, too."

Cranford's jaw jutted out. "She will not be happy."

"I am not particularly happy now, Admiral." Isabella waved her hand through the air, striving to look commanding and imposing, a true Fortunaro, even as her heart was racing with a kind of sick dread. "Proceed. Tell me what you were going to tell Captain Lord Greaves."

The admiral's eyes narrowed, accepting her challenge. "Very well, ma'am. If you insist, then you will hear. I have this evening the freshest news from Monteverde."

Isabella clasped and unclasped her hands restlessly in her lap. "My family? You have news of my family?"

"Your family is as safe as is possible, under the circumstances. Your father and brother are in exile with a small force in Parma, awaiting the opportunity to reclaim the country."

"That will not take long." Isabella nodded with a show of confidence. "You see, there are still those loyal to my father."

"But not enough, ma'am." Cranford tightened the sash on his dressing gown, tugging the ends hard. "Not nearly enough, not even if you believe the ridiculous drivel that the Marquis of Banleigh wrote for you. That sort of rubbish won't help your cause, you know, not in these times."

"I had nothing to do with that!"

"No matter." He cleared his throat. "I regret to inform you, ma'am, that England has decided it is in our best interests to withdraw support for your father's regime, and to grant it instead to the new government, forged by members of the Trinita."

Isabella gasped with shock, nearly overwhelmed by what the admiral was telling her. "But to support a pack of traitors over my father—over the Fortunari! Villains who have sworn to kill them, and have tried to kill me! You cannot do this, not after all my family has done for England!"

"It was a political decision, ma'am, carefully made and reasoned." The admiral's voice was hard as flint, in sharp contrast to his frivolous, flowing clothing. "We must consider the benefits to our entire populace and military forces, not to a handful of foreign individuals. We believe that the new government will have a better opportunity of countering Buonaparte than your father ever could."

A *foreign individual:* there it was, spoken aloud, what he'd always called her in his mind.

"But surely our generals will find a way to—"

"The generals and the army have sided with the Trinita. It appears your father's supporters are limited to his courtiers, and the few of his lords who have chosen exile with him. England's diplomatic relations with your father, ma'am, are now officially at an end."

"Damnation, I cannot believe you have told her in this way." Appalled, Tom was standing, his arms tensed at his sides. "You show no concern for her feelings, her welfare, her future—"

"I have done exactly as the princess wished, Greaves," Cranford said evenly, as if expecting this reaction. "I am only telling her the truth."

"The truth." She forced herself to take a deep breath, then another. Think, she ordered, think, *think*. She couldn't afford to faint or weep with hysterics. She was still a Fortunaro, wasn't she? "My father asked his ally for sanctuary for me, protection for his only daughter, and this is how your honorable country answers."

"I am sorry, ma'am," Cranford said, too automatically to be sincere. "It could not be helped."

"Sorry." She stood, as straight and tall as she could, refusing to let the admiral look down on her. "If your country's diplomats have ceased to support my father's regime, Admiral Cranford, then I must end our relationship, as well. You cannot scorn a Fortunaro and expect no consequences."

The admiral's uneasy smile showed his surprise. "Here now, ma'am, it's not as if I'm tossing you out on the streets."

"How kind," she said, unable to hide her bitterness. "How generous. Especially after you'd no compunction about casting my father away like yesterday's fish."

"You cannot remain at my sister's house, of course," he said quickly. "Other arrangements must be made."

"Oh, of *course*," she repeated, her thoughts rushing ahead to clear her initial shock. She must leave London at once, and she must rejoin her family in Parma as soon as she could. And God help her, she must do it all with the jewels. She would have to return to Berkeley Square as soon as possible to make sure she could retrieve the petticoat with the rubies from the canopy without anyone else's knowledge. "I would not wish to outstay Lady Willoughby's hospitality."

"Hospitality, hell," Tom thundered, striking the table beside him with his fist. "Everywhere she turns in this town there's someone bent on killing her. Where in blazes is she supposed to *go?*"

She glanced at him swiftly, grateful and pleading at the same time. As much as she loathed the admiral at this moment, he was still Tom's superior, and she did not want him to say things on her account that he might later regret.

"Don't, Tomaso, please," she said in low, urgent Italian. "Let this be my battle."

"Together, Bella," he said firmly. "I'm not going to abandon you now when you need me most."

"I'll find my way," she said, though she hadn't the faintest idea how. "I'm a Fortunaro."

"A Fortunaro, with a Greaves. That should answer the Trinita well enough."

"I won't let you destroy your future for me, not when you—"

"I do not know what you are saying, ma'am," interrupted the admiral sharply. "But you have no right to speak to one of my captains in that manner."

She glared at him furiously. "And you, Admiral, have no right to tell me what I can and cannot say to Captain Lord Greaves!"

"I do, ma'am, when you choose to insult one of my officers," he said, his own temper scarcely in check. "Because you are no longer under the navy's protection, you are also no longer the responsibility of Captain Lord Greaves. He has acquitted himself with honor and resourcefulness in this most difficult assignment, and he will be rewarded with new orders in the morning."

"No," she whispered, refusing to believe. How could he order Tom away from her? How could he turn love into an *assignment?* "No!"

"No." From Tom the single word reverberated through the room, as emphatic as his fist had been against the tabletop. "I'm not done with this assignment, sir. I will not abandon the princess any more than I'd leave a ship adrift in the middle of the sea."

The admiral looked at him sharply. "Consider what you are doing, man. Refuse a posting once, and there's no telling how long it will be before another will be offered."

Isabella shook her head with despair. She knew how much he loved the service, and how much he'd longed for another ship to command. How could she ever hope to compete with that? How long would it be before he'd blame her for what he'd lost, and his love would turn to hate? "Oh, don't do this, Tomaso, I beg you, not for me!"

But Tom stood firm, if anything standing taller, straighter, more resolute. "I know the consequences, sir. The gentlemen in Whitehall have long memories. But I must also live with my own conscience."

The admiral grumbled ominously. "Then it's a damned foolish conscience, Greaves. You pulled yourself back from death's very grip, and for what? To toss everything away for some foreign woman? Is she really worth that much?"

"To me the princess is worth infinitely more, sir." He bowed and came to stand beside Isabella, resting his hands on her shoulders. "I've always tried to act with honor, sir, and God help me, I'm not going to stop now. Come, lass. The sooner we leave town, the better."

For what was likely to be the last time, Isabella nodded to the admiral and swept from the room on Tom's arm. But on the stairs, she lost her confidence, and at last the tears she'd kept back all evening spilled down her cheeks. Once there'd been a time when she would have delighted in a lover who'd make such sacrifices for her; she would even have expected it. But not now, and not Tom, and her heart nearly shattered from the awful responsibility of what he'd done for her.

"Oh, Tomaso, what have you done?" she asked in a feverish whisper. "You've given up everything for me, and what do I have to offer to you in return?"

"Love," he said, his voice rich and steady and without any doubt at all. "That's what you've given me, Bella. Love."

"Then may all the saints in heaven have mercy upon us," she whispered, closing her eyes as he bent to kiss her, "and pray that love will be enough to make up for the rest."

Darden slumped in the seat of the closed chaise, watching Admiral Cranford's house with only his flask for company. The chaise was carefully parked at the end of the street, where he could see without being noticed himself. He'd learned he had no stomach for spying—he was tired and bored and his head hurt abominably—but just as he'd decided he'd guessed wrong and that Greaves and the princess had returned directly to Berkeley Square, the front door opened. Light spilled down the steps to the cab waiting at the curb, and in the brightness a man and a small woman with her head covered hurried from the house.

Eagerly Darden leaned forward, his hand on the latch. Though he couldn't see their faces, of course it must be them. Who else would be leaving this particular house, at this particular hour, and in such haste? All he wanted now was the chance to explain himself to the princess—his dearest muse, the woman he wished for his wife!—to tell her how he wasn't really the coward he'd seemed, and to beg her forgiveness. It wouldn't take more than a minute or two.

Yet as he saw the way the princess clung to Greaves's arm and the care with which Greaves helped her into the cab, Darden felt his courage slip away once again. He couldn't talk to her the way he wanted with Greaves present. He'd have to see her alone, and instead of joining them now, he sat back and watched as their cab drew from the curb and rattled down the street.

He groaned, once again disgusted with himself. But as he reached up to order his driver to leave, he saw something more that made him pause. Another cab pulled from the shadows, racing after the first. A dark-haired man in rough clothes was leaning from the window, intent on the chase, and excitedly calling to the two other men behind him. Though Darden couldn't make out his exact words, he heard enough to realize those words were in Monteverdian Italian. He was sure they were more of Pesci's men, just as he knew the princess was once again in danger because of him.

Darden swore, his heart pounding in his chest from what he'd just witnessed. If only he'd a pistol or a rifle, he could try to stop them, but alone and unarmed like this he was useless. What he'd give now to know for certain she was safe! He fumbled for his flask, desperately trying to figure what he should do next.

Yet suddenly he realized there were two more people on the street, as well. A tall man and a small woman, most likely servants from their dress, had come from a side door of the admiral's house, and now were hurrying away on foot, in the opposite direction from the one taken by the two cabs. Darden had a quick glimpse of the man taking the woman's hand to lead her, and the woman lifting her face to gaze up at him, her face inside the brim of her ugly sugar-scoop bonnet lit by a scrap of candlelight from a window. Then the pair slipped between two other houses and vanished into the night.

But though his heart twisted at the sight, at least Darden had his answer. For now—for him, for another day—his muse was safe.

Chapter Fourteen

"Not much further, lass," Tom said softly, taking care not to use her name in the remote chance someone overheard. "We're almost to the river steps, and once we find a boat, you shall ride in style the rest of the way."

He was proud of this plan, especially since he'd contrived it with so little warning or preparation. Switching clothing with the Cranfords' servants, then sending them away in the cab as decoys on a roundabout journey to nowhere had seemed an extreme precaution to the admiral—until from the windows of the house they'd all watched the second cab follow. It had been the last favor the admiral would grant, and Tom knew it had been given for his sake, not Isabella's.

Thanks to that ruse, he and Isabella would now have perhaps another precious hour to get a good start on whoever was chasing them. Given that Isabella was a princess, Tom was counting on those pursuers to expect her to travel in the luxury of a private coach to some great country estate, and not to consider sailing in the spartan anonymity of a little boat to the cottage his family had used for fishing expeditions.

Of course anyone who knew *him* would expect him to head to the water, the way he always did, but Tom was also counting on his own preferences being judged hopelessly inconsequential beside those of the princess.

But it was still an excellent plan. Together they could stay at the lodge as long as they wanted. Tom was hoping that once the news about the Fortunari downfall was commonly known, then the Trinita would lose interest in Isabella, and she'd be free to do what she pleased. And what happened to her—and him—after that was even less certain.

This day, this night, and nothing more.

And why the devil did she have to keep saying that?

"At least now you're more warmly dressed, thanks to the Cranfords' kitchen maid," he said, satisfied with the rough linsey-woolsey that was part of her disguise. "Silk's fine enough for ladies, I know, but it can be chilly on the river, especially by night."

"No wonder, considering how wretchedly cold your climate is. I cannot imagine what your English winter must be like, when this is summer." She tugged at the apron strings tied primly twice around her waist, likely the first time in her life she'd worn such a garment. "But I do intend to leave off these hideous woolly stockings once we're back at Berkeley Square. They're giving me blisters because they're so coarse."

"It's far too risky to stop at Berkeley Square." He shook his head, surprised she hadn't understood that already. "We're going directly to the Whitehall steps, and hail a boatman from there."

"No." She stopped abruptly, pulling her hand away from his. She had to face him squarely to be able to see him from inside that tunnel-like brim of her bonnet. "We must go back to Berkeley Square. I cannot leave London until we do."

"Be reasonable, Bella. That's the first place anyone would look for us."

"But I *am* being reasonable!" she protested, her voice rising to a wail of stubborn despair. "There are certain— certain belongings I must have with me, and cannot leave behind!"

"Not so loud, pet." He glanced about uneasily, hoping she hadn't wakened anyone in the houses around them. The streets were narrow here, the windows all dark for the night. The last thing they needed was for her to rouse the watch with some sort of foolishness about these "belong- ings" that couldn't be left behind. "Lady Willoughby will keep your belongings until we return. I know you've no love for the woman, but she's not about to put your trunks out on the pavement for the dustman."

"But she won't know—she *can't* know!"

"She already does," he answered firmly, taking her hand again. They had to keep going; they couldn't stand here in the street all night. "Or rather, she will, soon enough. I've already written a message to her from the admiral's house, to be delivered in the morning, telling her we've been un- expectedly called away. Come, Bella, we've dawdled here long enough."

She pulled free again, shaking her head furiously. "I must return to the house, Tom. I don't have a choice."

Before he'd answered, she'd turned away, determinedly walking from him.

"Damnation, Bella, wait," he said, grabbing her arm to stop her. "You don't even know which direction to go!"

"Then I shall stop," she said, "and ask the way."

"No, you won't. Look at me, Bella. *Look at me.*"

She didn't look. She glared.

"Now tell me what the hell is worth risking your life and mine to retrieve."

Her mouth was a tight, defiant line, but her eyes were contradictory, too bright, as if she might begin to weep again. "I can't tell you."

"Why in blazes not?" he demanded. "I've just about ruined myself for you tonight, and you can't tell me?"

"It's—it's a state secret," she whispered miserably. "From Monteverde. It's not mine to tell, not even to you."

He stared at her with disbelief. "What is it? Papers? Maps? Bonds?"

But she only shook her head. "I've already said too much, and after I swore I'd never say a *word*. Please, Tomaso, please. You must understand!"

"A state secret. Hell." He didn't understand. He doubted he ever would. But he did love her, the more fool he, and if this infernal *belonging* mattered so very much to her, they'd go. "Very well. We'll go back. But you must be as fast as you can, Bella, or I swear I'll leave you behind."

For the last time, Isabella climbed on the chair and pried the tacks from the top of the bed's canopy. While Tom had gone to his rooms to gather a few of his own things, she couldn't count on him to be gone long. She dug her knife into the heads of the tacks, not bothering now to be neat. Even though she could see the muslin lining to the canopy had not been disturbed, she still whispered a little prayer of thanks and relief as she peeled back the fabric and saw the petticoat with its treasure still hidden safely beneath. Swiftly she pulled it from its hiding place and slipped back down from the chair to the floor.

She'd forgotten how heavy the petticoat was with the coins and jewels stitched inside, the deadening weight pressing down around her hips and legs. Heavier still was the weight on her conscience, knowing that once again Tom had trusted her, a trust she most certainly did not deserve.

With a sigh she tied and knotted the petticoat's tapes around her waist, then shook her thick, borrowed servant's gown over it. Critically she glanced at her reflection in the looking glass, turning back and forth to make sure the petticoat didn't show. No one would ever guess the Fortunaro jewels were hidden beneath that coarse linsey-woolsey, which was exactly what she'd hoped.

But how long would she be able to keep such a secret from Tom as they traveled together? And how much longer would she wish to, no matter what she'd promised her mother?

"You are ready, lass?"

She started, not expecting Tom to rejoin her so quickly.

"Exactly as I promised, Tomaso," she said, giving him her brightest smile so he wouldn't noticed the guilty heat that flooded her cheeks. She retied the stiff, plain bonnet that made her feel like a horse with blinders, and over her arm she looped the small basket with a few other things she'd hastily gathered—a hairbrush, clean stockings, shifts, handkerchiefs—and joined him at the door. "You see I can be every bit as prompt as you."

"You found whatever it was you wanted?" He frowned down at the size of her basket. "That doesn't look large enough for even one of those tiaras."

"I'm not bringing even one," she said, taking his arm. She kept her voice low, not wanting to wake anyone in the house. "I won't need them where we are going, and besides, if we are stopped, a tiara would be very difficult to explain."

He smiled, pleased that she'd made such a practical choice. "The explanation would be easy enough. Dressed as you are, any stout watchman would assume you'd stolen the tiara from your mistress, and were now making your escape to the nearest pawnshop."

"Better a thief than a princess," she whispered as they hurried down the back stairs. "At least an English thief has a trial before she's judged and sentenced, which is more than a mere princess seems able to expect."

They left the same way they'd entered, through the kitchen and out the back door to the narrow alley that ran behind the grand houses. Only a weak quarter moon hung in the sky to guide them, and Tom had not wanted the fuss or bother of carrying a lantern. The streets were very nearly empty, and the only others they saw were as determined not to be noticed as she and Tom were.

After a lifetime of always being the center of attention, this trying hard not to be noticed was an odd sensation. She felt free and unfettered, like a pony that had managed to jump the fence. She could almost *be* that ordinary young woman she'd seen with her sweetheart at the theater—except that she was anonymous only through a disguise to deceive the men who wished to kill her, her sweetheart was carrying two pistols and a knife beneath his coat, and she herself had a king's ransom sewn into her petticoats dragging at her with every step.

"How much farther, Tomaso?" She'd lost any sense of time and distance, though her blistered feet were telling her she must have walked more in this night than she usually did in a month. "I know you are accustomed each morning to marching miles and miles and *miles,* but I am not, and—"

"We're being followed." His voice was low, muted with tension. "Keep moving. We're almost there."

"Who is it?" She forgot the blisters on her heels as the fear she'd felt earlier in the theater came rushing back with a fresh edge. Without thinking, she turned to look over her shoulder.

"For God's sake, don't let them see your face!" He jerked her back around. "It could be one of your Monteverdian bastards, or only an ordinary footpad. I don't know for sure, and it really doesn't matter. All that concerns me now is that we reach the river, and pray there's a boatman hunting for a passenger at the bottom of the steps."

They dodged between pyramids of stacked barrels, darted across another street, and suddenly the river was before them, a wide, glistening strip of pewter gray in the muted moonlight.

"Down here." Tom pulled her through a break in the iron railing, to the top of a long, steep flight of stone steps leading to the water. There was no railing, the stone was slick with moisture beneath her shoes, and she clung to Tom's arm, terrified she'd slip. If she fell into the water, she'd vanish and sink straight to the bottom, the weight around her waist like a brick tied to the neck of an unwanted kitten.

"Our luck's changing, lass. There's a wherry below, waiting as prettily as if I'd ordered it."

She'd been too worried about slipping from the steps to think of the boat, but now when looked up, she saw the narrow boat with the single oarsman pulled alongside the last step. The man was sitting low over his oars, the bright spark of his pipe glowing before his whiskered face and a lantern in the stern. To Isabella the wherry seemed very small and insubstantial, perhaps fourteen feet long at best, and hardly the sort of vessel she wished to trust her life to.

"Ahoy there," called Tom softly to the boatman. "Are you looking for a fare?"

"If you be lookin' for crossing, sir, then I be lookin' for a fare," the man said. "Climb aboard, sir, and tell me where you an' the lady be bound on this fair evening."

"East," Tom said, volunteering no more just yet. Without a thought, he clambered into the boat and turned to hold his hand out to Isabella. "Come now, lass, there's no time to waste."

But Isabella could only stare down at the ever-changing gap between the boat and the step that she had to cross, yawning black water ready to swallow her up.

"I cannot do it, Tom," she whispered miserably. "I'm afraid."

"You, Bella? You're never afraid of anything." His hand reached for her, even as he looked up the embankment, scanning the top for whoever had followed them. "Now, lass. It's dangerous for us to linger here."

"But what if I fall in?" She had a vivid, terrifying image of the water clutching at her, pulling her down, closing over her head and never letting go.

"If you fell in, you'd float, same as everyone else," he said, "and then we'd fish you from the water and pull you in."

"But what if—"

"Damnation, Bella, *now!*" He leaned forward and scooped her into his arms and swung her into the boat at his feet, where she landed with an undignified little shriek. The stiff brim of the bonnet slipped over her eyes like a blindfold. As she tried to push herself upright, she heard an odd *plop* in the water near her ear. At once Tom drew one of his pistols from his coat and moved between her and the shore, shielding her. Another odd sound, this time a crack that sent needlelike splinters of wood shooting past her. With a grunt the boatman shoved clear of the step with his oar, deftly maneuvering the little wherry into the current.

"They were shooting at us, Tomaso, weren't they!" exclaimed Isabella from the bottom of the boat as she pulled the bonnet off and realized what had happened. Two shots, two balls, one meant for her, one for Tom. "Oh, how *dare* they do such a thing!"

"They dared, and they did." Sitting back on the bench, Tom locked his pistol and helped Isabella up to sit beside him, his arm around her shoulders.

"But why do they want me now?" she cried softly in Italian so the boatman wouldn't understand. Once again she'd nearly been killed, and Tom with her. "They've ruined my family, and stolen my country. Isn't that enough?"

"Most likely they don't know all that yet, lass." The boat had caught the current and was racing over the water, the spray flying up in their faces. "I'm hoping when they do, they'll leave you alone. But we should be safe enough now that we're out of range."

"But how did they know it was us, Tomaso?" She was shaking, and she needed his arm around her to reassure her. She did not *feel* safe enough, not with gunshots flying about them in this cockleshell boat. "I thought we'd been so careful."

"Forgive me for askin', sir," interrupted the man at the oars. "But you be Cap'n Lord Greaves, don't you?"

"Hell." Tom sighed with resignation. "You see how much carefulness has gotten us, lass. Our names must be painted on our foreheads."

He shifted back to English. "Yes, I am Captain Lord Thomas Greaves."

The man at the oars nodded vigorously. "Then I am honored, Cap'n m'lord, most honored. Jonas Perkins, your servant. My brother was with you in the *Aspire,* gunner's mate Adam Perkins, if you remember him. I saw you when you was in Portsmouth, Cap'n m'lord, an' I knew you at once when you hailed me on the steps."

"Perkins!" Tom grinned, and from the delight in his voice, Isabella wistfully realized once again how much he'd loved his ships and crews, and how much he was giving up for her sake. "Of course I recall Perkins! A good man, and an excellent gunner. Have you heard from him? How is he?"

"Well enough, I warrant. He'd only th' best ever to say of you, Cap'n m'lord, only the best." The man nodded solemnly. "So where be you bound this night, you and th' lady?"

"Just east of Greenwich, there's an inn on the water called the White Roebuck—"

"Oh, I know it well, Cap'n m'lord. The blades do love it for the turtle soup. I'll have you and th' lady there in no time."

"But you must not tell anyone you've seen us." Pleading, Isabella leaned toward the man, her hands clasped before her. "Please, please, I beg you, or that—that person who was chasing us before—"

"You have my word on it, miss." He nodded, tipping the pipe in his mouth for extra emphasis. "For the cap'n here, I'd forget my own name. I'll be silent as death, miss, silent as death."

"Thank you," she said softly, her words whisked away by the wind off the water. "I—we—are most grateful for your silence."

But not death. Please, please, not death.

The old iron key scraped in the lock, and Tom had to press his shoulder against the door to make it finally swing open. Although he and his brothers each had a key, his had not been used in so long that he was thankful it still turned. The early-morning sunlight filtered in through the diamond-paned windows of the cottage they called Willow Run, and though at first glance everything seemed orderly enough, the rooms smelled musty and closed-up, with a faint overlay of mouse and wet hunting dog.

He held the door for Isabella, then set her basket and the hamper of food from the White Roebuck on the table. The cottage was small and old-fashioned, with this single large room serving as kitchen and great hall and dining room all together. Two small bedchambers opened off this, while a ladder led to the loft, with four more cots for extra guests. The furniture was an unmatched jumble, outmoded and mended castoffs from other houses, with the only decoration provided by the bawdy cartoons and prints his father had favored, and tacked directly onto the walls.

Willow Run was a bachelor haven through and through, with Isabella likely the first female—let alone a princess—to have crossed the doorstep. Tom himself hadn't been here for at least ten years, and seeing it now with fresh eyes made him question his own decision to bring her here.

"Poor Bella," he said sheepishly. "Each place I bring you to is farther and farther from the palace where you belong."

"Not any longer, I do not." She dropped heavily into an ancient armchair, letting her head drop back against the cushions. Her hair was trailing down, unpinned and tangled from the wind, and her skirts blotched by the river water. Earlier she had dozed in the boat, her cheek resting on his shoulder, but now her face was pale, and he didn't need to see the dark circles beneath her eyes to know she must be exhausted. "So this, then, is how the sons of grand English earls live in the country?"

"Only when they wish to be free from their English countesses for a fortnight or so." He braced his hands on the arms of the chair and leaned down to kiss her. "Family lore says my great-grandfather acquired Willow Run at the gaming table. The lore likewise says my great-grandmother believed my great-grandfather must have held the losing hand, to be saddled with such a monstrosity."

"It's not a monstrosity," protested Isabella mildly, making the effort to arch up the tiniest amount for that kiss. "It's not a palace, no, but it is not a monstrosity, either."

"That was a quotation, not my opinion. I have only the fondest memories of this place. My grandfather, and then my father, would bring us boys here to fish in the river and muck about on the pond, and generally do whatever we pleased."

She smiled up at him wearily, her hands dangling limp over the arms of the chair. "Is that why you have brought me here, Tomaso? To do what you please?"

"Only because what pleases you, pleases me." He kissed her again, striving to please them both.

"I *am* pleased." She made a happy, purring sound. "And I feel safe here, Tomaso, for the first time since I left Monteverde. I'm not sure why, but I do."

"So do I." He did, too. There was something about how the cottage had settled into the landscape over the past two hundred years or so, the oak trees and honeysuckle vines growing over it as the corners of the beams and bricks softened, that gave the old house a sense of permanence, and also a sense of sanctuary. Not even the chimneys were visible from the road, and a visitor had to know where to look to find the path to the door. In another generation or so, Willow Run would be overtaken by London's voracious expansion, and become no more than another old house squeezed among the new terraces, but now—now it belonged to them.

"Safe or not, you must be famished," he said. "What would you like for your breakfast, Your Royal Highness?"

Her smile turned bittersweet. "Let me be only your Bella while I'm here, Tomaso. And thank you, no, I'm not hungry, not at all."

He stood up, concern on his face. "I've everything you could possibly want in that basket, lass. I paid dearly for the privilege, too, having the Roebuck's cook stop her other work to pack it for us."

"I'm sorry, Tomaso." To his surprise, her dark eyes suddenly turned watery with tears, and she bowed her head. "I'm sorry you had to pay for the food, and hire the boat, and go back to Berkeley Square, and have people fire guns at you for no reason, and—and I'm so very sorry for *everything*."

"Oh, Bella." He crouched beside the chair so their faces were level, and brushed back the tangle of curls from her cheek. "What kind of nonsense is this, I ask you?"

"It's not nonsense. Tomaso. It's the truth." She snuffled, trying to keep back the tears. He passed her his handkerchief, and she took it reluctantly, dabbing daintily at the corners of her eyes instead of her nose, where it was needed.

"You see how it is," she continued, "even now with your—your handkerchief. You are always thinking of how to look after me, how to please me, and yet what have I given you in return?"

"I'm not keeping tallies, Bella," he said as patiently as he could, which was, under the circumstances, surpassingly, amazingly patient. "I love you, and you love me, and that's reason enough, isn't it?"

"But how can that *be,* Tomaso?" The tears clung in her lashes like dewdrops, her voice wobbling unsteadily with every word. "When I think of the risks I've put you through, the dangers you have faced because of my foolishness and—and *ineptitude*—oh, love, if anything had happened, if anything does happen, I will never, never be able to forgive myself for it!"

"Listen to yourself, sweetheart." Gently he stroked her cheek with the backs of his fingers. "Listen to how you've changed. You're scarcely the same princess that I first met, charging into Lady Willoughby's drawing room with all guns blazing."

"Do not tease me, Tomaso." She sniffed, squeezing the handkerchief into a soggy ball below her very red nose. "I am so the same. Who else could I be?"

"When I first met you, you would have shown no more concern for me than if I were a drop of water in the Thames. All you could consider was how greatly the world—particularly the English world—had misunderstood and abused and ignored you, and how much we all owed you by way of compensation."

"I did nothing of the sort!"

"You did," he declared. "Consider that boatman with the wherry. When I first met you, you would never have asked him for his silence, pretty as you please. You would have threatened him with the darkest Monteverdian prison plus drawing and quartering if he didn't obey you at once."

She narrowed her eyes at him, a flash of that old haughtiness returning. "You make me sound as if I've become a weak and spineless little creature, fit for little beyond mewling and fawning and groveling in the chimney corner."

"What you've become is less Fortunaro, and more Bella." With her hands in his, he raised her gently from the chair to her feet. "You've stopped behaving as if the sun and moon and all the stars above must rise and set around your charming small person."

"That is because I've learned they don't." The sadness in her voice as she looked up at him was genuine, as was the regret. "It has been a vastly humbling experience, Tomaso, to be forced to realize I am no longer the center of anything."

"You are for me," he said gruffly, feeling suddenly self-conscious. Other times when he'd tried to tell her how he felt, how much she meant to him, she'd been less than encouraging. She hadn't exactly rebuffed him—she was, after all, still here with him—but she hadn't let him talk about any kind of lasting future together, either. "The center of things for me, I mean."

"Tomaso." She smiled up at him through her tears, her nose red and her expression soft and muddled and impossibly dear to him. "No wonder I love you so much."

"As you should." This was a better response than he'd hoped, encouraging enough that he slipped his hands around her waist to pull her close. She always liked that; there was never any rebuffing when it came to kissing. "Seeing as I love you, too."

"What a keen eye you have, Tomaso," she murmured. "You don't even need a spyglass, do you?"

"I never have," he said. "And what I can see now is that you need to rest. You've two rooms to choose from, you know, though you can go up the ladder if that's your fancy."

But as soon as he slid his hands from her waist along her hips, she abruptly pulled away and turned her back to him, as if she suddenly could not bear that familiar touch from him. Just when he thought he truly knew her, her moods would shift like this, leaving him behind in a fog of confusion.

"What the devil is the matter now, Bella? What have I done?"

"Nothing, Tomaso." She was running her hands restlessly up and down her skirts, almost mimicking what he'd wanted to do. "Nothing at all."

"Then what in blazes am I—"

"No." She turned back to face him, those same skirts fanning stiffly out around her. The coarse linsey-woolsey gown that she'd borrowed from the servant didn't float over her body and legs the way her usual silk and muslin ones did. Instead this gown hung heavily, the thick folds ungainly and ungraceful, and he resolved that when this was done, he'd make sure she'd never have to hide herself away in clothing like this again.

"We—we must talk," she said haltingly. "We cannot put it off any longer. We must talk."

He stared at her, incredulous. "*Talk?* Bella, what have we been doing all this time if not talking?"

"But not like this," she said unhappily. "Oh, Tomaso, though I do not wish it, I must at last tell you the truth."

Chapter Fifteen

"The truth?" Tom looked at her warily, so obviously bracing himself for the worst that Isabella's resolve almost failed. "What are you trying to tell me, Bella?"

How could she explain how dishonest she'd been without hurting him? Where, really, could she begin? "I never willfully planned to deceive you, Tomaso. Please, please, understand that. It wasn't my secret to tell."

"Your secret."

All the expression was vanishing from his face, replaced by a flat, blank dread that made her feel sick to her stomach.

"Damnation, Bella, you're not married, are you?"

"Oh, no, no," she said quickly. There wasn't any going back now. "You are the only one I love, Tomaso, my first and only lover."

"Thank God for that much. So what in blazes is—"

"This." She shoved aside the skirt of her gown to untie the petticoat, her fingers fumbling with nervousness as she unknotted the strings. The weighted linen fell to the floor with a muted clunk. She stepped free of the puddled petticoat and swept it up in her arms, spreading it out onto the table. She took a kitchen knife from the table's drawer, and before she could change her mind, she began slicing into the fabric, carefully slashing a slit into the first stitched pocket. She gave the pocket a little shake, and one of the rubies slipped into her hand.

"There." She held the gem up to the light for him to see, the intaglio lion sparkling through the facets like red fire. "My first secret, and oh, there are so many more here to follow!"

He whistled low, impressed. "A ruby? You have been carrying rubies in your petticoat?"

"Not ordinary rubies," she said, pride still creeping into her voice despite everything else. "These are the Fortunaro rubies, the royal jewels. They have been in my family since my ancestors carried them off from the emperor of Rome."

"Looted them, you mean." Tom touched the petticoat, noting all the little bulges and bumps there were to mark the stones hidden inside. "They belong in the Tower for safekeeping, not in your linen. How many of these are there, lass?"

"There are sixteen lion rubies," she said, slipping the stone into her palm and covering it protectively with her other hand. "Then there are some lesser gems, too, still priceless, but without the same history, as well as the Fortunaro gold coins, minted from heathen gold brought back hundreds of years ago from the Holy Lands."

He lifted the hem of the petticoat from the table, gauging its weight. "You brought all this with you on the ship from Monteverde? And no one else *knew?*"

"Only Mama," Isabella said quickly. She couldn't judge

his mood, or his reaction, either, which unsettled her even more. "It was her idea. She said no one would think to look at me for the jewels, nor would they dare attack an English warship, with so many men and guns."

"Oh, they would have if they'd known." His face was turned from her, his voice oddly impassive, as if they were speaking only of what to have for tea or supper. "English warships are attacked with considerably less provocation than a princess with a ransom in jewels tucked under her skirts. But I still cannot believe this of you, Isabella."

"I had no choice, Tomaso," she said as firmly as she could. The gem in her closed hand felt cool and hard against her fingers. "These are the most important symbols of power the Fortunari have left. They could never be allowed to go to the French, or to the Trinita, either. That was the reason I came here instead of staying with my family in Monteverde, and I owed it to them to do what was right."

"You did," he said softly. "But what did you owe me, Bella?"

"That is why I am telling you—showing you!—now," she said, her words tumbling over one another in nervous haste. "After what we have survived together, it only seemed—"

"You should have told me before this," he said, not bothering to hide his bitterness. "Perhaps not in the beginning, when you didn't know whether to trust me or not, but damnation, Bella, I thought by now I meant more to you!"

"You do," she said, wondering how she could ever explain what she'd done so he'd understand. "But it's more than that, Tomaso. It's my family, and I'd sworn to Mama that I wouldn't tell anyone, not even—"

"Not even me." He shook his head, struggling to hold back the full force of his temper. "Didn't you realize that your little secret increased the danger a hundredfold? Not just to yourself, but to the Willoughbys and their staff and Lady Allen and her guests, even the prince? Hell, you put every innocent person within ten feet of you at risk because you'd sworn not to *tell*."

"You are being ridiculous." She raised her chin defiantly, her own anger simmering now that he insisted on being so—so pigheaded. How could he not see that by confiding in him, she'd made as great a sacrifice as he had when he'd passed on a new command? "I was the one they hunted, because I am the Princess di Fortunaro!"

"I'll grant you were a pretty prize for the taking, Bella, but *this* is what they really wanted, and what they'd kill us all to get."

Before she could stop him, he caught the hem of the petticoat and whipped it to the floor, scattering gold coins across the old flagstones. With a little cry she dropped to her knees, scrambling to gather up the rolling coins in her hands.

"So that is how you truly are, even now," Tom said, looking down on her. "Always the treasure first."

"That's not true, Tomaso," she said furiously, "not at all!"

"But it is," he continued, so relentless she couldn't mistake how much she'd hurt him. "So many things make sense now. Now I understand why you were so distraught when your bedchamber was ransacked, why your first concern was for jewels. Why the devil would you give a damn about your tiaras when you had these to fuss over? And now I can see why we had to return to Berkeley Square last night, even though we were nearly shot for our trouble."

She flushed. "You make it sound as if I'd planned it all."

"Not quite," he said. "Not even you could have done that. Oh, and the river, too. No wonder you were so afraid to fall in. If you had, you would have sunk to the bottom like you'd an anchor tied to your legs, wouldn't you? An anchor of cursed gold."

"So then why do you think I told you now?" She sat back on her heels, the coins in her lap, and shoved her hair back from her face. She could not believe he was saying such things to her now, and she could feel her temper rising in defense. "If you are so clever, then tell me why!"

"What, you want me to say that, too?" He shook his head, his expression growing darker by the moment. "Then I will, Bella—no, Your Royal Highness. You'll forget this little sojourn in England ever happened, and you'll forget me."

"I will not!" she cried, her outrage spilling over. "I will not, Tomaso!

"And I say you will," he said, unconvinced. "Look at you. You'll take your coins and your baubles that mean so much to your wicked old family, and you will return to Monteverde, and pretend that nothing has changed—not in your country, not in your life, not in your heart. If you have one, that is."

"Whatever became of our life together? Each day, each night?"

"I don't know. Perhaps it was never there to begin with."

"And I say it's there still, if you will stop being so cold and reasoning and English, and admit what your heart is saying to you." She scrambled to her feet, flinging the coins that she'd gathered to the floor as she seized his hands. "I told you my secret and broke the trust of my family because I love you, Tomaso! I love you, and you love me, and you are a fool if you refuse to believe it!"

His fingers grasped her hands, jerking her closer. "Then prove it," he said. "Stay in England, and marry me."

She gasped, too stunned to answer. Not even in her most fanciful daydreams had she let herself consider such a possibility. She didn't dare. The Fortunaro bloodlines must always be considered first. All her life she'd been trained to think of marriage as duty, as politics, as a way to cement her family's power. Her parents would be horrified by even the idea of an English husband so far beneath her. To marry for love was unthinkable.

Until now.

She searched his face, searching for the words to tell him how she felt. His jaw was dark with stubble, his blue eyes were weary, and the rough, ill-fitting servant's clothes he'd borrowed were far from his usual Navy perfection, but he had never looked more handsome or more dear to her. She pulled her hands free of his, turning away as she struggled to think. He was asking her to give up everything about her past and her life for him, a past and a life that already might well be lost to her forever.

But in return he was offering her his hand, his heart, his name. She would forever be his wife, his Bella, Lady Thomas Greaves instead of Her Royal Highness, and be done with palaces and intrigues and tiaras and rubies sewn into her petticoat. Their children—their children!—would be free to climb the trees and play in the stream outside this cottage, free to shout and get dirty and do whatever they pleased instead of being model princes and princesses.

And she could marry the man she loved, and be happier than she'd ever dreamed possible.

"Marry me, Bella," he said again, his voice a hoarse, urgent whisper in her ear. "Be my wife. I'm calling your bluff, lass, and you damned well better say yes."

"Why should I?" she said, clinging to the last bit of her anger as she turned to face him again. "Because you order it? Because you say I must?"

"Because it's right," he said. "Listen to your own heart, Bella. You can decide this for yourself. We'll have not one day, one night, but a lifetime of them. Damnation, I love you, and if you love me as you claim, you'll marry me."

Her hands were shaking as she placed her palms on either side of his face, holding it so there'd be no chance he'd look away from her.

"Yes," she said with a fierce joy. "Yes, Captain Lord Greaves. Because I love you, I will marry you, and nothing—nothing—will ever change my mind."

His only answer was a deep, wordless growl as he swept her into his arms and carried her away from the rubies and the coins and her past, and to the bedchamber and the future they'd share together.

Darden sat at the smallest table in the back of the inn to discourage any of the other patrons from sitting with him. He was too on edge for company, nor did he want to risk babbling more than he should to a stranger. With great deliberation, he ran the thumb of his glove along the rim of his glass before he drank from it. The White Roebuck might be the height of fashion for travelers along this part of the river, but it was far below his usual standards, and he wanted to make that as clear as he could to all around him.

Not that any of them would notice such a nicety. The taproom was crowded with revelers of every sort, from common laborers from the fields to sailors and wherrymen to foppish young gentlemen with overdressed milliners on their arms. The fiddle screeched like a caterwauling cat, and the laughter and drunken singing was enough to destroy the soul of a man of feeling like himself. Only his muse could make him suffer so; only his dear Isabella could draw him from the city to a den such as this.

The notice in the newspaper had been succinct: "After attending the theater at Covent Garden, Her Royal Highness Princess Isabella of Monteverde has withdrawn for a sojourn to the country." Most people who read that would imagine the princess as a guest at the grandest of country houses, perhaps even traveling to Brighton as a guest of the prince at his gaudy pavilion.

But Darden knew better, because he knew Tom Greaves. With the princess in his keeping, there was only one place they'd go to escape their misfortunes in London, and that would be Willow Run.

Darden sipped his brandy, trying not to recall his only experience at the family's cottage. The old earl had invited him once—from pity, Darden had always thought. Because he wasn't particularly good at the roughhouse games favored by the earl's four sons, he'd retreated to the stable to amuse himself. But when Greaves and his brothers had caught him idly swinging one of the dogs from a rope to see if it could fly, they had tied the same rope through Darden's breeches and suspended him from the oak tree, letting him hang there screaming and cursing for punishment until the earl himself had come to cut him down.

No, Willow Run had not been a favorite place of his childhood, any more than Greaves had been a favorite friend.

But Darden was sure he could find the way back to the shabby old cottage, even after so many years. He hadn't quite figured out what he'd do once he got there, how he'd separate Isabella from Greaves long enough to speak with her alone. But he would do it, and this time he wouldn't falter. He'd come this far, and he wasn't going to turn back now.

There was some sort of fuss near the door to the inn, and with halfhearted interest Darden leaned forward in his chair. Through the haze of tobacco smoke, he could see an elderly man leaning on his cane, followed by a small, dark lady in a black cloak, her exceptional beauty dimmed by obvious exhaustion. Though Darden could not hear their conversation over the din, it was clear that they were arguing, the lady in particular gesturing dramatically. At last the innkeeper appeared to have his way, and the ill-matched pair were shown to a table and bench close to Darden's own. Now he could overhear them, and to his surprise they were speaking in Italian—low, angry, aristocratic Italian.

"You know we decided it is better these people do not know who you are," the older gentleman was saying. "Not until we can first discern how the English regard us."

The lady snapped open her fan, an extravagant arc of painted ivory and black lace. Her profile was maddeningly familiar to Darden, a memory he couldn't quite place.

"But you must agree, Romano," she continued, "that the captain of that shameful boat had no right to abandon us here in this—this *place*."

The gentleman gently waved his hand through the air, striving to calm the lady. "The captain did what was necessary, Your Majesty. The boat was taking in too much water to continue, and for your own safety and convenience he put us ashore to wait at this inn while he made his repairs."

"This *inn*." Her voice would have withered dirt. "This *sty* is more accurate. I ask you, Romano. How am I to find my dearest daughter in London if I must be made to *languish* in such a dreadful spot? I knew I should never have sent Isabella alone to such a barbaric country. She is too gentle, too tender for such a rude place, and besides, she lacks the basic cleverness necessary to deal with the English. I knew the moment she had sailed that I'd made a hideous mistake."

"Which is precisely why we have made this journey to find her, Your Majesty," Romano said, his voice slow and soothing. "Soon, very soon, you shall be reunited with Her Royal Highness, I assure you."

"Forgive me for interrupting, Your Majesty." Darden bowed deeply, striving to contain his excitement. "But if it is Her Royal Highness the Principessa Isabella di Fortunaro that you seek, I believe I can assist you."

The queen didn't answer, merely staring at him as if he were the lowest insect imaginable.

"Might I ask your name, sir?" Romano was slightly more polite, but only slightly.

"I am Ralph Darden, Marquis of Banleigh." Darden bowed again. "Your servant, ma'am. I have had the honor of your daughter's acquaintance, and can count myself as one of her few true friends in this country, especially now that she is in such danger."

"Saints in heaven!" The queen gasped, pressing her hand to her bosom. "My daughter is in peril? How? Why?"

"I believe she is safe for now, ma'am, thanks to the selfless devotion of her friends." Darden nodded modestly as he reached for the quick courage in his glass. All was fair in love and war, wasn't it? To come across his princess's mother like this was the rarest gift of fate. It wouldn't hurt to have the queen on his side, and if he had to steal a bit of Greaves's glory to do so, why, who would know? "In fact, the princess is in hiding very near to this spot."

The queen rose, sweeping her cloak around her as she snapped her fan shut. "Then take us to my daughter at once, Lord Darden. At once!"

Chapter Sixteen

Isabella's dream was short but terrifyingly intense.

Her mother's fingers were like claws on her wrist, dragging her down the longest hall of the palace, their images reflected over and over in the row of tall gilt-framed mirrors. Isabella's heels slipped and slid across the marble floors and tangled in her skirts and her arm was jerked so hard it hurt clear to her shoulder. Yet though she cried for Mama to slow and let her catch her breath, she only quickened the pace, giving Isabella's arm an extra jerk for emphasis.

"You have shamed us, daughter," she said, hissing like an angry dragon. She was prepared for court, her hair dressed high and powdered white and her glittering red skirts held out stiffly on either side by panniers, with a long train flicking behind her like that same angry dragon's tail. "We put our trust in you, and this—this!—is how you betrayed us!"

Isabella tried to protest, but when she opened her mouth no words would come out, as if her mother's fury were a curse that had left her mute, or maybe, simply, she'd no explanation that this dragon version of her mother would accept.

But before she could decide, they'd come to the throne room, the walls lined with enormous frescoes in which generations of Fortunari mingled with ancient pagan gods and goddesses. To Isabella's horror, the paintings came to life, the huge figures thumping their painted swords and scepters on the marble floor and scowling their displeasure down upon her, and she gasped and shrank back.

Mama gave her an impatient shove. "Tell them what you have done, Isabella. Tell them why you betrayed them all."

The dream-Isabella was quaking with fear, yet at last she dared to find her voice to face those angry ancient Fortunari looming over her. "All I wanted was love...."

She woke with a jolt, wild-eyed and clutching at Tom's bare arm. The room was dark and disorienting, the sheets and pillows on the bed smelling of mildew, and it took a long moment for her to recall that they were at Willow Run, and no longer in London with the comforting glow of the lights in the streets. No wonder it was so dark, and so strangely quiet, too, here in the country.

She took a deep breath, struggling to control her racing heart. It was done, over, she told herself firmly. It wasn't real, but only a dream, and even the worst dreams didn't have the power to hurt you once you were awake, especially when they were fueled by her own uncertain conscience.

She curled closer to Tom, and he shifted in his sleep, slipping his arm protectively around her waist. She shouldn't feel guilty about marrying him, or being happy. He loved her, and she loved him, and not even a thousand years of her dead ancestors in a nightmare could change that. She sighed and closed her eyes as she nestled against Tom, relishing the closeness and security that she always found with him. No, nothing was going to scare her away from Captain Lord Greaves.

But there—there was the knocking again, and her eyes flew open. This wasn't a nightmare, and it wasn't the giant painted Fortunaro in the frescoes thumping their swords at her. This was real.

"Tomaso?"

"I heard it." He was already rolling out of the bed, tugging up his breeches and reaching for his pistols and the belt with the long sailor's knife in what seemed to her to be the same instant. "You stay here, lass. I'll go be the lookout."

"I will not stay here alone." Now she was out of bed, too, groping about the floor in the dark for her clothes. Finally she gave up and pulled the coverlet from the bed, wrapping it around her like a musty head-to-toe cloak. She pulled her loose hair free, letting it fall down her back. "You did that before, when the thieves came to my room at the Willoughbys, and I'm not going to be left behind again."

A little spark showed he lit the candle in the lantern by the bed. "You'll be safer back here." He glanced at how she was dressed, or rather, undressed. "Especially garbed like that."

"I won't stay here alone, Tomaso." After the nightmare, there was no way under heaven she'd do that. "I need to be with you."

He smiled over the lantern. "And I need you, too, sweetheart."

She grinned back, dipping a little curtsy in her makeshift robe. "And if you try to leave me behind, Tomaso, I'll follow."

"You are a trial, Bella." He sighed, swiftly checking the

flints on the pistols. "Very well. If you must come along, then keep to the shadows behind me. Likely it's only some stray animal, anyway."

But the knocking came again, at the front door of the cottage, and neither of them believed it was an animal.

"Take care, love," she said softly. Pistols and a knife, but he hadn't bothered with a shirt: if that didn't tell her he believed in the danger, than nothing would.

"Oh, lass," he said, his grin now lopsided as he tucked one of the guns into his belt. "We've come this far. I'll hardly do anything foolish and risk losing you now, would I?"

Yet she wasn't so sure as she hurried after him, her bare feet making no sound. He carried the lantern in one hand, a bobbing light through the darkness, and a pistol in the other, while Isabella scurried after him, hugging the coverlet tightly around her as she ducked beneath the ladder. She told herself that villains like the Trinita didn't bother to knock, that she and Tom were likely in no real danger, yet as she huddled obediently in the shadow of the ladder, she still whispered a little prayer to keep him safe.

With the pistol in his hand cocked and ready to fire, Tom pressed close to the door so whoever was on the other side couldn't see him through the nearby window. The knock came again, louder, more full of bluster.

"Who goes there?" called Tom in his most commanding captain's voice. "Give your name, or be gone."

"It's Darden, Greaves," came the muffled reply from the other side of the door. "Will you open now, and not keep me moldering on your infernal doorstep?"

Isabella frowned. Darden? Here? It made no sense. But how had he tracked them to here? Uneasily she pulled the coverlet higher over her shoulders, the security and peace she'd felt since they'd come to this little cottage rapidly evaporating.

"Don't you know the hour, Darden?" asked Tom, making no move to unbolt the door. "Hardly the proper time for calls."

"What I have to say to the princess can't wait," said the marquis. "She's there with you, isn't she?"

Tom swore softly. "Who else is out there with you, Darden?"

"Who else?" He was nervous, stalling, which made Isabella nervous, too. "Why do you think there's anyone else with me, Greaves?"

"I'm not a fool like you, Darden. I can hear them shuffling about beside you. So who the devil are they?"

A face suddenly appeared at the window not far from the door, pressing close to peer inside. Ghostly pale in the lantern's light, the features were distorted by the uneven old glass and broken up by the tiny diamond-shaped panes.

But it was enough for Isabella, who did not know whether to believe her eyes, or fear she was once again in the nightmare's grasp.

"Mama? It cannot be, not here, not now," she whispered hoarsely. *"Mama?"*

"I say, Greaves, you really must open," Darden said. "I've Her Royal Highness the Queen of Monteverde here with me, and it doesn't do to keep—"

So it *was* her mother, and with a little cry Isabella rushed to the door, pulling frantically at the lock to open the door.

"What in blazes are you *doing,* Bella?" demanded Tom as he tried to pull her aside. "Have you lost your wits entirely?"

"It's my *mother,* Tom," she sobbed. "I saw her through the window, and now Darden says it's true! She's come for me, I know it, I know it!"

At last the lock gave way, but as she tried to pull the door open, Tom held it with his shoulder, and she howled in protest.

"No, Bella," he warned. "Darden's played us false before. You have no reason to believe this is your mother, other than—"

"Isabella? Daughter?" came the voice in Italian from the other side of the door. "Open that door at once, I say!"

"You see, it *is* my mother, Tom!" she cried, and pulled the door open. "Mama!"

She would scarcely have recognized the woman on the cottage doorstep, the Marchese di Romano beside her. It *was* her mother, but her mother much changed, smaller, older, more haggard than Isabella could ever have dreamed. Gone were the jewels and the richly embroidered gown, the elaborate hair and artfully painted face. Instead her mother wore a plain dark traveling gown and cloak, and her severely pinned chignon was actually streaked with gray.

Much changed on the outside, yes, but not within.

"Isabella." Her face contracted with shock and disapproval as her gaze raked Isabella from her bare toes to the top of her disheveled hair. "What has become of you, daughter?"

Without waiting for Isabella's reply, the queen turned on Darden. "You *said* she was safe. You *assured* us she was with suitable friends, in good keeping, and yet here she is, the Principessa di Fortunaro, a slattern dallying in the hayloft with some baseborn English stable-boy!"

"Forgive me, ma'am." Darden ducked his head miserably. "Affairs have clearly been, ah, altered since I received my last assurances."

"Mama!" Too late Isabella realized how she must appear to her mother. "Mama, this is not what it seems, not at all! This is Captain Lord Thomas Greaves, Mama, and he is a good, fine, honorable gentleman, the son of an earl, and the man who has protected me and saved my life over and over. We are in disguise to evade enemies, Mama. That is why we are dressed like this."

Tom looped the lantern on an iron hook beside the door, uncocked the pistol in his hand and bowed. "Your Majesty, I am honored."

But the queen refused to notice. "Isabella, you have not only betrayed my trust in you, but you have ruined yourself in the process. Who would have you after you have debased yourself with this?"

"Mama, please!" Her mother hadn't been changed at all by what had happened, but Isabella was stunned and ashamed by her callousness. How could she be so rude and unfeeling toward Tom—toward anyone?

"'Disguise,' ha. Since when has nakedness been a disguise for any decent person? If ever I needed more proof that the world is in an immoral, disgraceful shambles, then you, daughter, are it."

"It's not disgraceful, Mama, and neither are we!" Isabella cried, shamed for her mother's sake, and because it was Tom, her Tom, the sting of her self-absorption seemed extra sharp. Why couldn't she have been born to an ordinary mother, instead of a beautiful queen who placed her rank before everything else?

"I love him, Mama," she continued, "and he loves me, and I have agreed to marry him, and remain here with him in England. Now please, come inside, so we—"

"So you can put the kettle on and make me a nice dish of tea, like every other good English wife?" Her mother sniffed with disdain, her eyes narrow. "I prefer to remain here under the stars in the sky, Isabella, rather than beneath the roof of your sinful hovel. *Marry* him, indeed."

"Yes, ma'am, marry," Tom said, biting each word as he fought to control his temper. "I love your daughter, and I believe I can make her as happy as she will me."

"Oh, happiness and love," said the queen scornfully. "Next you shall speak of Cupid's darts and Hymen's bower! Have you ever heard such nonsense, Romano? What trumpery on which to base a marriage!"

Isabella listened, aghast. It was her nightmare all over again, only instead of painted ancestors to show their disapproval, she had Darden and Romano clearly wishing to be anywhere else.

But there was another difference, too. Tom had told her she'd changed, and now—now she realized how exactly right he'd been.

"Now cover yourself, Isabella, so we might leave," her mother was saying, "and we shall do what we can to redeem this—"

"I'm sorry, Mama, but I am staying here," she said, surprising herself with how firm she could sound as she linked her arm into Tom's. "You cannot make me leave against my will, and my will is to marry Captain Lord Greaves."

"Do not be preposterous, daughter." Her mother snapped her gloved hand through the air, as if to swat aside

Isabella's objections. "Collect your effects—you do recall which particular effects I mean, you careless girl, do you not? Your father expects them back with him, you know, and as soon as possible. Or have you tossed our family's legacy into the river along with your virtue?"

"You mean the jewels, ma'am!" blurted Darden, his face glowing with excitement. "The Fortunaro jewels!"

Isabella gasped, too stunned to speak. The Fortunaro jewels were at this moment sitting in a willow-basket on the table near the kitchen hearth, wrapped in an oversize napkin beneath a humble layer of cheese, bread, and a roasted chicken, with a bottle of cider on top. But no one except her mother and now Tom were supposed even to know the jewels had left Monteverde. How could Darden possibly have guessed such a close-kept secret?

"You are mistaken, Lord Darden," Romano said severely, tapping his walking stick for emphasis. "The Fortunaro jewels would never have been given into the princess's safekeeping. That is far to grave a responsibility for a young lady."

Tom nodded. "True enough, Darden. If the princess had anything like that in her possession, I would have seen them by now, wouldn't I?"

The queen laughed derisively. "Given your familiarity with my daughter's petticoats, I should hope you have."

"You do not deny it, then, ma'am?" Eagerly Darden leaned forward, his palms pressed together as if in prayer. "The great Fortunaro rubies are indeed here in England? Here in the care of the dear princess?"

"She's not dear to you, Darden, nor will she ever be," Tom said sharply, slipping his arm around Isabella's cov-

erlet-shrouded waist to reinforce his point. "And you heard
this wise gentleman here. How could the princess have had
anything to do with a pack of old jewels?"

Darden made an exuberant flourish with his hands, the
ruffles on his sleeves fluttering in the lantern's light. "Ah,
Greaves, but the Fortunaro rubies are no more ordinary
jewels than Her Royal Highness is an ordinary princess."

"And how we thank you, Lord Darden," called a man's
rasping voice from the dark, "for leading us so generously
to both!"

At once Isabella turned toward the voice, toward the
sweeping branches of the old willows that gave the cottage
its name. The light from Tom's lantern barely reached so far,
just enough for her to pick out the three men. The one in the
middle was bent with age or illness, leaning heavily on a cane,
but the two others who flanked him were large and strong,
the faint light glinting off the pistols in their raised arms.

And saints in heaven, those pistols were aimed at *her.*

"Pesci!" cried Darden, his eyes wide with shock that
matched Isabella's own. So much for their sanctuary, their
safe retreat. Beside her, Tom swore, and Isabella knew that
in any other circumstances, he'd be throttling Darden, and
for once she wouldn't blame him. "How did you follow
me? How did you come?"

"By river, my lord Darden, the same as you." The old
man's cackle turned into a wheezing cough. "You took no
care to hide your path, my lord. You could not have made
it any easier for me or my men if you'd handed us a map."

"Who *are* you, you wretched man?" demanded the
queen, drawing herself up imperiously straight. "What do
you want?"

"Once I would have wanted you for my amusement, my revenge, and your pretty daughter, too." The man's regret sent a fresh chill down Isabella's spine. "But now all I can seek are the Fortunaro rubies."

Isabella grabbed her mother's arm. She'd already glimpsed the too-familiar little triangle hanging proudly from the men's shirts, and she understood the threat, even if her mother refused to. "Mama, don't do this, I beg you."

But her mother shook her off. "You—you are one of my subjects. I can hear it in your accent. I am your queen, and you must obey me."

Pesci shook his head. "Once I was your subject, and once you were my queen. But now, Monteverde belongs to the people, to the Trinita. Everything has changed, you see."

"No, it hasn't," insisted the queen. "Now put those guns away, I say, before someone is injured."

"But that is the point of guns, isn't it? To injure someone?" The old man picked his way slowly closer, shoving aside the trailing willow branches. "Which is why, Captain Greaves, I must ask you to toss yours on the ground."

With obvious reluctance, Tom did, the dull metal of the pistols shining in the grass.

"Now let the women go free," he said, gently pushing Isabella behind him to protect her with his own body. "Neither the princess nor her mother know where the jewels are hidden."

"No!" cried Isabella, squeezing around him. "I won't let you do this, Tomaso, not to save me. By all the saints, I swear Captain Lord Greaves knows nothing of the jewels, *signor*. He is only being gallant because he—he loves me."

"Bella, don't," said Tom, his voice so full of warning and

love that she could have wept. "There's no better reason for telling the truth."

She raised her chin, not letting herself meet his gaze. For his sake, she *must* be brave. She was still a Fortunaro, and she still had the heart of a lioness, didn't she? She'd been so afraid that the rubies would cause her to drown, but she'd never guessed they'd finally drag her down like this.

"Don't listen to him, *signor,*" she said, clutching the coverlet more tightly. "I am the one who brought the rubies from Monteverde to England, hidden in my clothing, and I am the only one who knows where they are now."

Pesci smiled, a death's head grimace. "What a wise, pretty child, to tell me the truth. For once, Darden, what you said was correct, yes?"

Darden stepped forward, reaching for Isabella's hands, but when she kept them clasped, he let his own drop awkwardly before him. "I never meant to betray you, my dearest princess. I only wanted to give you my esteem, my devotion, my love."

Pesci laughed again, that dry, cruel cackle. "Oh, Lord Darden never knowingly played you false, Princess. He's not clever or brave enough for that."

"That is nonsense, *signor,*" snapped Isabella, unable to contain herself any longer. It wasn't just that the man had insulted Darden; he was contemptuous of all of them, and no matter what the risk, she'd had enough. Her coverlet dragging behind her through the dewy grass, she approached the three men, challenging them. "*You* are the true cowards, hiding behind your blessed Trinita. You say you stand for freedom, but I say you're only greedy bullies, eager to steal whatever you can."

"You misspeak, Principessa." The old man scowled. "What you have described are the Fortunari, not the Trinita."

He nodded, and the man to his right lunged forward and grabbed Isabella by the arm, hauling her back.

"Let me go!" she cried, yelping with pain as the man's fingers dug into her wrist. Her first impulse was to break free, struggling to twist away as her bare feet tangled in the coverlet. Then she glimpsed the pistol in the man's hand, a pistol that could easily kill her, or Tom, or her mother, or any of the others, and instantly she went still.

"This is better, Princess," said Pesci with approval. "You'll gain nothing by fighting us, you know. You should have learned that by now, yes?"

She didn't answer, not trusting herself to say something that would not get her killed. Panting, she shoved her hair back from her face and looked at Tom, his face grimly murderous as he stood with his arms tensed at his sides. He'd been that close to racing to her rescue, and, unarmed as he was, that close to being shot by one of Pesci's men.

The old man grunted, watching her with rheumy eyes as he fingered the little triangle at his throat. "So where are the rubies, Principessa? Are they squirreled away in the house, or hidden in one of these trees?"

She looked back at Tom, her heart aching from the distance between them. *Think,* she ordered herself, *think, think what to do next!*

"Perhaps." She swallowed hard. "But I will tell you only if you give me your word, *signor,* that the others go free."

That made Pesci smile. "You would place any value in my word?"

"Then swear by something that matters to you," she said quickly. "Swear by that triangle around your neck."

Instantly the old man's expression became solemn as his gnarled fingers tightened around the three bound twigs. "Very well. By the Trinita, these others will go free once you tell me where the rubies are hidden."

"Daughter!" called her mother sharply. "Do not tell him! Those jewels are your heritage—they *are* the Fortunaro! No one here is worth them—no one!"

Isabella hesitated, her focus once again returning to Tom. He nodded, the slightest possible sign of agreement. Yet what was he agreeing to? Surrendering the rubies to save their lives, or keeping the Fortunaro treasure safe?

"Or perhaps the jewels are not so very far away." Pesci came closer, his red-rimmed eyes greedy and intent, so close that Isabella turned away from the foulness of his breath. "You said you'd brought them to England hidden in your clothing. Are they still there now, sewn in that coverlet you are clutching so dearly?"

Shaking with anticipation, he reached for her with his clawlike hand, ready to snatch the coverlet from her naked body.

"No," she said, trying to back away while the other man held her tight. *"No!"*

Abruptly Pesci gasped, an odd, rattling gurgle, then clutched both hands to his chest, letting the cane drop to the ground, as he finally, forever, toppled over. It was then Isabella heard the gunshot, the bright flash from the corner of her eye. Distracted, the man holding her relaxed his grip just enough for her to jerk free.

She bent down and snatched Pesci's cane from the

ground, and with a furious yowl she swung the cane as hard as she could at the knee of the second gunman, just as his gun fired. He swore, and through the stinging cloud of acrid gunpowder smoke he grabbed for her. But before his hand could reach her, he snapped backward, the pulpy red blotch of the gunshot bursting from his chest.

Another shot, and another; she'd lost count now, ducking low and praying she wouldn't be hit, too. Yanking the coverlet back over her shoulders with one hand, the cane still in the other, she turned to look for the other gunman. But he, too, was down, sprawled face first in the grass, one leg twitching while the rest lay still, too still for anything but death.

And then, just like that, it was over.

"Bella!" Tom dropped the smoking pistols from his hands and swept her up into his arms, holding her tight, reassuring himself as much as her. "Bella, Bella, my love, you're not hurt!"

"Of course I am not hurt," she said, with a long, shuddering breath as she hugged him back. She was shaking with excitement, and now with relief. "Oh, Tomaso, I'm so glad you were not hit, either!"

"No," he said, breathing hard. He leaned back, hungrily searching her face as if he could never see enough of it. "You're safe now, love. We both are."

"Look at him, the evil one," said her mother, her face hard with hatred as she stood over Pesci's body. "Darden thought he'd shot the old devil, but there's not a mark on his wicked carcass. Who would have thought he'd a heart to fail?"

She reached down and tore the triangle from the dead

man's neck and threw it as far as she could, then turned and spat on his chest. "May you already be burning in hell, old man, and stay there in the flames for all eternity!"

Isabella turned away, unable to share her mother's vindictiveness. She had been too much a target of the Trinità to want revenge with more violence, more hatred. All she wanted now was peace.

"You'll be safe now," said Tom softly, understanding. "Pesci was the leader here in England. Without him, there's nothing left."

She nodded. With the rush of excitement fading, she felt so exhausted she might have slipped to the grass if Tom hadn't held her.

"The others?" she asked. "Darden?"

"Romano escaped unharmed. They'd no interest in him. But as for Darden…"

Tom's expression was sorrowful, and Isabella knew. She twisted free and hurried to where old Romano was bending beside the marquis, the red stain on Darden's white shirt blossoming like a gruesome flower. His eyes were already glazing over, his soul nearly gone, but with a final effort they held steady as Isabella dropped to her knees beside him.

"I—I *was* a hero," he gasped. "For you, Princess."

"I know," she said softly, taking his chilling fingers. "I know."

And then, like that, he too was gone.

Without a word, Tom raised her to her feet. Shaking, she squeezed her eyes shut, her cheek pressed against his chest. This night, this much hatred and death—it was all too much, and for what? He would always be her true hero, her true love, but there would also be a place in her memory for poor Darden, and what he'd done for her.

"Isabella." Her mother had composed herself, her beautiful features again serene as she drew her fan from inside her cloak. "You do have the rubies, don't you?"

Isabella turned, separating herself from Tom's embrace. "Of course I have them, Mama, though now I wish I'd tossed them into the river for all the sorrow they've brought this day."

"That is the way of the Fortunaro rubies." Her mother smiled. "They say their color grows a deeper crimson with each drop of blood shed for them."

"Then you take them back, Mama," said Isabella with a little catch in her voice. "Back to Monteverde, or Parma, or anywhere other than here. I want nothing more to do with them."

"I will." Her mother's eyes glittered. "But you've done well to guard them this long, daughter. You are a Fortunaro at heart, no matter what reckless path you follow."

Isabella reached for Tom's hand, her fingers linking into his. "I have already decided, Mama."

"I thought as much." Her mother studied her over the top of her fan, her eyes as hard as the rubies she'd reclaimed. "Everything has changed in this foolish world of ours. Nothing is as it should be any longer. This man has stolen your maidenhead and saved your life, and now you will tell me you have no choice but to stay here with him."

"I love him, Mama," said Isabella. "I love him. Why is that so difficult to understand?

Her mother sniffed with disdain. "If you remain, daughter, I can promise you nothing in the future. When the Fortunaro return to power and your father regains his throne, there will be no place for you. Any children you bear to this Englishman will be no better than bastards in Monteverde. Is this love of yours worth that?"

Isabella nodded. Mama would no more understand her choice than Bella could understand her mother's reasoning.

"Hah. You always were a willful child." Her mother sighed, and bent forward, kissing Isabella on her cheek. "I suppose there's little left now for you but to marry your English rascal, and make yourself as happy as you can in this dreadful country."

Isabella tried to smile, knowing this was as close to a blessing as her mother would ever give.

"You heard your mother, lass," Tom said, drawing her gently back into his arms. "Marry me, and I'll make you happy, even in this dreadful country."

"Yes, Tomaso," said Isabella softly. "Yes, yes, yes."

And to Isabella's endless delight, they did, and she was, day after day after day.

* * * * *

FALL IN LOVE WITH THESE HANDSOME HEROES FROM HARLEQUIN HISTORICALS

On sale September 2004

THE PROPOSITION
by Kate Bridges

Sergeant Major Travis Reid
Honorable Mountie of the Northwest

WHIRLWIND WEDDING
by Debra Cowan

Jericho Blue
Texas Ranger out for outlaws

On sale October 2004

ONE STARRY CHRISTMAS
by Carolyn Davidson/Carol Finch/Carolyn Banning

Three heart-stopping heroes
for your Christmas stocking!

THE ONE MONTH MARRIAGE
by Judith Stacy

Brandon Sayer
Businessman with a mission

www.eHarlequin.com

HARLEQUIN HISTORICALS®

If you enjoyed what you just read,
then we've got an offer you can't resist!

Take 2 bestselling love stories FREE!

Plus get a FREE surprise gift!

Clip this page and mail it to Harlequin Reader Service®

IN U.S.A.
3010 Walden Ave.
P.O. Box 1867
Buffalo, N.Y. 14240-1867

IN CANADA
P.O. Box 609
Fort Erie, Ontario
L2A 5X3

YES! Please send me 2 free Harlequin Historicals® novels and my free surprise gift. After receiving them, if I don't wish to receive anymore, I can return the shipping statement marked cancel. If I don't cancel, I will receive 6 brand-new novels every month, before they're available in stores! In the U.S.A., bill me at the bargain price of $4.69 plus 25¢ shipping and handling per book and applicable sales tax, if any*. In Canada, bill me at the bargain price of $5.24 plus 25¢ shipping and handling per book and applicable taxes**. That's the complete price and a savings of over 10% off the cover prices—what a great deal! I understand that accepting the 2 free books and gift places me under no obligation ever to buy any books. I can always return a shipment and cancel at any time. Even if I never buy another book from Harlequin, the 2 free books and gift are mine to keep forever.

246 HDN DZ7Q
349 HDN DZ7R

Name	(PLEASE PRINT)	
Address	Apt.#	
City	State/Prov.	Zip/Postal Code

Not valid to current Harlequin Historicals® subscribers.

Want to try two free books from another series?
Call 1-800-873-8635 or visit www.morefreebooks.com.

* Terms and prices subject to change without notice. Sales tax applicable in N.Y.
** Canadian residents will be charged applicable provincial taxes and GST.
All orders subject to approval. Offer limited to one per household.
® are registered trademarks owned and used by the trademark owner and or its licensee.

HIST04R ©2004 Harlequin Enterprises Limited

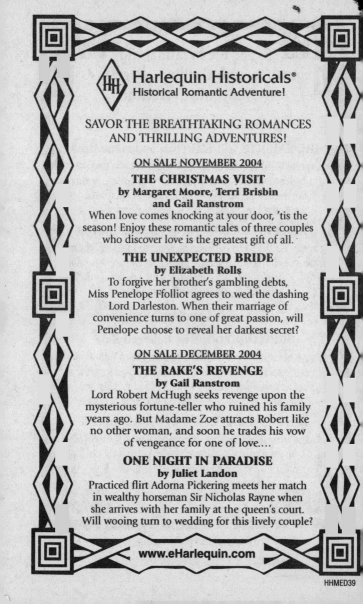